CUPID'S REVENGE

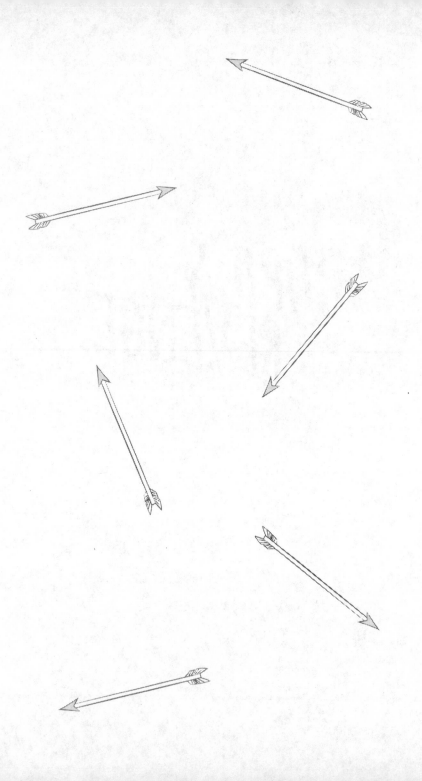

CUPID'S REVENGE

WIBKE BRUEGGEMANN

FARRAR STRAUS GIROUX
NEW YORK

Farrar Straus Giroux Books for Young Readers
An imprint of Macmillan Publishing Group, LLC
120 Broadway, New York, NY 10271 • fiercereads.com

Our books may be purchased in bulk for promotional, educational, or business use.
Please contact your local bookseller or the Macmillan Corporate and Premium Sales
Department at (800) 221-7945 ext. 5442 or by email at
MacmillanSpecialMarkets@macmillan.com.

Library of Congress Cataloging-in-Publication Data is available.

First edition, 2024
Book design by Maria W. Jenson
Printed in the United States of America

ISBN 978-0-374-31402-6
10 9 8 7 6 5 4 3 2 1

Dedicated to everyone who lost the one they loved the most.

And to their friends who helped them through it.

CUPID'S REVENGE

Act I

Scene 1

I would like to state for the record that it was never my intention to fall in love.

I was going to stay way away from all that, even after what happened in church. And maybe even after that, but you know Cupid: He'll get you when you least expect it.

The whole thing was kind of Teddy's fault, because if it hadn't been for his ridiculous plan, I'd never even have known about the existence of Katherine Cooper-Bunting.

I'd reluctantly agreed to help Dad clear out the spare room for Grandad, but not five minutes into the endeavor, my phone dinged. I put down the bin bag I was holding and squeezed the phone out of my shorts pocket.

"It's only Teddy," I told Dad somewhat unnecessarily. No one else ever messaged me.

> You need to come over pronto and wear a cute dress.

> Why are you insane?

> I'll explain.

The thing is, when you've been friends with Theodore Booker forever, you kind of don't question these things.

"Teddy is having some sort of emergency," I said.

Dad rolled his eyes. "Fine. Go. But hurry back, I can't carry that dreadful filing cabinet by myself."

"Why do we even have it?"

"Everything used to be on paper before the internet. Bills, bank statements—you wouldn't remember," Dad said, and started ripping up A4 sheets and putting them in the recycling bag.

I quickly changed into my short florally summer dress (flowers equal cute, right?) and, not bothering to put on shoes, walked over to Teddy's house.

We'd been neighbors all our lives; our parents are—well, were—literally BFFs, and Teddy and I were born only four months apart. And even though our mothers insist this was merely a coincidence rather than the result of meticulous reproductive planning, we knew the truth.

We were Teddy and Tilly, brother and sister but not.

The moment I walked through the creaky gate, his front door flew open.

"Come in, come in," Teddy said, gesticulating manically.

"I'm coming. What's the matter with you?"

"Here's the story," he said, and looked at his phone. "It is now sixteen forty-seven. At seventeen hundred hours, Katherine Cooper-Bunting is going to arrive for her last piano lesson before taking a summer break, and we have to find out what she's doing for said break, so we can accidentally on purpose

4

run into her, so I can ask her out, because I'm fiercely in love with her."

"Who the hell is Katherine Cooper-Bunting? And why have you literally never mentioned this fierce love?" I asked.

"It was a silent kind of fierce love. Plus, I haven't really seen her in person for a couple of years, and let's just say there's an almost ethereal difference between fourteen-year-old her and the now-sixteen-year-old her."

"Ethereal," I repeated, nodding, hoping he knew how crazy he sounded.

"I'm also fueled by testosterone," Teddy said, and flexed his biceps as if they had undergone a gigantic transformation since he'd turned sixteen. "Why are you laughing, Matilda?"

"Because you being fueled by anything apart from Haribo is literally disturbing. Also, you're wearing a Care Bears T-shirt."

"Hey, don't ever mock the power of the Care Bears. This is Love-a-Lot Bear, by the way."

"Can you put on a Testosterone Bear one instead, maybe?"

"Ha ha, hilarious, Tilly, I'm finally a joke even to you," he said, and led me into their narrow front room. "I thought you'd be really pleased at me making a conscious effort to move on from Grace."

I looked at him.

We hadn't talked about Grace in the longest time.

"Um, Teddy, why don't you just ask out this Katherine

Cooper-Something? Then we don't have to stalk her. Because you realize that's weird, right?"

"Bunting. Cooper-Bunting. For a number of reasons, all of which I could explain to you if time wasn't of the essence right now, but it is with—no!—eleven minutes until her arrival. Are you listening to me?"

"I always listen to you."

"Here's the plan. She's one of those punctual types, which means that at exactly seventeen hundred hours, she's going to knock on the door. Mum is going to come and open the door, at which point we'll have approximately fifteen seconds of 'Hello, Mrs. Booker,' 'Hello, Katherine,' before the front door will shut, at which point Katherine Cooper-Bunting is going to see me casually leaning against the doorframe here, and you're going to sit in the green chair over there, and you're going to laugh like I've just said the funniest thing you've ever heard."

"Have you hit your head recently?"

"Fine, Tilly. Forget about it—you don't have to stay."

"No, I'm staying. Sorry. Continue."

"Right, go and sit in the chair. I'm getting Rachmaninoff. You'll be holding him. I'll also grab a hoodie or something."

Approximately forty-five seconds later, Teddy, now wearing a lumberjack-style long-sleeved thing I'd never seen on him before, carried the screaming, three-legged Rachmaninoff into the room and plopped him onto my lap. The cat then proceeded to shout at me, like I had something to do with him being torn away from whatever he'd been busy with.

"Sorry, mate," I said, restraining him.

Rachmaninoff growled and tried to bite me.

"Fuck off!" I hissed, and held him down.

Teddy disappeared again, and when he came back, his violin in hand, I knew he'd lost his mind for real this time.

Both of us were born into musical families, but neither of us had inherited the musician gene, which was the cause of unspeakable embarrassment for our parents. Mum and Dad gave up on my musical education pretty early, but only because my older sister, Emilin, was already a genius on the piano. But because Teddy's an only child, his parents literally didn't want to believe how utterly useless he was and made him take Grade 2 violin exams when he was twelve and all the other kids were, like, six. When he couldn't get through the theme tune of *The Flintstones*, they took him home and never spoke of it again.

"Teds, why this setup?" I asked, still wrestling with Rachmaninoff, who was trying to full-body launch himself off my lap.

"Girls like guys with cute animals," he said, nodding at the still-screaming cat from actual hell.

"And I'm here because?"

"Because, seeing me with another woman will make me immediately more desirable. Especially if that woman is clearly appreciating my company, hence why you're going to LOL."

I raised my eyebrows at the violin.

"Every girl likes a musician. Also, it indicates I'm good with my hands, which, you know, is a really good quality. Sexually speaking."

"Ew!"

"And she absolutely doesn't have to know that I'm not a musician."

"What if she asks you to play together?"

Momentary terror washed across his cute little face, but it was all too late, because—

Knock

Knock

Knock.

"Hell and damnation," Teddy panic-whispered, and turned around on the spot for no reason. "And you have to call me Theodore."

"The fuck?" I whispered back, and then his mum walked past.

"Hi, Tilly."

"Hi, Amanda."

"Are you all right, Teddy?" his mum asked him after spotting his violin.

Then she opened the front door, and the next fifteen seconds played out as predicted, all "hello, hello," as did the closing of the door, Katherine Cooper-Bunting's sudden presence in the hallway, and us appearing in her direct line of vision.

What happened next happened fast.

Teddy was suddenly frozen to the spot, but being the reliable friend I am, I remembered that I was expected to laugh hysterically, and so I threw my head back and made a noise I'd never made before, which scared the shit out of Rachmaninoff, who screamed, bit me (which was okay because, apart from a leg, he's also missing all of his teeth), and threw himself off me, before hopping out of the room and disappearing down the hallway surprisingly fast for a cat with only three legs.

Everyone kind of stood back to let him pass, but nobody spoke until Teddy's mum looked at Teddy and went: "Why on earth are you wearing my blouse?"

I caught the shortest glimpse of Katherine Cooper-Bunting, who may or may not have been smirking, but who left the scene quickly with Teddy's mum, and less than a minute later, we heard her limbering up her fingers with a bunch of featherlight-sounding scales.

Teddy still hadn't moved.

His eyes looked enormous.

He didn't blink.

"I feel like this could have gone better," I said quietly, so as not to startle him.

He cradled his violin like a doll and slowly slid down the doorframe until he was sitting on the floor.

"Why *me*?" he asked, and then looked up. "What if there's literally only that one person out there for us? And what if it was Grace? I'm too young to know I'm going to die alone."

"Teddy—"

"I actually think about that a lot."

"I don't believe that. And not all is lost," I said. "Maybe catch her after her lesson, hey?"

"Or maybe I'll just go to my room and never come out again."

"I don't think you should do that," I said, and got off the green chair. "I'm sorry I ruined it."

"You didn't. I'm stupid. I've completely forgotten how to behave in real life. I mean, it's not TikTok, is it? You can't kind of just do it again and post it when it's perfect. Real life really sucks . . . You look nice, by the way."

"Thanks. And you should at least say hello to her. I mean, if your love is still fierce."

"I'm such a joke."

"Blame the hormones, I always do. I better go. Dad and I are doing up Grandad's room."

"Oh shit, I knew that. Sorry for dragging you away. You okay?"

"Yeah, I'm okay," I lied. "See you, Teds."

"She's beautiful, though, isn't she?" he whispered, and looked up at me as I stepped over him.

"I didn't really get a good look at her; I was too busy laughing at nothing. But she's probably not beautiful enough for you to have an existential crisis."

"Does she remind you of Grace?" he asked.

"I don't know."

"Life's so hard," he said, and plucked the strings of his violin. "And this is unbelievably out of tune. Like my insides."

In the background Katherine Cooper-Bunting played something entirely too cheerful.

"On that note," I said. "See ya."

I left him moping and went home, where I changed back into my shorts and T-shirt.

Dad and I proceeded to take the filing cabinet apart and eventually carried it down the narrow stairs, one heavy drawer at a time. I was literally sweating, and every time I bumped my shins against the metal, I resented the whole situation a bit more.

We also got rid of a couple of chests of drawers and some moldy suitcases. We'd booked for the council to pick everything up, and when all was outside and on the curb, Dad printed off a reference number that I had to stick to the furniture. I was sellotaping it to one of the drawers of the filing cabinet when I saw Katherine Cooper-Bunting leave Teddy's house, turn right, and walk toward me.

She looked at me, recognized me even though at that point I looked like my normal scruffy DIY self again, and said: "Hi."

Then she stepped into a ray of the early evening sun that shone through the narrow gap between our houses, and I watched it fall like a golden caress across her perfect face.

She blinked and smiled, then kept walking.

"Hi," I said, but she was already gone.

Scene 2

The next day was a Saturday, which meant that Mum was teaching ballet at Arts Ed, Dad had a matinee and an evening performance at the Royal Opera House to conduct, and Teddy's mum was teaching piano in their living room while Teddy's dad taught violin lessons via Zoom in the bedroom.

Teddy's dad used to play the violin at the Royal Opera House, and he and Dad would usually have breakfast in town together before work, but then there were loads of job cuts, and Teddy's dad was made redundant, and he and my dad completely fell out over it, which is kind of understandable, but also really stupid because it's not like it was my dad's fault. Anyway, Teddy's dad was so furious about it that he stopped speaking to my dad, and because my dad hates this song called *The Lark Ascending*, Teddy's dad would literally play it at all hours just to piss him off, and then my dad would run through the house raging, going: "Fucking David, fucking lark, fucking Vaughan fucking Williams."

Mum would watch him with her neutral face and do a little demi-plié or something.

She and Dad met when they both worked at the English

National Opera. Like, over twenty years ago. Mum was a principal dancer and danced the role of Coppélia in a ballet of the same name, and it was Dad's first conducting job, and when asked how they ended up together Mum always answers: "Well, you know what they say. The only way to get the orchestra to play the right tempo is by sleeping with the conductor."

Big laughs.

Always.

Cringe.

Legend has it that Emilin is a direct result of their tempo-driven union, because she was conceived in my mother's dressing room seconds before the half-hour call for *Swan Lake* that Christmas.

Which is why she got the musical gene, I reckon.

I was conceived in my parents' marital IKEA bed five years later, which explains a lot about a lot.

When I tell people about my family, they're always like: "It must be amazing growing up in such a musical household"—but let me tell you, amazing it is not.

It's weird. Because we literally don't speak the same language.

For example, when you ask a normal person how they are, they're usually like: "I'm well, thank you." Even when they're not.

In my family, when you ask, for example, my mum how she is, and she's feeling good, she'll do a casual double pirouette then breathe the gentlest of kisses against your forehead before floating out of the room, sometimes backward, and on tiptoes.

My dad will hum something relevant and look into your eyes either enthusiastically or annoyed, or with whatever emotion the piece he's humming is supposed to convey.

In short, these people aren't normal.

Which is why they can't do normal things, like unblock a drain or wire a plug. I, however, being a normal person, can do all of that. I mean, it's all on YouTube, and not exactly rocket science, but when Mum and Dad were kerfuffling around the spare room earlier that week and contemplating whether or not it needed to be painted, I was like: "Let's just paint it. I can paint it."

And then, justifying their shortcomings as both humans and parents, they were like: "That's great, Tilly, because that way you'll have something to do, and you won't have to spend your summer like the passionless, planless loner you are."

My parents genuinely believe that people who don't dance or play an instrument have nothing going on in their lives and therefore simply can't wait to do shit like pull giant clumpy hairballs out of the drain of the family bathroom, or paint the spare room for Grandad, who's only moving in because Dad's guilt about having been absent for his mother's untimely death is so great that he can't see the truth, which is that we won't be able to cope with looking after an old man with Alzheimer's.

But nobody ever listens to me.

Dad took me to B&Q first thing to buy paint, where he was being no help at all because he literally doesn't even know the difference between a matte paint and a gloss, even though the clue is 100 percent in the title.

"Tilly, just be careful with it. The fumes are poisonous," Mum said, not even looking at me on her way out of the house and throwing a pack of particle filtering masks that we still have stacks and stacks of in my direction.

An hour into the endeavor, and Teddy was sitting in the middle of the floor, drinking a cup of tea, wearing a mask like a party hat.

"Does she not realize paint is no longer toxic?" he asked, and I knew it was a rhetorical question, because, as I said, our parents know nothing about normal things. "When's your grandad coming?"

"As soon as the paint's dry and they've delivered the bed."

"Oh man."

"I know." I sat down on the floor opposite him and took a sip of his tea. "Did you come to help? Because I've got another roller."

"I came to tell you the good news, actually."

"There's good news?" I asked, and looked around the room that would soon be my grandad's new home. Possibly his last home. Except it wasn't his home at all, it was just a room. And he'd have to sleep in it all by himself, which must be so odd after you've shared a bed with the same person for forty-odd years. Not that he'll know. I mean, at the beginning, yes, but at the end, he won't. At least that's what I read about dementia and Alzheimer's. In the end, people know nothing and no one.

Teddy reached for my hand and squeezed it.

"I'm sorry, Tills."

"Yeah, me too. Anyway, what's the good news?"

"Forget it."

"No, tell me. I'm sorry for being all negative."

"You're not negative—you're sad. It's different."

"I'm okay."

He smiled his cutest, full-dimpled Teddy smile at me, then lifted up his eyebrows in the most idiotic way, which made me laugh.

"It's about Katherine Cooper-Bunting."

Ethereal in the evening sun, I thought, and then realized that this was what made her completely unlike Grace, who'd been the world's greatest goofball.

"Let me guess. You're getting married," I said.

"You're so funny. No, but I found out from Mum that Katherine Cooper-Bunting is going to do amdram this summer, and apparently everyone can try out for it, which means we're going."

"Why would we want to do amdram?" I asked. Because the last time we were onstage was in the Year 1 Nativity play, where Teddy played the donkey and I was a shepherd, wearing a tea towel for a beard, and when we sang "Little Donkey," Teddy cried.

"Because we have to get in with Katherine Cooper-Bunting."

"*I* don't."

"No, you do. Because if you're there too, me declaring my undying love for her won't be so awkward."

"I'm thinking it'll be more awkward," I said, but he wasn't listening to me.

"The auditions are at the Clapham Social Club on Thursday, and Katherine Cooper-Bunting told Mum that you have to prepare either a monologue or a song."

"I'm not doing it."

"Tills, all we have to do is learn a few words. Or you can sing, I guess."

"Read my lips," I said, taking his hand and squeezing it. "Nooooo. I'm not doing it. You can do what you want, but I have no desire to be an actress."

"I think it's called actor now."

"And what happened to us vowing to never date a creative? Do you want to turn into our parents?"

"Well, actors aren't really creatives, are they? I mean, they just say words other people have written for them, and they go and stand where they're told to go and stand. They're idiots, actually."

"And you want to be fiercely in love with an idiot?"

"She's a beautiful idiot."

I just looked at him.

"I'll help you find a girlfriend in exchange," he said.

"I don't want a girlfriend."

"Fine," Teddy said. "But you obviously don't have to try out. Just sit with me, okay?"

"No."

"Please, Tilly, pleeeease," he said, and made sad puppy eyes at me, and I wondered what Grace would want, and so I was like: "Fine!"

"I owe you, Tills," Teddy said, and we high-fived.

"You can grab the second roller now and help me paint," I told him.

"Yes, ma'am," he said, literally bouncing to his feet. "I'm going to have to do some reading and learn a monologue."

"Just do the one you studied for drama GCSE."

"I don't know. It was about masturbation."

"Ew! Was it?"

"Yeah, the character wanted to cover the whole world in his jizz."

"Ew, ew, ew! Don't ever speak to me about that again."

"I should learn something romantic. You know, in case we have to audition in front of each other. Not that jizz isn't romantic."

"EW!"

"Well, you're a lesbian, so you *would* find that gross. I wonder if anyone's ever written anything romantic about jizz. Like, 'Ode to Jizz' or something, you know, like that poet guy. Keats?" Teddy asked.

"Stop it!" I said, and pressed the saturated roller against his arm, leaving a huge splatter of paint.

"Whyyyy?" Teddy cried.

"Because I said to stop it. I think testosterone is eating your brain," I said. "Maybe puberty is like Alzheimer's, except you recover."

"I just can't stop thinking about her, you know?"

I watched him dip his roller in the puddle of paint on the tray.

Then, in perfect rhythm with the up and down of the roller on the wall, he kept saying: "Kathe-rine. Kathe-rine. Kathe-rine."

I dipped my roller in the slushy paint and listened to the moist, squelchy sound it made.

Katherine, my brain thought, and I literally jumped.

Scene 3

"And that's why, no matter what happens, you'll always come first," Teddy stage-whispered to his imaginary co-star. "And I mean that in every possible way, Saffi. You"—dramatic pause—"are always going to come"—dramatic inhalation followed by held breath—"first."

Teddy stared into the silence, and just when I thought he may have forgotten his lines again after all and I glanced down at the script, he stood facing the imaginary audition panel (me, sitting cross-legged on my bed), nodded his head, and said: "Thank you very much."

"No, thank *you*, Mr. Booker," I said, and clapped. "Don't call us, we'll call you."

Teddy shook himself like a wet dog and plopped down next to me.

"Why am I so bad at this? Honestly, what if I forget, like, every other sentence? Tills, you're going to have to read along and prompt me."

"Why did you choose this if you can't remember it? And, seriously, 'You will always come first'?"

"It's all part of my genius plan. I'm going to kill two birds with one stone. I'm going to impress the director so I can get a part, and at the same time I'm giving Katherine Cooper-Bunting the opportunity to fall in love not only with me, but also with this character—what's his name—Darren. Who is also me."

"So this is, like, some monologue mating ritual in which you, disguised as Darren, promise to always make Katherine Cooper-Bunting come first?"

"It's an immediate confession of the depth of my love and devotion."

"It's disturbing."

"Just FYI, Tilly, when you're a man having sexual relations, the woman coming first is literally the most important thing."

"Please stop talking."

"And I need Katherine Cooper-Bunting to know that I know that. And that it will be my pleasure to always make her come first."

"Please leave."

He smirked at me.

I rolled my eyes. "And where did you gain this knowledge?" I asked, because he so clearly wasn't done talking about it.

"Well, Matilda, where *do* you gain this knowledge when you haven't been allowed to leave the house because a global pandemic coincided with your sexually formative years?"

I looked at him.

He looked at me.

"Fan fiction," he said.

"Ew," I said, because: Ew!

"No, Tilly, don't be so judgmental. Fan fiction is"—he opened his arms and looked up at my ceiling like he was looking for the words—"everything."

"Ew! What kind of fan fiction? And if you say Care Bears, I'm never going to speak to you again, because that's just wrong."

Teddy held up his index finger.

"No, but let me say that there is Care Bears fan fiction, and I have read Care Bears fan fiction, and I may even have written Care Bears fan fiction, but I'm only into the adventure stories in that universe and would never indulge in Care Bears porn."

"Oh *God*, that's so distressing."

"I said no Care Bears porn!"

"So, what, then? Elves and dwarves? OMG, Lord of the Rings, right? You've always fancied the pale woman. Isn't it all a bit, like, wrong?"

"They were all pale. And, okay, guilty as charged, and I'm not gonna lie, I did stumble across one where Gandalf did the most unspeakable thing to Frodo Baggins, but that's why you should never just search for 'Lord of the Rings.' You have to set filters."

"You read it, though, didn't you?"

He spread himself out on my bed like a starfish.

"EW!"

"Why are you shocked, Tills? Everyone's doing it. Besides, you can choose whatever pairing you like. It's even, like, cross-genre. If you want, I don't know, Arwen—her name is Arwen, by the way—to have sexual relations with Batman, you could probably find that. And I don't know who writes these stories, but let me tell you that the woman always comes first. And if there's a scene where two people are having sex and they orgasm not only simultaneously but literally two seconds into it, the comments are savage, because that happening the first time you're with someone is apparently an urban sex legend made up by men who don't know how to make a woman come and don't really care either, and so everyone usually makes the woman come first, and usually with cunnilingus."

I literally snorted then and burst out laughing, because Teddy was the absolute last person on earth I'd ever expected to ever say "cunnilingus."

"Who's going to come first when I have sex?" I inquired, after wiping tears of hilarity off my face.

"That's a really good question, Matilda. Let me read up on it and get back to you."

"Please don't."

"Oh, come on, it's fun. And no one's hurting anyone, and besides, everyone's fictional. And let me tell you, some of the sex scenes are really well choreographed. Like, you can imagine exactly how it's done. Which is why Katherine Cooper-Bunting is a very lucky woman. And I need her to know that."

Ew, I thought.

"Good for you," I said.

Teddy got up, stretched, and picked up his monologue.

"Right. I'm just going to say it again and again and again. Maybe I'll remember it by tomorrow. Actors are like parrots."

"You're in fierce love with a parrot?" I asked.

"I'm actively trying to move on from Grace," he said. "I thought you'd be pleased for me."

"I'm very pleased for you," I told him. Because I was.

"We have to be there at twelve tomorrow," Teddy informed me. "I tried to find out more about it online, but there's nothing. I hope Katherine Cooper-Bunting wasn't lying."

"Why would she lie? Also, it's just amdram."

"It's not too late to prepare a monologue yourself," he said, and winked at me.

"Over my dead body. Do you know where the place is? Are we busing it?"

"Battersea Rise."

"Fine. We should probably leave at eleven thirty."

"Eleven fifteen," he said. "I'll meet you outside."

"All right. See you, stud."

"See you, loser. And you really should read some lesbian fan fiction. Maybe that'll get your juices flowing."

"My juices are flowing; I just don't fancy anyone."

"Tills, you have to get over Mrs. Pearson. Because you can't marry your English teacher."

"I don't want to marry anyone. And I was only in lust with her for, like, two weeks in Year Nine. You're the one who's not over it."

"Well, so let's look forward not back," Teddy said. "I don't know about you, but I want a fulfilled sex life that includes another person. It's all well and good fancying someone in silence, but I'm not willing to just masturbate for all eternity. Anyway, I better go. See you tomorrow." He winked at me from the doorway and waved goodbye.

"You're so gross, Teddy!" I shouted after him, and I heard his chuckle from halfway down the stairs.

"It's okay to just want sex, you know, but you don't have to be all dramatic about it," I shouted, just in case he was still in earshot, which I don't think he was.

"Besides," I added quietly, looking at my reflection in the mirror, "isn't cunnilingus a bit personal?"

I didn't actually mind masturbating.

Scene 4

Turned out they were going to deliver Grandad's special bed the next day, which made me so glad I'd agreed to go to the audition with Teddy, because I really didn't want to be in the house for it.

And I know it sounds stupid, and it's just a bed, but it felt like all the things I'd dreaded were finally happening, and if you could get away from your worst nightmare even if it was only for another minute, wouldn't you?

The paint was kind of dry, but I told Mum and Dad to have the people not put the bed up against the wall just yet, and Mum was like: "It's got wheels anyway, it'll be easy to move around."

I don't know why it hadn't occurred to me that it would have wheels, because hospital-style beds always have wheels for obvious reasons, but suddenly the thought of being in charge of the person in a bed like that made me feel all vomity.

I as good as ran from the house, and luckily Teddy was early as usual, which was why we got an earlier bus and got to the place in Clapham half an hour before it was supposed to start.

Now, I'd never been inside one of those social clubs, and I'm not sure what exactly I was expecting, but the place looked like a love child of a church hall and one of those local old man pubs that fly the England flag.

It smelled like the toilets in the changing rooms on the athletics field at school: a mixture of wee and feet and bleach, cheap air freshener and stale cigarette smoke, and of course Teddy had an episode about it all straightaway, like: "This was a huge mistake, and we have to leave immediately."

"Is this OAPs only?" I asked, because Teddy and I lowered the average age by at least sixty years.

"This was clearly a cruel joke," Teddy said, and tried to turn me around by my elbow.

"How was it a joke? It's not like Katherine Cooper-Bunting told you about this. She told your mum, and why would she lie to your mum?"

"People lie for the stupidest reasons. Oh my days, is that bust Winston Churchill . . . ? What I meant was, it's a cruel joke by the universe."

"You think the universe has time for this? With everything else that's going on?"

"I don't know, Tilly, but the universe hasn't exactly been kind to me," Teddy said, and kind of power walked us back toward the exit and past the toilets. Seconds before we cleared the threshold, Katherine Cooper-Bunting strode in, and the only way to avoid a head-on collision was for me to hold my arms out and physically stop her.

"Whoa," she said, and came to a standstill.

Her eyes were blue, and I watched her pupils contract.

"Sorry," I said, looking at the faintest cluster of freckles on the bridge of her nose.

She looked first at me, obviously, because I was touching her. Then, when I let go of her, she looked at Teddy, and she suddenly clearly figured out who we were, and she was like: "Oh, hi."

Teddy stood there like an idiot, not like a hero in a sexy fan fiction mash-up, and my hands were tingling from touching her.

"You're Teddy, right?" Katherine Cooper-Bunting asked, but it clearly wasn't actually a question. "We've never officially met."

"It's Theodore, actually, and yeah, I know, it's my mum— she likes to keep work and home separate even though she obviously works at home, which makes it a bit tricky, but you know what I mean."

"I'm Katherine," she said, and Teddy went: "Oh, are you? I mean, I had no idea. This is Tilly, by the way, but we're not together."

I shrugged, and Katherine Cooper-Bunting looked as if she was about to say something when—

"Thespians! Listen up!" a voice boomed through the hall, and all three of us jumped. "First of all, welcome, and thank you for coming out today. For those of you who don't know me, I'm Brian, and I am the director. I'm also a professional actor."

"In his dreams . . ." Katherine Cooper-Bunting whispered,

and snorted quietly. "He's done nothing since playing Mr. Toad in the national tour of *The Wind in the Willows* thirty years ago."

"Harsh," I whispered back.

Katherine Cooper-Bunting shrugged. "Tragic truth, more like. It's not his fault. He's a character actor. It's limiting," she continued, still whispering and gesticulating like she was desperate for me to get the point she was trying to make.

"Please, everyone, come to my desk and write down your name and contact details, and I will arrange"—and when he said "arrange," he rolled the *r* ridiculously—"you all in alphabetical order for your audition."

"I resent that," Teddy said to us. "What if I'm first?"

"Maybe now's the time to adopt a stage name," I suggested.

"I don't mind going first," said Katherine Cooper-Bunting. "But you're Booker, aren't you, and I'm Cooper-Bunting."

"Are you?" Teddy asked.

"What's your last name?" Katherine Cooper-Bunting asked me, and I was just like: "Oh no, I'm not auditioning. I'm only here for emotional support. Why is everyone else so old?"

Katherine Cooper-Bunting shrugged again and put her bag on one of the knackered-looking plastic chairs.

"I guess all the theater kids are down at Stagecoach," she said. "And who else has the time to come to rehearsal every day for a month in the middle of the day? Normal people are working."

"Good point," I said.

"Everyone!" Brian shouted, and clapped three times. "We've

lost our pianist, so for those of you who've prepared a song, I'm terribly sorry, but you're going to have to do it 'a cappella' today. That means unaccompanied."

I looked at Katherine Cooper-Bunting.

"I don't do musical theater," she said, like it was an abomination.

"What do you mean we've lost him?" asked a severe-looking Irish woman, who was leaning on the cordoned-off bar. "I've brought you a song, Brian. We need a pianist. What's happened to Gordon?"

"I thought you'd heard," Brian said. "It was in the paper, Maeve. Gordon's dead."

Teddy clutched his chest, Katherine Cooper-Bunting looked at me and I looked at her, and I was trying not to laugh, which was literally just awful, because poor Gordon, but you know when your body has some sort of hysterical reaction to unexpected information?

"No!" Maeve exclaimed, and crossed herself. "He was only at the shop a few weeks ago. What happened?"

"Oh, daaaaaarling," Brian said three times louder than strictly necessary. "You're going to think I'm joking, but I'm not joking. He had a bad case of food poisoning."

"Food poisoning?" Teddy whispered.

"Who gave him food poisoning?" Maeve cried, and when no one said anything, she shouted: "Well, he sure as hell didn't get it from anything he bought from me!"

"They reckon he had a dodgy prawn cocktail at the Stag," Brian informed her. "You know he always ate fish on a Friday."

"Bloody Catholic stubborn old fool!" Maeve shouted. She looked at the heavens, crossed herself again, and rushed over to Brian to hear more.

"Who eats actual prawn cocktail?" Teddy whispered.

"At a pub," Katherine Cooper-Bunting added.

"One down already," I whispered. "Poor Gordon," I quickly added.

"What a stupid way to go," Katherine Cooper-Bunting said.

"And all because he was a good Catholic."

"Death by prawn cocktail."

"Life's literally so cruel," I said.

Katherine Cooper-Bunting rummaged around in her massive shoulder bag. I watched her pull out a tube of Carmex, unscrew the red top, squeeze a blob onto her fingertip, and apply it to her lips.

I licked mine.

She screwed the top back on, threw the Carmex back into the bag, and smiled at me.

I swallowed.

I looked at her freckles again.

And then I thought about their future children. Her freckles and Teddy's dimples.

Heartbreak central.

Katherine Cooper-Bunting did a double take over my shoulder and wrinkled her perfect nose.

"You've got to be kidding me," she mumbled, and narrowed her eyes. I looked behind me and saw that two girls had just walked in. "That's Olivia. She's Stagecoach's poster child. She's also my nemesis. Why is she here?"

I didn't know which one Olivia was, but because Katherine Cooper-Bunting had said "Stagecoach" and "poster child," I could pretty much guess she didn't mean the one wearing a pair of worn-out Converse, shorts, and a My Little Pony T-shirt, but the one who'd rocked up in nothing but a black sports bra and matching leggings, who had perfect hair and the longest fake eyelashes in the observable universe.

"I didn't know she frequented the library," Katherine Cooper-Bunting said.

"The library?" I asked, and leaned a bit closer to her because I could, and I looked at her lips that were still glistening in the awful fluorescent light and smelled of cherries.

"I thought the library was the only place this was advertised," Katherine Cooper-Bunting said. "Why? How did you hear about it?" she asked, and looked at me, then Teddy, who was smiling at her like a stupid puppy instead of a man on a mission who had fierce love and a sexual master plan.

"We actually heard about it from a mutual friend," Teddy bullshitted, finally joining the conversation. "Who isn't here today," he continued, and because he sucks at lying, I knew immediately this would escalate. "Because he's dead," Teddy concluded.

Katherine Cooper-Bunting and I looked at him, and he huffed a nervous laugh.

"I'm obviously joking," he said, and flapped his arms like he didn't know what to do with them.

"This was advertised at the library," Katherine Cooper-Bunting said. "And I obviously wanted to do it because of the West End thing. I also wanted to do real theater for once in my life and not Stagecoach."

Teddy and I looked at each other, and he shrugged, but with his eyes only.

"I thought this was only amdram," I asked.

"Yes," Katherine Cooper-Bunting said, suddenly so surprisingly in my face that I took a step back. "But if you're rubbish, you won't get a part. Not like at Stagecoach, where everyone gets a part even when you suck, because your parents have paid for it."

Teddy looked at her like he'd never seen her before in his life, and I wondered if his fierce love was being tamed by her somewhat strong opinion on something boring.

"What?" she asked. "If you want to be a successful actor, you're going to have to put yourself out there. And at our age, we really can't waste any more time."

"Yeah, I totally agree with you," Teddy said. "I mean, that's exactly what I said. Isn't that exactly what I said, Tills?"

"That's exactly what you said, Theodore," I replied, and nodded violently. "Which is also exactly why we're here, isn't it? Which is why you two should go and put your names down, and I'm going to find somewhere so I can just sit and look pretty."

"You're always pretty, Matilda," Teddy said.

When he walked off with Katherine Cooper-Bunting, I heard him say: "Tilly's basically my sister."

I rolled my eyes at no one.

Scene 5

Okay, so you know how you sometimes see something on telly, and it's so unspeakably cringe that you have to actually either change the channel or leave the room?

Like the first few rounds of *Britain's Got Talent*. Imagine that, but worse, because no one has edited it to make it in any way watchable.

Brian decided to go in alphabetical order by first names because "we're all friends here, daaaahlings," and an old man called Charles performed a song called "Some Enchanted Evening," and it was not only severely out of tune but also grossly out of rhythm, due to the lack of musical accompaniment—something the next people, a geriatric husband-and-wife duo called Daniela and Thomas, were more cross about than was strictly necessary.

Brian kept saying: "I'm not here to judge your singing but the way you perform your song," but I think we all knew he was just saying it because he didn't want people to hate him.

Anyway, Daniela and Thomas had prepared the main song from the musical *The Phantom of the Opera*, you know the dramatic one, like, daaaaaaaaaa-da-da-da-da-daaaaaaaaa, and they insisted they could absolutely not do it without the music, and so they ended up playing the song on her phone and singing along to it while acting out the scene.

And let it be said that I have never felt that degree of vicarious embarrassment ever in my life, and if Teddy had as much as looked at me or breathed in my direction, I would probably have never stopped laughing.

I think everyone else was also too mortified to even snicker, and when it was finally over, Teddy grabbed my hand and did not stop squeezing it until Brian called the next person to the stage: Katherine Cooper-Bunting.

The silence in the room when she took the stage was electric.

Or maybe my ears were still ringing from "The Phantom of the Opera."

She shook a strand of hair off her face, zeroed in on Brian, and went: "My name is Katherine, and I will be performing Lady Macbeth from *Macbeth*."

Teddy grabbed my hand again and squeezed, but so suddenly that two of my bones knocked against each other.

"Ouch!" I whispered, and then *he* told *me* to be quiet.

This much was clear even before she opened her mouth: Katherine Cooper-Bunting had not left the house that morning to get over a lost love, or with cunnilingus on her mind, or to get away from her grandfather's actual deathbed arriving.

She hadn't even come to have fun.

She'd come to perform Lady Macbeth, and she was going to do it well, and she was going to get a part in whatever this was, because she was going to do "the West End thing" and become an actor.

I hadn't even ever seen this level of determination in Emilin, who won, like, every piano competition, and the one time she came second, she had an absolute meltdown on the tube, where she ripped up her certificate in a blind rage and threw it in front of an approaching Northern Line train when we changed at Kennington.

"Out damn spot, out I say!" recited Katherine Cooper-Bunting in a voice that aged her ten years at least, and the room collectively leaned forward in their shabby chairs.

When she was done, everyone clapped, and I watched her walk off the stage and back toward her seat like she hadn't even done anything, when, only moments earlier, I'd absolutely believed she'd killed a man in cold blood and had lost her mind over it. And you know how you never understand anything anyone is saying when you read Shakespeare? Well, it sounded like English when she said it.

Teddy gave her a thumbs-up, and she pulled a funny face at him and blushed a blush I followed all the way down her neck and chest, and which then continued to run down my own body, and I think I must have looked at her like a thirsty person who'd just discovered water.

Katherine, I thought, and wondered if I could ever call her by just her first name, before coughing my heart back into its normal rhythm.

"You all right?" Teddy asked.

I nodded, but I couldn't look at him.

Next was a tone-deaf woman who sang a song called "Three Coins in a Fountain," then came the loud Irish woman, Maeve, who performed Helena Bonham Carter's song from *Sweeney Todd* about bad pies, and despite not having a piano, she sounded really great. Halfway through it, Katherine Cooper-Bunting looked back at us and whispered: "She's a butcher in real life," and Teddy and I went: "Eek!" at the same time.

Next was a guy I'd clocked when we walked in, but had since forgotten about, mainly because I thought he wasn't there to audition, but because he was someone's grandson.

He looked like he was probably our age.

He wore skintight black jeans despite the absolute heat, and a black T-shirt that had the arms cut off, and his hair was long and blond and unbrushed.

"Hello," he said in an Eastern European accent. "I am Miroslaw. I am Polish, and I am doing *Lithium*."

And then he launched into this monologue that kind of rhymed and was about a person who had mental-health issues, and it was so amazing, and so completely weird, and because of his accent, which was not only Eastern European but also American, I couldn't really understand everything he was saying, but it didn't matter, because it was all in his face and in the way he said the words.

Katherine Cooper-Bunting, who was sitting one row in front of us and to my right, clutched her chest, and I was like, maybe she's actually a perfect match for Teddy, because he's always been, like, compassion central, which is why I reckon he identifies so much with the Care Bears.

The girl Katherine Cooper-Bunting hated, Olivia, even wolf-whistled at Miroslaw, and I think he was really pleased, but you know when people are trying really hard to not show it, and they kind of have to fight their own smile?

Olivia was next.

She strode confidently onto the stage, faced Brian, and went: "My name is Olivia, and I'm going to perform Lady Macbeth."

Katherine Cooper-Bunting didn't move in her seat, and Olivia actually looked over at her and laughed, and then was like: "Only joking, mate. LOL, as if. I'm going to be singing a few bars from 'As Long as You're Mine' from the musical *Wicked*."

And for a moment I was thinking, *OMG, help, this is going to be really awful again*, but it was anything but, because Olivia could sing.

You know when you hear people, and you know they're professionals? Like, it was insane. I'd never heard the song before, but at the end she went into some fancy riff and really opened her mouth, and it was just astonishing, and even as she was still singing, we were literally clapping and whooping, even the old people.

Teddy just went: "Yeah, I mean, that was flawless." And then he slow clapped and nodded his head until Olivia was back at her seat.

"No wonder she and your girlfriend are rivals," I whispered in his ear.

"I know," Teddy whispered back, still looking at the stage, which was by now empty. "At least they won't hate us, because we're literally no competition. I don't even think we're the same species. Compared to them we're, like, plankton."

Next, we had to endure a monologue by a man called Steven, and because he said his memory wasn't so good anymore, he'd written it down, but the reading wasn't very good either, because as well as bad memory, Steven also had bad eyesight and couldn't read his writing.

Then it was Teddy's turn, and he grabbed my arm for a second, and his hand was all cold and clammy.

"Kill me," he whispered.

"Remember that you're doing it for love," I said, which obviously didn't make it at all better, because he kind of glanced at the back of Katherine Cooper-Bunting's head and audibly dry-swallowed.

"I want to say for the record that this is literally the worst moment of my life," he said to me, and gave me his phone with the text for the monologue.

"Grace-face would be so proud," I said, and smiled at him.

"I know," he replied, and walked forward and onto the stage.

The thing was, the way all his limbs are generally gangly kind of really helped the performance, and when he forgot his words twice, all I had to do was throw in the next word or two and he was back on track, so all in all, I have to say it definitely could have been a lot worse.

He chickened out of doing the dramatic breathing thing he did when we rehearsed it in my room, but it was really good anyway, and everyone clapped, but there was no wolf-whistling.

Teddy bowed so dramatically that his nose almost hit his kneecaps before walking off the stage like an overexcited puppy.

Brian was like: "Thank you, thank you, thank you, everyone. I will have a think and then I'll let you all know by Sunday. Please give yourselves a huuuuuge round of applause."

On our way out, Katherine Cooper-Bunting smiled at Teddy and gave him the thumbs-up, which made him literally trip over his own feet.

Then she said goodbye to me and touched my arm, which made my pulse literally trip over itself.

I imagined Grace linking arms with me, shaking her head gently, whispering: "Don't even think about it."

Scene 6

Grace was hit by a car when we were thirteen.

It happened right at the end of our road. Not the main road end, but the end that leads onto the road that runs along Tooting Bec Common. The one with the speed bumps where there's a twenty-mph speed limit.

Apparently, the car that got her wasn't even going fast, but the driver just didn't see her. Grace was wearing a helmet and everything.

We'd always been in the same year at school, and Grace and Teddy and I had been basically inseparable from day one.

After she died, Teddy told me he'd been in love with her.

It broke my already broken heart into even tinier pieces, and I always thought that watching Teddy's heart mend one day would somehow also mend mine.

So, yeah, I needed Katherine Cooper-Bunting. For Teddy.

When I got home, the bed had arrived.

It was exactly what I'd imagined, a heavy monstrosity on wheels with cage-like railings you could bring up to prevent the person from falling out.

I stood in the doorway, and I wondered what Grandad would look like in it.

When he's dead.

Or almost dead.

I wondered what he would actually die of. Because Alzheimer's itself obviously doesn't kill you. Usually pneumonia does. Or other infections.

My biggest and most gut-wrenching fear is that one day in the maybe not-so-distant future everyone will be at work, and because "oh, Tilly can watch Grandad—she's got no life," I'll be alone with him, and that's when he'll die.

I know this sounds awful, but at least when Grandma died I didn't have to watch it. It's easier losing someone that way, I think.

Grandma was in Scotland, and we weren't allowed to visit because of the pandemic. And she was in hospital, and people in hospitals know what to do when someone's dying. But how are *we* supposed to know what to do with a dying person?

And the thing about Grandad is, I just can't imagine him dead. Because everything about him is majestic. He's like a great big elephant.

Have you ever seen a dead elephant? Not in real life, obviously, but on a David Attenborough show? It's the saddest thing. This giant deflated corpse, lying on the ground in the middle of nowhere.

I walked into the room, and I picked up the bed's remote that lay on the brand-new pillow.

I pressed one of the buttons.

The backrest came up slowly.

"There you are," Mum said. She was carrying sheets, but when she saw what I was doing, she put them down. "Tilly, I don't think we'll be needing all this technology for a while, so why don't you put the bed back down for now."

"A majority of people with Alzheimer's die because when they eat or drink it goes down the wrong hole and then they get pneumonia. So sitting up in bed while eating and drinking is vital."

"Yes, but we won't be needing that tomorrow, Tilly."

"When are you going to familiarize yourself with the bed, then, Mum? When he's in it and can no longer get out?"

Mum ignored me.

"Let's flap all these barriers down, too," she said, and her bony little hand started yanking at the metal, but it wouldn't give, obviously, because that was the point of barriers.

"You have to loosen the slidy catch underneath," I said. She fumbled for it, and I could see her hands were shaking.

"Mum, come on. Here, let me do it," I said, and did it. "I hate this room. It looks gross, like, sterile. Like in a hospital."

"Tilly, I can't help that right now, all right?" Mum said, and put the pillow into the pillowcase in a really complicated way. "When your grandfather gets here with all his things, we'll be able to decorate. But I don't know what he'll want in here, and so I can't really do anything about it."

"I just don't understand why he can't have a normal bed for now. I mean, you just said he's not going to need this straightaway. It's like . . . he's going to look at this and know he's going to die in it."

Mum pinched the bridge of her nose.

"How would *you* like it?" I kept talking because I knew she wanted me to stop and go away. "If Dad had died, and you had to move from your home into this tiny room that has a remote-control bed in it? He knows he's losing his mind, which must suck already, but imagine being reminded of it every second of every day with this awful ICU-like bed. It's cruel, Mum."

Mum just looked at me.

"This is the bed they recommended. And we all agreed to do this. You agreed, too, Tilly, remember?"

I left her there, shaking out the sheet, being all super aggressive, and went to my room.

It's funny, really, how during the height of the COVID pandemic, we were concerned about Grandad because he's old and he's got Alzheimer's. But then Grandma caught COVID, even though she was fifteen years younger than him, and in perfect health. She got it so bad so fast that it only took her a week to die. None of us, including Grandad, ever got to speak to her again.

And we couldn't even go to the funeral, because it was in Scotland. Only Emilin went.

The thing with Grandad's Alzheimer's is that he needs regular medication, and of course when you've got Alzheimer's, you're not likely to remember that, and so he had to have a nurse visit him every day, but it became clear that he literally couldn't do anything for himself, because he'd never had to do anything for himself in the first place because Grandma always did everything. In fact, Grandma always did everything for all of us, and because we knew she'd haunt us from beyond the grave if we just dumped Grandad in a home, we decided as a family that he should come and live with us.

Grandad wasn't happy, because he didn't want to leave his house or Edinburgh, and so it was phone calls, phone calls, phone calls, or Zooms with Emilin there, too, and every time, someone would end up shouting, or crying, or both.

One night Dad was literally weeping and telling Grandad that he'd never forgive himself for not having broken the rules and driven up to Edinburgh when Grandma was starting to feel unwell, and how Grandad should stop being such a stubborn old bastard; besides, he could come to work with Dad whenever he liked, which would be a lot better than sitting "all by your bloody self in bloody freezing Edinburgh," which "would make you lose your bloody mind even quicker, Dad!"

Oh, yeah, FYI, Grandad's a musician, too.

Pianist.

Like Emilin.

She's his favorite.

Shocker.

I'd dreaded the day of Grandad's arrival since the moment we agreed he should move in. It felt like a constant uncomfortable pressure in my core that I knew would never go away, and the only thing that made it at all bearable was the fact that the day of his arrival wasn't that actual day.

But now it almost was.

"Tilly," Mum said, appearing in the doorway. "When Emilin brings your grandad here, her boyfriend is also coming to stay."

"The oboe? Boring."

"Would you mind sleeping in Emilin's room when they're here? She only has the single bed."

"Ew! I don't want them to have sex in my bed."

"Tilly!" Mum said, her face going from the normal neutral to instantly super annoyed.

She never talks about sex, you see, apart from the "the only way to get the right tempo is to sleep with the conductor" story of utmost hilarity, ha, ha, ha, which is why I bring it up whenever possible.

"No way, Mum. There'll be other people's sex stains on my sheets. Gross. All those juices."

"They can change the sheets," Mum said, ignoring my comment, but flinching when I said "juices," which pleased me.

But then I was like: "Why do I always have to give up everything for other people? She could have had a bigger bed, but she wanted that stupidly giant electric piano in her room. I chose to have a nice big bed. It's not fair."

"Emilin doesn't even live here anymore."

"Exactly! I live here, and I want to be able to sleep in my own bed."

"They're staying for one night. And they're driving all of your grandad's things, including your grandad, all the way from Edinburgh. Honestly, I'm not asking you to—"

"Fine," I said, except I didn't say it—I sort of barked it.

"Jesus Christ, Tilly," Mum said, now proper huffy.

I heard her go downstairs, and when I knew she was well out of earshot, I shoved my pillow over my face and screamed until I felt nothing apart from my vocal cords about to snap.

Then I got out my phone and found a fan fiction website.

I looked around for a while trying to decide which lesbian fictional ship I should board, but I literally couldn't think of one, and when I looked at pairings in general, I found that there was too much choice. You know, like when you're at a buffet and because there's so much of everything, you're literally not even hungry anymore.

Then I thought about Katherine Cooper-Bunting lying on a table, naked and smiling, saying: "Good evening, Tilly."

I shook myself, got out my phone, and messaged Teddy.

How's your research going re:

who comes first in lesbian sex?

I'm so glad you're asking, Matilda.

Because I have an answer for you.

?

It appears that the person
initiating is the one to come last.

Got it.

You're welcome.

I let the phone slip out of my hand and fall onto the floor,
then immediately picked it up again so I could find Katherine
Cooper-Bunting on social media.

I typed her name into IG.

Her picture came up immediately, and all I wanted was based-
on-real-life, hot-and-sweaty fiction that featured Tilly Taylor and
Katherine Cooper-Bunting, in which I'm doing the honors.

Then I imagined Grace, leaning in my doorway, looking at me.

And the really weird thing was that she suddenly didn't look
thirteen anymore.

She looked like us now. Sixteen. And she was shaking her
head at me.

Scene 7

You know how some people have a face like a slapped arse?

That's my sister Emilin, which is why she annoyed me unspeakably even before she'd left the van and said anything to anyone.

The oboe had called when they were fifteen minutes away, and Mum, Dad, and I ran outside to locate and block a parking spot.

Normal people would wave or something, wouldn't they, but Emilin didn't even properly acknowledge us, but was all serious and passive-aggressively parallel parking.

All right, the van was big, and she'd been driving it since, like, six in the morning, but still, what's wrong with her?

Also, I hadn't seen her in person for literally ages, and did she hug me when she got out? Nope.

She didn't even hug Mum and Dad.

As soon as she opened the van door, she was like: "Help Grandad down, guys, this is his bag with his medication, this is the folder with all his documents," blah blah blah, you know, all with utmost urgency, like she was the first paramedic arriving at the scene of some horrific accident, instead of a person who is the sister/daughter of the people standing on the road, and whose job it is to just play the stupid piano.

You see, that's one of the reasons why Teddy and I vowed to never date creatives. Their self-importance is so staggering that you'll only ever be second best. And second best is literally the most disappointing thing you can allow yourself to become.

Unless you're like my grandmother, who was confident enough to not give a shit and would graciously stroke their egos because she knew they were all basically idiots.

We all lined up to say hello to Grandad, and when it was my turn to hug him, I was shocked at how old he looked.

Like, he was falling in on himself. He was all bony, and his rib cage was visible in a freaky way through his nice shirt. He'd also spilled tea or coffee down his front, and in the past he would have changed his shirt straightaway, but in the present maybe he hadn't even noticed.

I swallowed a huge lump in my throat and hugged him.

He smelled like an old person, stale and sad.

"Let's get you settled, Grandad, and get you a nice cup of tea," Emilin said, and pulled him away.

We followed them and left the oboe to start unpacking the van, and when we were in the house, Emilin was like: "Do you need the toilet, Grandad?" and Grandad didn't say anything, just glared at her like she was no longer his favorite.

"Look, it's right here," Emilin said, completely ignoring his discomfort, opening the door to the tiny downstairs loo and pulling on the cord to switch on the light. "No need to lock the door—I'll keep watch," she said, and stood there.

The rest of us just froze.

You see, we're not one of those families who talk about their bodily functions. Like, ever.

When I got my period, Mum was all weird and whispering to me about pads and tampons for five excruciating minutes, calling it "Aunt Flo," and then she literally never mentioned it ever again.

From then on, the pad and tampon stash was always refilled as if by magic, and since Mum didn't believe in physical pain, she never acknowledged me telling her about having period pain, and because I literally never got a reaction out of her, I eventually just stopped talking about that aspect of my life.

And now we had all communally witnessed my grandad being led to the toilet, and I felt complete emotional agony over it, but obviously I wasn't the only one because, in a typical fight-or-flight reaction, everyone dispersed really fast. Hearing someone on the toilet was the absolute worst thing that could happen to us, both individually and as a group, and three seconds later I was saying hi to the oboe and carrying a giant box inside that was labeled SHEET MUSIC. Because if there was one thing we needed in our house, it was more sheet music. Joking. Obviously.

The oboe followed with a box of CDs.

"Where does all this go?" I yelled.

"Put it in the living room for now," Mum yelled back.

On my way back out to get another box, I ran into Grandad, who was just coming from the toilet, and he was like: "Can I help?" and I was like: "No, why don't you go sit down?" and then he went: "Thank you, Sarah," which was Grandma's name, and I don't know why I didn't correct him.

Dinner was just as painful.

I didn't eat the lamb because one night I randomly felt so fundamentally sorry for every single creature in pain that I honestly just couldn't bring myself to eat another bite of anything that had ever lived. Mum, who had zero emotions about food at the best of times, accused me of overthinking, and when I bit down on a pork chop, a mental image of a pig with tears running down its pink and slightly dirty cheeks flashed into my mind, and I actually physically gagged. Dad then shouted at me for being hysterical, and I shouted at him about the pig's sad eyes, and then I ran upstairs into my room and cried.

"Could you pass the mint sauce, please?" I asked, pouring it over my potatoes and mushing it all together, which turned out to be totally disgusting, but I ate it anyway, while Emilin gave us a forty-five-minute lecture on Grandad's pills.

He got all agitated at one point when he couldn't figure out how to cut his meat, so Emilin just cut it for him without commenting on it, and I watched Mum watch it, and I watched Dad trying to not watch it, and I just thought: *This isn't going to work.*

After dinner Emilin took Grandad to the toilet again, and

when they came back, she sat him down on the piano bench and pulled up a chair for herself.

She opened some music, and the next thing I knew they were playing together.

How is that possible?

How can a person not be able to work out how to use a knife and fork, and play a four-handed Mozart thing not twenty minutes later?

I mean, I'd obviously read about it, but seeing it in real life made it real, and it was scary, and I hated it.

I went to bed early because I couldn't be in the same room with anyone anymore, but who can sleep at nine, especially in the middle of summer?

I was lying there, in Emilin's stupid, tiny bed, looking at the ceiling, thinking that it's all well and good taking in an elderly relative, but the fact was that Mum and Dad didn't even enjoy looking after their own children, so why did they think that looking after Grandad was something they could do?

I had to go for a wee, and I listened for ten minutes to make sure I wouldn't run into anyone. I opened the door so quietly, tiptoed to the bathroom, but Emilin must have had the same idea, and so we super awkwardly ended up in the narrow hallway together.

"Go," she whispered.

"No, you go," I whispered back.

"Fuck's sake, Tilly, just go."

"No, you go."

"Why do you have to be so difficult all the time?"

"You don't know if I'm being difficult, you're never here. I'm actually exceedingly generous."

She glared at me in an annoying way.

"That's *my* bed you're probably about to have sex in, or already had sex in, and you're welcome."

"You're such a child, honestly," Emilin hissed.

"Fuck off," I said, and went for the bathroom door, but she stopped me by pulling my arm.

"Ouch!"

"That didn't hurt."

"Did too."

"Tilly, listen to me," she said, and it was clearly no longer about her having sex in my bed. "You need to keep an eye on things here."

"What?"

She came too close into my personal space, and I was going a bit cross-eyed looking at her face, and I wondered which one of us was the prettier one these days.

"You need to really keep an eye on Grandad," she whispered.

"How am I supposed to do that? I've got school."

"Right now you've got summer holidays. And you're doing fuck all as usual."

"You don't know that. Have you even asked me? No, of course you haven't, because all you've done since you arrived was talk about yourself and lecture us about Grandad."

"Maybe if you opened your mouth every once in a while and contributed to a conversation instead of running away and locking yourself in your room, I wouldn't have to ask you."

"No one cares about what I have to say. You never did. I'm not one of you."

"What are you on about? We care. But you don't care about anything. All you ever do is sit there and sulk or try to annoy Mum. The only person you really talk to these days is Teddy. It's not healthy, Tills."

"Fuck off."

"I know you miss Grace; we all do—"

"You don't know anything," I said, because she didn't. "And why do I have to be the one to keep an eye on Grandad? I'm not his carer. They need to get him a carer."

"And when we were little, they should have got us a nanny, but they didn't. Instead, we had to sleep over at Teddy's house, or they shipped us off to Edinburgh at every opportunity."

"That's not the same."

"Of course it is. Grandma was the mother Mum could never be for us, and, Tilly, we owe it to her to look after her husband now."

"But—"

"Just pull your finger out. Everyone knows you're not a fan of hard work, but you can keep an eye on Grandad—it takes nothing. All you have to do is make sure he eats, drinks, goes to the toilet regularly, takes his pills, and doesn't wander off. How is that a chore?"

"If it's not such a chore, then why don't you cancel your dumbass touristy summer lunchtime recitals no one even pays you for anyway, and stay here?"

"Because I have commitments."

"Only to yourself."

"Why do you always have to be so hostile?"

"Why do you always have to be so condescending? It's not my job to look after Grandad. I don't know how. And I'm terrified he's going to die."

"He's not going to die," Emilin said, and looked at me the way Dad had looked at me after the pork-chop incident.

"We're all going to die," I said, pushing past her and into the bathroom.

I had a wee, then decided to brush my teeth again, and I took ages on purpose, because I wanted to annoy her. But when I came out, like, ten minutes later, she wasn't there anymore.

I went into her room, lay on the tiny bed, and picked up my phone.

Before I could think about it, I was back on IG, looking at a picture of Katherine Cooper-Bunting.

I took a screenshot, cropped it, and saved it on my phone.

Scene 8

I never spoke to Emilin again before they left, just stood on the curb, not waving, still livid that she tried to guilt me into taking charge of Operation Grandad and then ridiculed my fear.

The moment their van turned onto the main road, I went out into the garden, where Teddy was waiting for me in the rhododendrons.

I'd successfully detached the back of the fence from the post so I could slip through and meet Teddy in their garden inside the giant bushes.

As I breached the outer branches—it was hard getting inside with them now in full bloom—a paper airplane hit me in the head and crash-landed.

"Ouch!"

"How's your grandad?"

I shrugged.

"Have a look at the flyer," Teddy said, and nodded at the crashed plane. "Get it? Flyer-flyer?"

"You're so hilarious," I said. I picked it up and started unfolding it. "What is it?"

"I went to the library, and luckily it was still up."

"Where even is the library?" I asked, and was immediately captivated by the blurry, brown-tinged headshot of a much, much younger Brian.

"Well, there's one on Mitcham Road—who knew?—and I went there, but they didn't have them, and so I looked on Google, found the library in Clapham, and ta-daaaaa."

"'*Cupid's Revenge*'?" I read, and looked at him. "'An evening celebrating theater's favorite songs and words of love.' Well, at least you hit the bull's-eye with your questionable 'you'll always come first' monologue."

"Keep reading, the worst is yet to come."

"'An evening to honor my dear husband, Malcolm.' Oh my God, he's dead—"

"Keep reading."

"'In aid of Acting for Others, a charity that provides financial and emotional support to all theater workers in times of need.' Well, that's cool."

"Keep going."

"'With a gala performance at the Criterion Theatre on August twenty-ninth.' Oh my God. This is what you auditioned for? Your parents are going to be so proud," I said, and looked at him.

"I can't go through with this, Tills," he said, and flapped his arms around ridiculously. "It's completely absurd to think I'm going to be on the stage of a West End theater. I only auditioned as a joke. And performing in a shabby social club in front of a bunch of geriatrics and, I don't know, Mr. and Mrs. Cooper-Bunting, is one thing, but this is, like, unacceptable."

"To be fair, you didn't actually audition as a joke."

"Fine," he said, and scratched his head. "But I definitely didn't go there so I can make my West End debut."

"So, what now?"

"So now I'm waiting for a sign from the universe. If I don't get in, I'm going to be spared the complete humiliation of having to perform in front of people, but my love life will once again be over before it has truly begun. And if I do get in, I'm going to have to ask myself if my love for Katherine Cooper-Bunting is greater than my fear of the aforementioned humiliation."

"I feel like you had this coming."

"I probably won't get in, though," he continued.

"I hate to tell you this, but you probably will get in."

"Because I was the only guy under sixty?"

"You weren't the only guy under sixty—there was that Miroslaw guy."

"He was intense. Was he also really good-looking? Did you see his pretty eyes?"

"A killer combination with his rugged Eastern European charm. But your monologue was actually very good."

"Thanks. But maybe I'm not part of Brian's creative vision."

"The man has to fill an evening," I said, pointing at the flyer. "And I doubt he'll be falling all over himself to put the seventy-year-old Phantom of the Opera in it. Daaaa-da-da-da-da-daaaaaaaaa," I sang. "And isn't that song a bit—"

"Rapey?"

"Don't say rapey."

"Creepy masked guy abducts young girl and leads her into his underground lair where she's confronted with a life-size doll of herself wearing a wedding gown. Were we, like, ten when we all went to see that?"

"Ew, yes. Although I have to admit I didn't really get how weird all that was back then. I just loved the costumes and the set so much. And the woman who played Christine."

"Mum and Dad would literally lose their minds if I was like: 'Please report to the Criterion Theatre on the twenty-ninth of August to witness my West End debut.'"

"I'll be the lonely only black sheep, then."

"I told you to audition."

"I don't want to be an actor. Also, I bet our parents look down on actors. You know, the parrot thing and actors not having an actual skill. I mean, *we* look down on actors. And besides, I wouldn't want Mum and Dad to be invested in me only because I'm on a stage."

"Ouch," he said, and clutched his chest. "That hurt."

"I'm sorry, that didn't come out right."

"It's fine. Imagine it, though. At the Criterion. Imagine me taking a curtain call with Katherine."

"It's just Katherine now, is it?" I asked, looking down at

Brian's way-too-young face again and back up at Teddy. "I think you've already decided to do it."

He grabbed his chest dramatically again and went: "My loyal heart."

I could imagine them together already, Teddy and Katherine Cooper-Bunting, standing in a single spotlight beam on an otherwise empty stage, and slowly drifting toward each other, then kissing, but not, like, friendly, but going at each other with open mouths, and the audience erupting into thunderous applause.

I licked my lips, looked at the flyer, folded it back into an airplane, and actually threw it at Teddy.

"Good luck with it all," I said, and turned to go.

"Wait. What do you think I should do?"

"You've clearly already mentally committed to Katherine Cooper-Bunting, or should I say, *Katherine*." And I kind of said her name in a super-breathy voice.

"Hey," he said. "Are you annoyed with me or something?"

Yes, I thought, and looked at him.

"No," I said. "There's just a lot going on at the moment."

When I carefully crawled out of the rhododendrons and back through the fence into the hot afternoon, I felt all wrong. Like I was a stranger in my own brain or something, and then, when I walked into the house, that felt all wrong, too, with Grandad's stuff still in boxes everywhere and him sitting on the sofa, just staring ahead, like someone who was waiting for time itself to dissolve him into nothingness.

I went up to my room, opened the window, closed the door, closed the curtains, and lay down on the bed.

I don't think I moved a single muscle until Mum asked me to accompany her to the big Asda by Clapham Junction hours later.

She was like: "We can get some stuff in bulk," which was something we never did. Like, ever.

Between the three of us, we usually picked up bits. We sometimes get deliveries, but Dad has to order them because Mum's so rubbish at food. She doesn't know how to buy it, prepare it, or consume it. Mainly because she's spent the majority of her life not eating like a normal person, because it was literally her job for decades to only eat the bare minimum of selected food groups in order to be alive, light as a feather, and at the same time strong as an ox and stretchier than an elastic band.

I'm not saying that all dancers have a questionable relationship with food, but Mum certainly does. She doesn't understand things like multipacks, or buy two get one free, and so on, which is why the trip to Asda was so highly unusual.

So, when we got there, she literally couldn't do it.

Instead of a bag of potatoes, she was putting, like, eight single ones into the trolley. Ditto four carrots. Four apples. Then she was getting into a proper frenzy and started chucking all sorts of random shit in the cart that made no collective sense whatsoever, and when she chose two kiwis, a lime, a leek, and a whole living coriander, I was just like: "What are you doing?" and she was like: "Grandad has to eat a healthy diet."

"Everyone has to eat a healthy diet. But it should be eatable."

She looked at the bananas she was holding like she was going to start a conversation with them, and so I quickly grabbed them and put them in the trolley before she could change her mind.

"Emilin said that we have to prepare every meal for him," I lied. I don't know why. I think I wanted to scare her.

"We'll all take turns with the cooking. It'll be fine," Mum said. But you know when you know they're wrong? "And on Fridays we'll get fish and chips. I know he and Sarah used to do that."

"Great, problem solved," I said, but under my breath.

We pushed through the dairy aisle, then perused the breakfast cereals, a place Mum had clearly never been to, because her face was all twitchy. She looked at everything in a really hectic way, and then chose Bran Flakes.

I got Frosted Flakes for me. That's another thing: When your parent doesn't do food, they really don't care what you do about it either.

When I thought we were done, Mum went down the toiletries aisle, and I was like: Please tell me she's going to buy tampons in front of me for the first time ever, but you know how they say you should be careful what you wish for? Well, she wasn't after tampons at all, but went to the adult nappy section and was like: "Emilin said the nurse said he should wear one at night. Just in case."

I looked at Mum, who then looked at me, and I pictured this

whole scenario in my head of my grandfather, the most dignified person I knew, wetting the bed. And it wasn't that I was put off by the prospect of having to change wee-stained sheets, but that I could be the one he'd have to tell, and then I wondered if that would be worse than finding an actual adult nappy in the rubbish.

I don't know what Mum was thinking in that moment, but I suddenly felt this red-hot panic rise up inside me, and I didn't know what to do, and so I just stood there and watched Mum put the pack into the trolley with her pale and bony yet elegant hand, and I felt almost sorry for her.

We didn't say a single word on the whole journey back.

The adult nappy situation got dealt with the way the arrival of my period had been dealt with: all hush-hush and cringe, and basically completely unacceptable by normal people's standards.

Mum made Dad take Grandad into the bathroom ("He's your father, Roger, not mine!"), and Dad whispered at him for what must have been the actual worst thirty seconds of both their lives.

It ended with a door being slammed and then I didn't see Grandad again for the rest of the evening.

I messaged Teddy about it, and he WhatsApp called me straightaway.

"That's intense," he said.

"I know."

"Imagine having to do that for your parents one day."

"I'd rather do it for strangers."

"Same. That's sick, isn't it?"

"Totally."

"I got in, by the way. *Cupid's Revenge*."

"Well, Cupid's revenge, indeed. All you wanted was to schmooze Katherine Cooper-Bunting, and now you're going to have to really go the extra mile."

I thought he'd at least laugh at my lame attempt at a joke, but he said nothing.

"What?" I asked.

"Please, Tilly, I know you have a lot on, and I'm sorry for going on and on about this, but will you just come to the thing? You know how rubbish I am at learning stuff by heart, and you can be my script girl or something."

"And just like that, all my dreams have been realized," I said to him, and looked at myself in my bedroom mirror. I was eyebrow central, so I picked up my tweezers.

"No, listen," Teddy said. "I've been thinking about the thing you said. About having to fill an evening. And unless Brian only has that Olivia girl and Katherine, and maybe the Polish guy, and that butcher woman, and that old dude who sang about the enchanted evening, it's going to be a bit shit, isn't it? But not just shit-shit, but cringe-shit. And I need you to be there to witness it."

"That would be such a loser thing to do," I said, and plucked one really long eyebrow hair out slowly, which hurt so much that my eyes watered. "Like I have no life or something, and nothing to do but watch you and a bunch of weirdos pretending to be people you're not."

"It's Monday to Friday twelve till four. What else are you doing?"

"I've got stuff to do," I said, and the plucking made me sneeze.

"Bless you."

"Thank you. Why are you so keen to have me there? I'm not going to help you with Katherine Cooper-Bunting, Teds—I'm telling you that right now."

"I need you!" he shouted.

"You're the one who fancies her, not me," I lied, putting down the tweezers and plopping down on my bed.

"I don't know how to talk to her."

"Why not?"

"Because I'm stupid. Come on, Tilly. You're a woman—you can help."

"I'm a woman who likes women," I said to him, because I obviously wasn't going to tell him the truth, which was that I couldn't stop fantasizing about her. "Which means I'm as awkward with them as you are. Maybe you need to find yourself another female BFF," I suggested. "A straight one."

"Where's Grace when you need her?"

"Well, no, because you loved her. She'd be no help to you with this."

"It's all her fault, really," Teddy said, and I think he was smiling.

"Bloody Grace-face. Dying on us."

"It was literally rude. Come with me tomorrow!" he pleaded. "You know you want to."

"I actually don't," I lied.

"Sleep on it?"

"Maybe. Bye," I said, and hung up.

Two seconds later, my phone beeped.

Meet you outside at 11:15, Teddy wrote.

Of course I wanted to go with him.

Katherine Cooper-Bunting would 100 percent be there, which meant I could at least look at her. Like, when you're a kid and you go to the posh cake shop, and your dad's all like: "You can look, but you're not allowed to touch."

"Life's so unfair," I said to the ceiling.

———

I had weird dreams that night about Mum and Emilin and periods, and Grandma coming back from the dead, and then I dreamed about Teddy and Katherine Cooper-Bunting making out in the rhododendrons, but suddenly I was literally eye to eye with Katherine Cooper-Bunting's nipple, which was what finally jerked me out of my half-awake stupor at three in the morning.

I took a deep breath, lay back down, and closed my eyes.

I was still half aroused, half disturbed, and I couldn't get back to sleep, and then I wondered how wrong it would be to masturbate now, because, yes, a good orgasm would probably make me fall asleep again, but at the same time, you can't masturbate when you're thinking about an actual person, can you?

But you know what happens when you think about not masturbating . . .

Scene 9

Fine, I'll admit it was probably the early morning orgasm followed by me contemplating Katherine Cooper-Bunting as I was pouring milk over my Frosted Flakes at breakfast that made me tell my parents I'd be attending rehearsals for a "West End cabaret type thing" with Teddy for the foreseeable future.

I obviously also knew this would have to make them think of arrangements in regard to Grandad, and I could see the wheels turning in Mum's head, and before she could come out with the obvious, which was making it my problem again by saying something like: "But what about your grandad?" I told them the cabaret was raising money for Acting for Others, at which point Dad looked at Mum, and both looked at me and went: "That's a great cause—well done, Tilly."

Dad even hummed "Land of Hope and Glory," and Grandad, who was sitting at the piano at the time, then started playing it and, because all the windows were open, you could probably hear it all the way to Balham. *Please, God, don't let everyone in our street think we're Tories.*

Teddy grinned from ear to ear when he saw me walking toward the bus stop. "Shut it," I said, and then he hugged me, stuck his tongue in my ear, and I was just like: "Get off!"

"Good afternoon, ladies and gentlemen, and a very warm welcome to *Cupid's Revenge*."

Brian beamed down at us all from the tiny stage at Clapham Social Club, and the room erupted into spontaneous applause, which clearly delighted him to no end, and he bowed like he'd done something spectacular.

"I am so utterly pleased about this project, and as you all know, it's for a good cause, as well as a love letter to my darling husband, Malcolm, who"—Brian took a deep breath, and Teddy took my hand and squeezed it—"after four long and agonizing weeks on a ventilator"—Teddy now squeezing harder—"made a full recovery."

"Shut up!" Teddy said, and then exhaled for ages.

Katherine Cooper-Bunting, who was sitting exactly where she'd been sitting during the audition, at two o'clock from us (we were also sitting exactly where we'd been sitting during the audition), turned round.

Teddy waved at her in a completely exaggerated way, all hands and elbows, like he hadn't seen her until that very moment, which was obviously bullshit, because he hadn't visually let go of her since she'd entered the room, and she wrinkled her perfect nose and turned back to look at Brian.

I felt a red-hot stab in my solar plexus, and then a gentle tingling radiated out into every nerve ending.

Katherine, I thought, and then I remembered that my personal fan fiction about us was one thing, but doing anything about it in real life was essentially the absolute worst kind of deep and unforgivable betrayal.

"You should congratulate her on getting in," I quickly whispered to Teddy.

"And sound like a condescending dick?"

"Maybe say you knew she'd get in or something."

Teddy looked around. "The tragic thing is," he whispered even closer to my ear, "I don't think anyone didn't get in."

I craned my neck in all directions, and he was right. Even the Phantom of the Opera and his wife were there.

"This is so bad," I said, and wondered how gutted Katherine Cooper-Bunting was about that.

"I haven't decided on the full program yet," said Brian, who'd put his glasses on and was looking at the tiniest of notepads, "because I want the opportunity to get to know you all a bit better—"

"You've known me forty-odd years!" Maeve heckled.

"I can't believe she's a butcher," Teddy whispered.

"Why not?"

"Because . . . I don't know."

"Because she's a woman, right? Why can't women be butchers? That's such a dumbass thing to think."

"No. I mean, imagine gutting and cutting up animals for a living."

"Well, someone's gotta do it. Or did you want to do it yourself?"

"Tills, if I had to hunt and kill and fillet my dinner, I'd be a vegetarian."

"I think you should meditate on that in greater detail and then make better choices."

"And I'm especially pleased to have so many young people joining us," Brian announced.

"Hear, hear," Teddy said in a moment of manliness, which resulted in everyone looking at us, and Brian looking down at his pad and going: "Theodore Booker."

Then Brian looked at me, at his notes, flicked back and forth between pages, looked up at me again and went: "I'm sorry, but you didn't audition for me, did you?"

And you know when everyone looks at you and it's not Zoom, so you can't just leave the room and regroup and come back like: "So sorry, Wi-Fi's shit."

I looked at Olivia because she was right next to Brian, and she was suddenly all aggressive-looking, like I was going steal her lover or her spotlight or something. I realized that her friend was there again, too, and so in that moment of acute panic, I did the thing the guilty or unprepared do in those situations: I pointed my finger at someone else, in this case the friend, and went: "She didn't audition, either."

Brian looked at me, smiled, and went: "No, but *they* are going to help us find and tailor the costumes."

And you know when you could just die?

With all eyes now on me, and Olivia obviously furious about me misgendering her friend in such a pathetic act of desperation, I made the final fatal error of looking at none other than Katherine Cooper-Bunting, who was smirking, and that's when I was like: What is language?

Teddy looked at me like I'd had a stroke, which would have been a much better excuse than nervousness followed first by ignorance, then stupidity, and he went: "Yeah, Brian, the thing is, I've got a very active mind, and sometimes when I'm really into a scene I can forget my lines, and we were wondering if Tilly here could be my personal script person. You know, it just helps to have someone on the book."

Brian, and everybody, looked at me, and I went: "I've got a photographic memory," which, luckily, wasn't even that much of a lie, because I kind of do have that.

Brian looked at me another moment, then shrugged and went: "I could use an assistant director," he said. "Which means you'll be everybody's script person. And you'll note down my stage directions. And if I can't be here, you'll oversee rehearsal."

"I—"

"Marvelous, we have a deal," Brian said before I could even think about it. "And you're Tilly, are you?"

"Tilly Taylor," I said, and looked at Olivia who still seemed a bit put out, but had relaxed significantly, probably because she knew I wasn't going to steal her anything.

Then Brian insisted the whole company (including the assistant director and the wardrobe person) take part in the ice-breaker exercise.

"All right," he said, clapping his hands to get our attention. "For the next ten minutes I want you all to really get to know one another, okay? But you're not going to speak. And don't just engage with the people you already know. That's not what this is about, okay? You're going to choose an animal that best represents you, and you're going to explore one another as these animals. You've got ten minutes." And then he started one of those actual ancient stopwatches no one's ever seen in real life.

I already knew the way he said "okay?" at the end of most sentences would grate on me.

I spent an awkward three minutes on all fours, kind of sniffing Miroslaw, who I felt drawn to as soon as I saw him roll his eyes. I think he was a goat, because he kept biting imaginary things and was pretend-chewing sideways.

I'd decided to be a horse, but only because I could literally think of nothing else.

Maeve made a big song and dance of lowering herself onto the floor, but Brian ignored her.

I was peacefully grazing in my pasture when I came across Teddy, who was bopping his head like a chicken, making clucking noises, even though I'm sure he was pretending to be a rooster. He pecked at me and whispered at me to fuck off back to my own farmyard, and I pranced, still on my hands and knees, back toward Miroslaw, who I saw rubbing his head against a table leg on the far side of the room.

I was intercepted by Katherine Cooper-Bunting, who was trotting across the filthy carpet like a prize dressage pony, and I decided I needed her to understand just how cringe I found this exercise, and I was just about to fall out of character and whisper something stupid about horsing around, when she came closer and closer, and suddenly we were just two horses who realized they were the same species and trapped in a petting zoo. She advanced farther and kind of inserted her nose in the crook of my neck and then she was sniffing me.

And all four of my horsey legs were suddenly made of jelly, and I let out a breathy whinny, which she answered by actually nose-butting me.

Instead of nuzzling her back like a good horse, I kind of scuttled on the spot all panicky, shaking my head as if someone was yanking my invisible reins, breathing in through my nose again and again and again to smell her.

Katherine Cooper-Bunting, suddenly blinking in a non-horsey way, and now very obviously regarding me like a person on all fours having some sort of erratic equine episode, wrinkled her forehead, snickered, and then had the absolute audacity to wink at me.

She turned round, wiggled her bum, and set off at a gentle canter.

The next person I looked at was Teddy, who had clearly witnessed the whole interaction, and my heart just stopped.

Act II

Scene 1

was obviously 100 percent completely mortified by the look on Teddy's face.

But I was also 100 percent completely aroused by Katherine Cooper-Bunting.

So much so that I wanted to throw myself at her in a horsey, full-frontal way, chest to chest, with my neck exposed, my hair wild, and foaming at the mouth.

I imagined Grace-face standing at the edge of the paddock, watching me, shaking her head in complete disbelief, like: What on earth are you doing, Matilda Taylor?

Which is why I decided it would be wise to avoid Katherine Cooper-Bunting for the rest of the afternoon.

I mean, not because of Grace, exactly, but because the image of her was clearly my conscience and, as I've said: Katherine Cooper-Bunting belonged to Teddy.

But that lusty tingling under my skin wouldn't go away, and I knew I absolutely had to see her just one more time before we went home, and so I conveniently timed my trip to the toilet to intercept her.

Does that sound creepy? Yes.

Would you have done the same? Of course you would have.

She must have been in a daydream, because she was smiling a huge smile that didn't fade even when she saw me, and I must have looked like a deer, or a horse, or possibly a mule in headlights.

"All right?" she asked, tilting her head sideways, and I was just like: "Yeah, fine," and then I went to wash my hands, and I looked at her through the mirror.

"How did you find this afternoon?" she asked.

Do you mean in general or when you almost licked my face? I thought.

"Did you get that I was being a horse?" I asked.

"I got that."

"Oh good."

"I really love those kinds of exercises. It's all part of the process, isn't it?"

I went: "Hmmm," and kind of up and down the octave to show enthusiasm and hide the fact that I obviously thought these kinds of exercises were complete bollocks because, let's be honest, how does it help Brian to cast a cabaret if he's got a bunch of kids and geriatrics crawling around on the floor, making animal noises, and most of them wishing they hadn't come?

"Anyway," Katherine Cooper-Bunting said, and smiled at me through the mirror. "See you tomorrow."

"Bye," I said, and looked back at her, and because I literally couldn't help myself, I raised my eyebrows at her and smiled.

She winked at me, scrunched up her perfect little nose, and left the toilets.

I felt heat rise from the hidden depth of my organs/soul and watched my face crack into an absurd smile.

I took a deep breath.

"What are you doing?" I whispered at my reflection, knowing perfectly well what I was doing.

I gave it another minute before I made my way to the bus stop where Teddy was waiting for me.

He was talking to Miroslaw.

"Are you waiting for the two nineteen?" I asked Miroslaw, and he nodded.

"I live in Balham," he said, and he pronounced the *h*, which was a bit cute.

"Miroslaw's only just moved to the UK," Teddy told me, and I was trying to read his face to see if he was going to be weird with me after witnessing me on all fours with Katherine Cooper-Bunting, but I couldn't make out what he was thinking.

"Why?" I asked Miroslaw. "I mean, why did you come to live here of all places?"

"My parents, they wanted a better life for me."

"Oh," I said. "Did you have a bad life? I thought Poland was really normal."

"Yes, but our village in Poland is still not very good for gay people."

"Oh," I said, and I know you shouldn't judge a book by its

cover, but I never in a million years would have thought he was into boys.

"I'm gay, too," I said to him, but then I regretted it immediately, because it was obviously also a reminder for Teddy. In case he'd forgotten my gayness. And my gay horsey nibbling interaction with the girl he fancied. "So, you're into theater, then?" I quickly asked Miroslaw. "Do you want to be an actor?"

"No," he said. "Definitely not."

"Oh," I said, and looked at Teddy, who looked at Miroslaw like he was part of the inner circle now.

"My mother, she sent me here."

"Why?" I asked.

"Because she thinks community theater is a great way to meet other gay people."

"She's obviously not wrong," I said, and kind of curtsied.

"Yes, but you are the wrong kind of gay for me."

"Rude."

"No, no. My mother wants me to find a boyfriend."

All three of us laughed.

"Well, maybe we'll find you the right kind of gay person. There're so many gays in show business."

"There are gay people everywhere," Miroslaw said. "But my mother was like: 'Go to the community theater—don't sit at home.'"

"I'm sorry you had to leave Poland," I said.

"It was a family decision. We came here just before Brexit, so we could get pre-settled status."

"Don't you miss your friends?"

"Yes."

"Well, the good thing is now you've got new friends," Teddy said, and put a hand on Miroslaw's shoulder, and I looked at them standing there—Miroslaw head to toe in black denim, Teddy in khaki shorts and a white T-shirt with a pink Care Bear on it giving us a thumbs-up and the slogan HANDLE WITH CARE—and I knew that I could under no circumstances pursue Katherine Cooper-Bunting.

Not even in a horsey way.

Miroslaw got off a couple of stops before us, and once he'd gone, I was talking to Teddy like nothing at all had happened earlier at the pretend farmyard, and you know how that never works but makes things even more awkward than if you weren't saying anything at all? And the more you try to be all normal, the weirder you sound. And because you know you sound like an idiot, you try to not sound like one and just talk. I went on and on and on about what had happened that afternoon, and then I repeated the whole conversation we'd literally just had with Miroslaw, and when he could bear no more, Teddy finally was like: "Yeah, I know, Tilly. I was literally there."

By the time we got off the bus, Brian had created a *Cupid's Revenge* WhatsApp group, and had told us: Well done for day one, thespians, and that he was looking forward to working with us and already had excellent ideas regarding the program. It would be something memorable and utterly stunning, darlings.

Seconds later both Katherine Cooper-Bunting and Olivia had messaged a kissy emoji and the words: Thank you for today, Brian.

"Imagine trying that hard to be the star of the show," I said, but Teddy didn't say anything, just stuffed his phone back into the big side pocket of his shorts.

When we got to my front door, I was like: "See you tomorrow?" And because I said it like a question, I think I finally acknowledged to him that something wasn't right, but Teddy just went: "Yeah, I'll see you tomorrow—why wouldn't I see you tomorrow?" But he still wouldn't look at me.

When I went inside, Grandad was in the living room playing the piano, and Rachmaninoff was sitting next to the bench, looking up at him and blinking huge cat blinks every once in a while.

"Hi," I said.

"Hello, Tilly," Grandad said. He stopped playing, and the cat growled.

"Your cat likes me," he said, and petted Rachmaninoff's head.

"He's not our cat," I said. "He lives next door. His name is Rachmaninoff."

"Ah," Grandad said, and I presume the next piece he played was by the composer Rachmaninoff, because he smiled down at the cat and pulled faces at him.

The cat meowed his approval.

My phone dinged in my pocket, and I got it out.

I thought it was going to be a message from Teddy saying "sorry for being weird just now," but it was an IG follow request from Katherine Cooper-Bunting.

My eyes went all blurry and so I ran up the stairs and threw myself onto my bed, but I didn't dare look at my phone again because it felt like Katherine Cooper-Bunting was somehow aware of my every move now that she had actively looked for me on IG.

I lay there and thought about our encounter as horses. Then I thought about her smile in the toilet.

I picked up my phone again and googled "How do I set up two of my friends?" but the list was too long and too extensive and too obvious, and so I just let my phone slide from my weak grasp and onto the floor.

When Mum got home, we made dinner together, a.k.a. we opened a packet of washed and ready-to-eat salad, shoved three potatoes in the microwave, and heated a tin of beans, and I told her what little I knew about *Cupid's Revenge*.

She was all like: "That sounds very good, Tilly. I'm really pleased you've finally found something you're passionate about."

Typical for her to exaggerate.

In her world, you couldn't just enjoy something. You had to be obsessed. It was all or nothing. Always.

"And you know," she continued, chopping cucumber into

the tiniest little cubes imaginable, "the people behind the scenes are just as important as the people onstage. They usually have much better and longer careers, too." And then she went: "I don't know why we've never thought about this before, but a lot of people like you work in stage management. And in LX. How do you feel about lighting?"

I rolled my eyes.

At all of it.

But mainly at the "people like you" part, which obviously meant lesbians.

I decided not to be offended, because OMG, like, I'm tired, but I chopped carrots with a lot more force than was strictly necessary. I also made the slices huge.

Rachmaninoff stayed for dinner, but instead of sitting on the floor like a normal cat, he shouted until we pulled up a chair for him, so he could sit at the table. Grandad was like: "No one likes to eat alone," and I was like: "He's not actually eating," and then Grandad gave him a baked bean, which the cat literally inhaled. Grandad was like: "And have you noticed that he has no teeth? It's got to be tough for a cat to not be able to kill its prey. He can't live on baked beans."

"I wouldn't worry about him," I said. "He gets wet food, and he always licks the jelly off first. And then he shouts for someone to put some liquid squeezy treat on the rest. He's really okay."

"Rachmaninoff's a bully," Mum said, and put a tiny piece of cucumber in front of him, and he nearly took her hand off.

When Grandad headed upstairs to have his bath and go to bed, with Rachmaninoff hot at his heels, Mum was like: "Remember, that's not our cat, Douglas."

Grandad just looked at her with such obvious underlying annoyance, and went: "Yes, I know. He lives next door. You told me this half an hour ago."

Instead of leaving it, Mum went: "I just wanted to make sure."

And Grandad went: "I'm not that forgetful yet. Jesus, Suzanne."

And Mum was like: "I'm sorry. Just make sure you don't lock him in your room, because he has to go home at some point. He's not allowed out overnight. He may not have teeth, but he's still a menace."

We watched them both ascend the stairs, Grandad shaking his head, and Rachmaninoff hobbling up on his three legs, chatting all the way.

"Your father has suggested your grandad should join a group that helps people with Alzheimer's," Mum said. "It's over Wandsworth way, and they play cards and board games, and you can do painting and all sorts of arts and crafts. Apparently all that helps the brain."

"He'll love it," I said. "Let's just hope he's already forgotten how much he hates board games."

"Do you think your sarcasm is helpful, Tilly?" Mum asked, and looked at me in such an annoying way that I wanted to scream. "We're not doing this for us, you know, but for your grandad."

"Are you?"

"Excuse me?"

"I know Grandad's only here because Dad's emotionally scarred because of Grandma dying alone, and he's clearly trying to rid himself of his guilt. But I'm telling you now that Grandad's going to literally hate going to a games afternoon. He knows that he's got Alzheimer's, so can you imagine for just one second how much he's going to hate playing stupid snakes and ladders with a bunch of people whose brains have literally deteriorated to the point where they don't know who or where they are? Have you met the man?"

Mum looked at me.

"And just FYI," I continued, "I'm not taking him there. I'm not his carer. Dad can do it. It's his idea."

"Your father has a matinee on Thursdays. And would it really be too much for you to take your grandad to a community center once a week on your way to your rehearsal and pick him up on your way home? He doesn't have anyone here, he's lost his wife, he's coming to terms with his disease—"

"Now you're trying to guilt me into this?" I asked. Because she was.

"Get out of my sight, Tilly. I don't need this from you," Mum said, and then she walked out into the garden.

I went upstairs and sat on the floor in front of my mirror.

"What a life," I said to my reflection.

Then I looked at my favorite picture of Teddy and Grace and me that I kept Blu-Tacked to the top right-hand corner. All three of us were on the rusty old merry-go-round on the playground on Tooting Bec Common. Teddy's mum took the picture literally seconds before Grace flew off it and landed a good ten meters away, facedown in the sand. We all look completely crazed.

Below was a picture of Grandma and Emilin and me at Tayto Park in Ireland.

It's one of those photos they take of you when you're on a roller coaster. Grandma is sitting between Emilin and me, and we both have our eyes closed and faces all squished up, but Grandma is screaming.

"You suck, Tilly," I said to myself.

Because of course I'd take Grandad somewhere and pick him up.

And, yes, I'd read in an online article that keeping socially active and trying new things was super important for people with dementia and Alzheimer's, but everybody knew that Grandad hated board games.

And then I thought, well, maybe that's why Mum's so arsy, because she knows it's a shit idea, but she doesn't have a better one.

LOL, to think that once upon a time I believed my parents knew everything.

I quickly checked whether Teddy and Katherine Cooper-Bunting were already friends on IG, but they weren't, which meant that I couldn't accept her follow request, because then Teddy would be cross if he checked.

I was wondering why didn't she send him one, too, and then my brain came up with a gazillion scenarios of what might have happened and was currently happening, and when my head was spinning from it all, I think I finally truly understood the need of there being parallel universes. Like, there had to be at least one where this situation wasn't hopeless. One where Teddy had ended up with Grace-face. Or where I found Katherine Cooper-Bunting appalling.

I decided to read some *Lucifer* fan fiction, but I couldn't really get into it, mainly because the women in it are all really old, and who wants to imagine old people having sex?

What I did learn, however, is that the whole #friendstolovers thing is a fan-fiction favorite, and I thought, fine, maybe I need to help Teddy and Katherine Cooper-Bunting on their #friendstolovers journey.

I reluctantly read a couple of stories, and the problem with that trope is that the transition always seems to happen within two paragraphs, which obviously makes it completely unrealistic. And, yes, I realize it's called fan *fiction*. But people in real life obviously won't get from a first kiss to having their tongue literally inside the other person in under five minutes. I mean, fair enough, if these writers didn't move it along, no one would ever read up to the good bit, which—and Teddy had been absolutely correct about this—was absolutely always one person on her knees giving "soul-shattering" cunnilingus.

I'd just started reading another #lesbian #friendstolovers #oralsex fanfic when my phone bleeped. It was Teddy.

> Do you fancy Katherine Cooper-Bunting?

I jumped off my bed, my movement so violently sudden that I saw black dots, then nothing but white, and the next thing I knew, I was lying on the floor, looking up at the ceiling.

I felt panicky sick.

I imagined Teddy's little puppy-dog face.

I imagined Grace looking at me, waiting for me to answer.

Which is why I didn't, even for a millisecond, contemplate telling him the truth.

> Of course I don't.

> Because I really like her.

You don't even know her, I thought—though when did I become the expert in all things Katherine Cooper-Bunting?

> You know I don't actually want a GF.

> Besides, she's not my type.

> You don't have a type.

> So don't worry about it. She's all yours.

I waited for him to message me back, but he went offline.

He was still offline fifteen minutes later. I was still on the floor.

Eventually I got up and had a shower.

Under the hot water I thought of Katherine Cooper-Bunting, who was exactly my type.

Scene 2

"Our bodies are our instruments, okay?" Brian boomed as he walked around and over us as we lay scattered on the disgusting floor at Clapham Social Club in the semi-supine position.

"It is our duty as performers to maintain them so that they perform at peak efficiency all day every day, but especially the moooooooment the curtain goes up. Again. Take a deep breath in through your nose, and let the air go all the way deep down into your belly. Hold it there for one, two, three, relax your jaw, and just let it out. Ahhhhhhhhhhhhhhhhhhhhh!"

You know when you're just like: *How did I get here?*

Teddy had been weird on the bus, still all mopey and giving one-word answers, and I was beginning to wonder if *Cupid's Revenge* was the worst decision we'd ever made. And when I say we, I obviously mean me.

I looked up at the ceiling, at the awful lights that looked like those at school, and saw there was flaky water damage in the corner.

I could hear the birds outside, someone lying somewhere behind me had already fallen asleep and was snoring, and

Katherine Cooper-Bunting and Olivia were out-sighing each other somewhere over to my right.

"You should do your vocal exercises daily and whenever you have a minute, okay? Your voice must be resilient. It must be healthy, and it must carry. You should avoid alcohol, nicotine, and dairy products."

I turned my head to look at Miroslaw, who was lying directly to my left, and I remembered that he was only here because his mother had told him to meet other gays.

I giggled.

He rolled his eyes.

I looked to my right and the person I'd misgendered and whose name I still hadn't learned rolled their eyes at me, too, which made me feel like, not only had they forgiven me, but that I was truly among friends, after all.

"Repeat after me," Brian said, and took a deep breath. "Dim drums throbbing, in the hills half heard."

I don't know if it was the way he delivered it or the throbbing bit, but the deep breath I'd just taken literally evacuated out of my nose and mouth at the same time. I pretended to cough, and I thought surely no one was going to say it back, but of course Katherine Cooper-Bunting and Olivia were on it like white on rice.

"Dim drums throbbing, in the hills half heard," they projected into the universe.

"And again," said Brian. "Dim drums throbbing, in the hills half heard."

"Dim drums throbbing, in the hills half heard," repeated the room minus whoever was still snoring, and myself, who was sort of just mumbling.

"Dim drums throbbing, in the hills half heard," said Brian, this time clapping on every syllable to urge us along.

"Dim drums throbbing, in the hills half heard," we repeated, now in rhythm.

I could make out Teddy's voice, and I was aware of my own, and I just thought: *If Grace were here, we'd be absolutely dead with laughter already.*

Soon the room became a pulsating beast of "Dim drums throbbing, in the hills half heard," and I was just wondering to what lengths people will go in order to get famous, when I looked to my right again, to find the person I'd misgendered had ceased chanting and was literally laughing so hard that they had tears running down the side of their face and dripping into their ear.

When they saw me looking at them, they laughed even harder, and then I snorted, which made us absolutely die, and when the others had finally stopped, all you could hear was the person who was still snoring, and us being all hilarity-snot and tears.

We introduced ourselves the moment we got up from the floor.

Their name was Robin.

"Nice to meet you," I said, and we actually shook hands.

"I hope I didn't sabotage your voice work there."

"I'm not sure this exercise is really for the assistant director and script person."

"Or the wardrobe person," they said. "Although you will be using your voice."

"Only if someone forgets their lines or where to stand."

"The throbbing ended me," Robin said, wiped their eyes, and did another cough-laugh. "Who comes up with that shit?"

"I bet Brian's a poet in his spare time," I suggested, and we laughed again.

Brian then told us all to have half an hour's break before he was going to lead us into an "afternoon improvisation."

Olivia approached Robin and me, and Robin introduced us like: "Olivia, Tilly; Tilly, Olivia."

"Nice to meet you," I said, but Olivia and I didn't shake hands.

"This is Miroslaw," I said, and pulled him into the conversation by his arm. "He's only just moved to England."

"Sorry about that," Olivia said.

"It's okay," Miroslaw said.

"I'm Olivia."

"I'm Robin. I'm they/them."

"Miroslaw. I am he," he said. "I am here to meet other gays."

"Sorry, mate. I'm straight," Olivia said.

"You've got a great voice," I said to her, and she was like: "Thanks," and then she looked at Robin, and was like: "Do you want to go to the shop?"

"Sure," Robin said, and shrugged, and then they looked at me and Miroslaw, and were like: "Do you want to come?" and I was like: "Sure," and as I said it, I looked around to see if Katherine Cooper-Bunting had noticed I was talking to her apparent nemesis and her nemesis's sidekick, and of course she had.

She quickly looked away, though, rummaged through her bag, got out a cardigan, and put it on before sitting down on one of the plastic chairs with her back to us.

I walked over to Teddy and said: "We're going to the shop. Why don't you ask you-know-who what she's doing?"

"Why don't you?" he asked, and looked at me all annoyingly challenging.

"Because I'm going to the shop with Robin and Olivia and Miroslaw."

"Just go, then."

"Why are you being so weird?"

"I'm not being weird."

"Yes, you're weird, and you need to stop it. I told you I don't want her. Nothing's changed since I told you that."

"She keeps looking at you," Teddy said, and my heart did a weird sort of cardiac hiccup.

"Probably because we got on really well yesterday, and today

I'm avoiding her like the actual plague, which is something I'm doing purely because I don't want you to think that I'm trying to steal your *girlfriend.*" And I sort of angry-whispered "girlfriend," which made Teddy angry-looking. "Teds, I'm not trying to cramp your style."

"Fine."

"So ask her the fuck to come to the shop with us all, and if she says yes, you can walk with her, and en route you can ask her if she's on IG, or if she has pets, or whatever, but please can you start acting like a normal person and stop being a total twat, because I haven't done anything."

He looked at me.

I looked at him.

"Why can't I talk to her like a normal person?" he whined.

"Because you fancy her," I said, and looked across to find her looking at us.

Heat shot from my insides all the way to my face and scalp, and my brain fizzed.

"Go," I whispered to him, and Teddy exhaled and then trotted over to where Katherine Cooper-Bunting was sitting and now drinking from a water bottle.

I watched him speak to her, I watched her look over at Robin, Olivia, Miroslaw, and then me, look back at him, smile and nod, and oh, my heart.

"Let's do one," Robin said to us, put on their backpack, and I followed them outside.

We walked together but sort of in a four and a two, with Teddy and Katherine Cooper-Bunting trailing fifty meters behind us.

From the looks that Olivia and Katherine Cooper-Bunting had given each other the moment our small group assembled outside, it was clear that they a) weren't friends, b) probably hadn't been friends for quite some time, and c) possibly actually never were friends to begin with.

We walked down to the Co-op on Northcote Road.

I wanted to go to the bakery section and get a cinnamon swirl, but Teddy and Katherine Cooper-Bunting were there and taking forever, and even though I wanted nothing more than to squeeze myself into the tight space between Katherine Cooper-Bunting and the basket of freshly baked buns, I resisted and went to the crisp aisle instead with Robin and Olivia, where we decided to share a big bag of Doritos.

I met Miroslaw at the checkout.

"What are you getting?" I asked.

"Meal deal," he said. "It's great. You get a sandwich and a drink and chips." He held up a bag of salt and vinegar Hula Hoops.

"We call them crisps," I said. "But those we call Hula Hoops."

"Are they good?" he asked.

"They're, like, standard."

"I'll try them."

I watched Miroslaw scan his items and get out a brand-new

bank card, and I just thought: *Imagine moving to Poland and having to open a bank account. And then imagine going to the self-service checkout machine in Poland and it being all in your face about loyalty cards and 10p bags. In Polish. And you having to press the right buttons.*

Robin and Olivia were already outside, and we passed around the hand sanitizer, and then Olivia went: "Mate, let's just go. They probably want to be alone anyway."

"You think?" I asked because I'm a masochist, and then I pulled a face that I hoped looked like I was utterly surprised by her observation.

"He's way too nice for her," Olivia said.

And I was like: "Is she not nice?"

Olivia was like: "Mate, when someone does Lady Macbeth in an audition, you literally know everything you need to know about them."

"She's not actually a murderer," I said.

"Doing that monologue is literally the most arrogant thing you could possibly do in an audition. Only people who're, like, actual celebrities get to play that part. She totally reckons herself."

Robin laughed and was like: "To be fair, you did a song from *Wicked*," and Olivia was like: "Yes, mate, but I didn't do the biggest song of the show. I could have done, but I didn't, because I'm *not* arrogant, innit?"

"Do you and Katherine go to the same school or something?"

I asked, and I felt all woozy saying her name like that out loud and in public. It sounded, I don't know, naked.

We'd arrived back at the social club and sat down outside the entrance on the crumbling wall.

"Cooper-Bunting and I used to do Stagecoach together," Olivia said, chewing Doritos. "I don't know why she isn't down there this summer. Her mum's one of the teachers, and Cooper-Bunting's, like, everyone's favorite."

"Interesting," I said, but kind of to myself, because hadn't Katherine Cooper-Bunting said the exact same thing about Olivia?

"No, mate," Olivia went. "She's literally the dullest person you'll ever meet. Trust me. Her father's a priest."

"He's a priest with the Church of England," Robin cut in, half laughing, half rolling their eyes. "You always make it sound like it's weird, and it's not."

"No, mate, it's weird. They have, like, a gazillion children," Olivia said.

"They do not," Robin said.

"No, they do not. She's one of ten or something," Olivia said. "And they're all dull."

"They are a bit dull," Robin agreed. "And Teddy looks like so much fun," they added.

Next to me, Miroslaw retched, and we were all like: *Are you okay?*

"This is shit," he said, pulled a disgusted face, and held up the packet of Hula Hoops.

"Salt and vinegar, mate," Olivia said.

"Do you not have this flavor in Poland?" Robin said.

Miroslaw shook his head. "It's disgusting."

"Welcome to the UK," I said, and offered Miroslaw the bag of Doritos.

He took one and ate it.

"This is much better, no?" he said, and smiled at us.

"I'd say," Olivia said. "Vinegar makes my throat go all scratchy. It's not good for my voice, innit. And let's face it, singin's, like, the only thing I'm good at."

"That's not true, you're good at loads of things," Robin cut in straightaway.

"Name one."

"Like . . . I don't know—"

"See?"

"Hair and makeup."

"Yeah, but I ain't going to beauty school and then earn fuck all at some shit nail bar or salon."

"Being a musician is actually really annoying," I said. "Because you're kind of surviving from one contract to another, and sometimes there's nothing in between."

"But if you're extra, you can tell people where you want to sing, what you want to sing, and how much you want to earn."

"All right, Beyoncé," Robin said, and we laughed.

"You'll see, bitches," Olivia said, and smirked.

Then they appeared, Teddy and Katherine Cooper-Bunting, carrying one of those crinkly brown bakery bags. It contained doughnuts, and Teddy was eating one. He was doing that thing where he's kind of chewing slowly and dragging his feet because he thinks that's making him look casual, when in fact it just makes him look like an unpaid extra shuffling along in the background of a show about the zombie apocalypse.

"All right?" Robin asked, and Teddy looked at them, then pointed at their shirt and went: "That's pretty cool, by the way."

We all looked at the My Little Pony patch on it.

"You a fan?" Robin asked.

"Let's say I'm familiar with the fandom," Teddy replied, like he was talking about an actual fandom. "Friendship is magic," he added, and Robin's whole face lit up.

"Friendship *is* magic," they said back, and then they and Teddy did an actual fist bump.

"I'm more of a Care Bears guy myself," he declared, and I grinned first at Robin, then Olivia, then Miroslaw, who was of course on the exact other end of the color palette, and then at Katherine Cooper-Bunting, who was licking sugar off her thumb and seemed to have no emotions at all regarding this conversation.

"Care Bear alert," shouted Robin, and then there was another fist bump. "I actually have an original Care Bear. Well, it's my mum's, but she's kind of given her to me."

"No way," Teddy said, and stepped closer. "Which one?"

"Share Bear."

"The best one."

"Sharing is caring," Robin said, and held out the bag of Doritos.

Olivia rolled her eyes at me, took the bag of Doritos from Robin, and shoved way too many into her mouth.

Two seconds later, the brown bag containing doughnuts appeared in front of my eyes.

"Doughnut?" Katherine Cooper-Bunting asked. "Since sharing is caring."

On my visual journey from the bag via her fingers, hands, wrists, arms, collarbone, neck, chin, and mouth to her eyes, I noticed a slightly darker freckle just on the side of her nose, as well as a couple of grains of sugar on the tip, and I swear I salivated and felt my insides quiver.

I looked at Teddy, who was looking at me, then back at Katherine Cooper-Bunting, and all I could do was shake my head, because I knew I could never actually say no to her.

Scene 3

"Today I noticed that Rachmaninoff has no teeth. Did you know that?" Grandad asked at dinner.

I looked at my plate and started stabbing singular peas onto my fork.

"We talked about that yesterday, Douglas," Mum said. "Do you remember?"

"Oh yeah? I mean, I was just wondering. Because it must be tough for a cat. They hunt, don't they? How can he do that? Without teeth?"

"His favorite food is actually the juice from a tin of tuna fish," I said.

"Brine," Grandad said.

"Whatever."

"How was rehearsal today?" Mum asked me.

I watched Grandad get back to his dinner, and I wondered what he was thinking about.

"I don't have to do anything yet. But I met a few nice people. Like, our age."

"Good. I was worried about you, you know. Since Grace, you haven't really—"

"Mum—"

"All I'm saying is that, you know, you haven't really been doing anything with your time, have you?"

"What, apart from school, which, I assure you, has been anything but boring with GCSEs and everything."

"You know what I mean."

Of course I knew what she meant, and it made me ragey: Just because I didn't have some sort of greater calling in life ("calling," what bullshit), it didn't mean that I lived in a heightened state of being either bored or unfulfilled or lonely, or all three.

And I'm sorry, but their "calling" was nothing but a distraction, anyway.

The whole thing with Grace, for example, Teddy and I really felt it.

We didn't just run away from it and play the piano until our fingers bled or bend ourselves into the shape of a pretzel for hours even though we were, like, fifty.

Everyone else decided to get distracted so they didn't have to feel it.

We felt it.

We felt every excruciating second of it.

Which, if you ask me, makes us superhuman, and not to be pitied by emotionally inept people like my parents, who can't face life and who hide behind their art. Or who can't be in their own company and doing nothing for five minutes without feeling lonely and unfulfilled.

"Because, darling," Mum was still saying, "I'm really glad you've got Teddy, obviously, but there's going to be the day when Teddy is going to, well . . . I mean, not like with Grace, God forbid, but you know, he's a lovely guy and, you know, he may meet someone and want to start a relationship."

I was back to stabbing peas, and I caught one at the wrong angle and it flew halfway across the room.

"Tilly, sit up and eat your dinner like a grown-up," Mum said, and tried to rearrange me by violently shaking the backrest of my chair.

"Ouch!" I said, even though she obviously wasn't hurting me. "I'm also a nice person, you know, and I may meet someone, too."

"And I want that for you, darling, which is why I'm really glad you're doing your play and that there are other people your age. That was all I was trying to say to you. Why do you have to be so defensive all the time? And for the love of God, can you please stop slouching like that? You're killing your back."

"I don't need my back," I said, but kind of not to her but to my plate.

After dinner, Mum and I did the washing up, and Grandad played the piano. Rachmaninoff hopped in through the back door, and Grandad picked him up and made him sit on the stool next to him.

"Never tell Amanda her cat prefers someone else's playing," Mum said to me.

"Why is he literally obsessed with Grandad?"

"I wonder if your grandad could teach the cat," Mum said.

"Imagine the cat becoming a better musician than Teddy."

"Well, Amanda always says Rachmaninoff is her best child."

"I thought parents weren't allowed to have favorites," I said, and Mum did one of those pretend laughs very similar to the one I did that day in Teddy's front room when Katherine Cooper-Bunting walked into our life. "And when someone accuses you of having a favorite child, you're supposed to deny it," I told her.

"Not favorite," Mum said, and put the cutlery away. "Best. Her best child."

"Please don't ever tell me how you really feel," I said, because OMG, like I didn't already know Mum and Dad think the sun shines out of Emilin's arse, but hearing it was something else entirely.

"Tilly, I've talked to your grandad some more about the dementia-friendly games afternoon," Mum whispered awkwardly.

"I think all games afternoons would be dementia friendly, don't you?" I asked, but she ignored me.

"He wants to give it a go," she said. "Will you take him? It's two buses, and I don't want him to get lost."

"I've got rehearsal."

"I'm teaching in Richmond, and I've already told you your father has a matinee on Thursdays at the moment."

"I've got rehearsal," I said again, but slower, in case she hadn't heard me, and because for Emilin this had always worked. *Sorry, Mum, I can't do that thing you need me to do that I really don't want to do because I've got rehearsal. But I'm sure Tilly is free because she doesn't have rehearsal because her life is empty.*

"I've got rehearsal," I said again, kind of mumbly, but Mum heard me and gave me one of those looks that glues you to the spot, and since I knew I'd never be able to stage a full-on Emilin-style meltdown with crying and screaming, all like: "I can't miss reheeeeeeeeearrrrsaaaaal," I was just like: "I'll tell Brian I'll be late."

"You're my best child," Mum said.

"Lies," I told her. "But I don't care. I don't need you people to love me to feel valued as a person."

And with that, I walked up the stairs, feeling oddly empowered yet completely empty.

I'd left my phone to charge in my room, and when I checked it, I had IG follow requests from Robin and Olivia, and a WhatsApp message from Teddy.

> Katherine has sent me a follow request on IG.

Katherine, I thought. It still sounded odd. And exciting. And terrifying.

> Told you to ask her to the shop. You're welcome BTW.

He replied straightaway.

> All her pictures are theater related.

And you're surprised because . . .

IDK, I thought she'd be one of those people with loads of friends. FYI, I also had a follow request from Robin, and all their pictures are with other people. And they also skate.

You skated for, like, 5 mins.

I wasn't bad.

You fell off and sprained your wrist.

But I was good for five minutes.

Do you think I should message Katherine?

About what?

I don't know. I could say something cute.

Like what? You're seeing her tomorrow.

I'll ask her to spend the break with me again.

Go wild.

Not just yet.

You know that saying about every cloud having a silver lining? Well, with Teddy and Katherine now connected on social media, I was finally able to accept her follow request, which I did immediately, and I also sent her a follow request, which she accepted not thirty seconds later, which felt like a second and all eternity at the same time.

Teddy was right about her pictures. One was of her outside the Apollo Victoria Theatre where they show *Wicked*, one was outside the National Theatre where she saw a show called *Present Laughter*. Then there was a picture of her at the Globe Theatre, standing in front of an empty stage, holding an umbrella because it was raining.

Her most recent one was of the book of *Macbeth*.

In one picture she'd posted late last year, she was wearing a plain white dress, kneeling on a stage, gazing up toward the heavens. The description just said, *Remembering Romeo and Juliet. #TBT*.

I stared at it for a good five minutes, counting every freckle on her perfect face, tracing the lines of her lips with my eyes, and then I remembered reading *Romeo and Juliet* for school, except, of course I didn't read it but watched the film instead, because, let's face it, Shakespeare's horrendous. There's the scene when Leonardo DiCaprio is all breathy and fighting his way through undergrowth because he's stalking Juliet on the balcony, and he's like: "And Juliet is the sun."

And then, with all the conviction of dim drums throbbing, I took a deep breath all the way into my belly, and I said: "Juliet is the sun!"

I looked at Katherine Cooper-Bunting's picture again and threw my phone across the room and onto the pile of dirty washing.

"Juliet is the sun," I projected so that even the little old deaf lady in the back row could hear me.

"Keep it down, Tilly," Mum said, knocking on my door, and I don't know why, but the whole thing suddenly made me laugh hysterically.

Like, I was not okay.

Scene 4

Cupid's Revenge was set to run approximately one hour and twenty-five minutes without an interval, and Brian actually cried when he told us about the program.

He was like: "It's been a dream of mine to do something like this, okay? Not only because I've been longing to see my darling husband's deepest wish of performing his favorite song in front of an audience fulfilled, but because I think we're doing something amazing here." (At this point his well-trained and regularly exercised voice started wobbling.) "The pandemic's been brutal for so many, and especially for so many people in our profession who've lost their livelihoods, and it's just wonderful that all of you are here and willing to give up your free time"— huge wobble followed by a few fish-out-of-water gasps—"and share your talent and your love and your enthusiasm."

He pulled an actual handkerchief out of his tracksuit trousers and started wiping his eyes, and I was like: *OMG*, and Katherine Cooper-Bunting clutched her chest, and Teddy looked at me like everything was my fault and whispered: "We're imposters."

I elbowed him in the side, and he dramatically threw himself to lie across the empty chairs next to him, and I just thought:

Maybe this acting thing is your calling, after all, and Katherine Cooper-Bunting was merely the person who delivered you to it.

Everyone seemed pleased with Brian's selection of songs and scenes, apart from Olivia, who was given the song "As Long as He Needs Me" from the musical *Oliver!*

She was like: "This song's about a woman, yeah, who gets abused, yeah, and basically goes on about how much she loves the guy abusing her."

"It's a classic," Brian told her.

"Yeah, which is why everyone'll hum along and then clap. It's wrong, mate."

"You know, Brian, she does have a point," Maeve said.

"She does, but it's a nation's favorite. You don't have to do it, if you d—"

"No, I'll do it," Olivia said, flicked her ponytail over her shoulder, and looked at Brian from under her enormously long lashes. "I'm not a diva, innit."

And then she took a deep breath and started singing, "As long as he needs me," at triple the necessary volume.

Brian cut her off by clapping his hands three times. "Thank you, Olivia."

"You're welcome, mate," she said, and I felt elevated by her sass, which is why I turned my head and stared at Katherine Cooper-Bunting until she looked at me.

She wrinkled her cute nose like: *What?*

And I just smiled and shrugged but kept looking at her, and she blushed spectacularly.

Then Brian put the program up on the shitty noticeboard and was like: "But, since this is a group effort, I think it would be great for everyone to attend all rehearsals, okay? Of course, I'll understand if you have other engagements, but don't just come in for your scene twice a week. And we'll need everyone to think about their own costumes, too. But Robin here is going to be on hand to help with suggestions and alterations, and they will be frequenting local charity shops for items and ideas."

Robin raised their hand, even though I'm sure everyone knew who they were already.

"If it's a nice day, you can even take your scenes outside and rehearse by yourselves. And, Tilly," he said—and I raised my arm the way Robin had—"will be able to help you in case you've forgotten your stage directions, okay?"

Weirdly, only then did it dawn on me that I'd agreed to accompany the Phantom of the Opera and his wife on every step of their musical-theater journey. Cringe.

And, speaking of them, Brian had decided to not go with their original song but had given them one from a musical called *Annie Get Your Gun* instead. And just the one song, nothing else, whereas most people were given two performances. Even "Some Enchanted Evening" Charles was given two songs, "Some Enchanted Evening" and one called "If Ever I Would Leave You."

Olivia had "As Long as He Needs Me" from *Oliver!* and "The Wizard and I" from *Wicked*, Katherine Cooper-Bunting got her Lady Macbeth and then a scene with Teddy from a Shakespeare play called *As You Like It*.

Miroslaw was given a Shakespeare scene from *A Midsummer Night's Dream* opposite Maeve, and Maeve was given that plus two songs—one of them being the bad pies song she sang at the audition, which has nothing to do with the love theme, unless you love bad food, but I wasn't going to question Brian.

Katherine Cooper-Bunting took a picture of the program and rehearsal schedule, and Olivia did the same not three seconds later, and then everyone was doing it, including me, and I was like: *Herd immunity may not have been a thing, but herd mentality certainly is.*

"And, daaaaaaarlings," Brian said, watching us all, "we'll rehearse the opening number every day, okay? Because I know not all of you are confident singers, and I really want it to be fabulous. You know, National Theatre fabulous, darlings."

"Not Stagecoach fabulous," Olivia said, smiling.

Brian looked at her, smiled, too, and went: "Well, you know, grown-up fabulous, darling."

I looked at Katherine Cooper-Bunting, who looked at Olivia, and I couldn't read her expression. Which I found intriguing.

"And, unfortunately, I still haven't found us a pianist, but I may pop into St. Mark's when we're done today to see if they have an organist who's feeling generous."

"We can't do anything without a pianist," Maeve said, and shook her head.

"I just said I'm working on it," Brian told her. "Don't get your knickers in a twist. Right, everyone, let's warm up. On the floor and get into the semi-supine position."

Maeve was like: "Argheweeee, Jesus, Mary, and Joseph," but lowered herself down, a lot more able than she made out.

I watched as everyone was positioning themselves, and I don't know if it was me or her or gravity, but Katherine Cooper-Bunting and I ended up lying next to each other.

"Take a deep breath in," said Brian. "And sigh your breath out."

I did.

The right side of my body was buzzing from the proximity of Katherine Cooper-Bunting.

"Another deep breath in," Brian said. "And sigh the breath out."

I suddenly felt like I hadn't taken a conscious breath maybe ever.

Like breathing hadn't been a thing. Like all I'd done for all of my life thus far was hold my breath.

I inhaled again and stretched my neck, my spine, my legs, and then my arms.

The fingertip of my index finger brushed against one of Katherine Cooper-Bunting's fingers.

When she didn't pull away, my heart started tottering like a spooked Clydesdale.

I looked at her, but this time she completely ignored me, just kept breathing in and sighing out, and I had absolutely no idea what to do with myself.

———————

During break we all sat under the big trees on the grassy bit on the other side of the road and ate our lunch.

Katherine Cooper-Bunting was sitting opposite me, next to Teddy. At one point, when no one was looking because we were all listening to Olivia telling us about her job at WHSmith and how she always has to sort the porn magazines even though she's not old enough to purchase them, which obviously is LOL, Teddy pulled a fun-size KitKat from his backpack and casually placed it next to Katherine Cooper-Bunting's tuna mayo and sweetcorn sandwich.

She looked at him, smiled, mouthed, "Thank you"; Teddy mouthed, "You're welcome"; and my stomach just dropped, and I got all dizzy. But not the slap-happy kind. The awful kind.

"Do you get porn magazines in Poland?" Robin asked Miroslaw.

"Yes."

"Even gay porn?"

"Gay porn is like drugs. You have to buy it from a person you know."

"Mate, if we get a van, we can drive that shit to Poland once a month and make a mint."

"Okay. I'm in," Miroslaw said, and we all laughed.

"I'll see you in a minute," said Katherine Cooper-Bunting, putting her gifted KitKat in her bag and gathering her rubbish.

"Mate, we've got, like, ten minutes."

Katherine Cooper-Bunting shrugged. "I want to go over my lines."

"Surprised you don't know them already," Olivia said.

"You already know yours," Katherine Cooper-Bunting said. "But musical theater isn't exactly Shakespeare, is it?"

I looked at Teddy like: *Are they going to have a fight?* but he wouldn't even look at me, and so I looked at Robin who rolled their eyes at me, and I realized that this was what those two did.

"No, mate, but when I go wrong, everyone knows it because everyone in the audience usually knows the words. But you can literally make up words, and they wouldn't know the difference."

"But has to be in iambic pentameter, no?" Miroslaw said, and we all stopped and looked at him, and he was like: "What? We have Shakespeare in Poland."

"Just FYI," Katherine Cooper-Bunting said, addressing Olivia specifically, "I don't give a shit if you make fun of me. All I care about is getting into drama school. And, unfortunately,

I can't just stand there and sing a song—I'm going to have to do Shakespeare. It's a requirement. And the thing is, if we can't audition in person for whatever stupid reason, at least I'll be able to send them the clips from *Cupid's Revenge*, instead of doing some shit self-tape in my bedroom at the last minute."

Olivia looked at her, and I thought she was going to come back with something super sassy, but she just shoved ready salted crisps into her mouth, never breaking eye contact with Katherine Cooper-Bunting, and finally she said: "You've got a point, mate."

"I'm so glad you agree."

"We should make an official video."

"We need to talk to Brian," Katherine Cooper-Bunting said.

"One hundred percent. But if we're filming it, I ain't doing that hymn to domestic abuse. I'm going full 'Defying Gravity,'" Olivia said.

"That's not really a love song, though, is it?" Robin asked, but it was clearly rhetorical.

"Mate, it's self-love. Which was fashionable, like, only five minutes ago. It's interesting how quickly people forget."

"I'll probably be able to film on the night," I said. "If we can get a proper camera from somewhere."

"My dad's got a camera," Katherine Cooper-Bunting said. "Because during lockdown all his services were broadcast live, and the church provided the tech. I'm sure he won't mind us using it."

"But will Jesus?" Olivia asked, and looked at Robin, clearly looking for laughs, but Robin gave her a death stare.

"See you inside," Katherine Cooper-Bunting said to all of us, and walked away.

Teddy shot up off the ground like a rocket and, like a puppy who hadn't yet grown into its giant feet, he bounded after her.

He caught up with her on the pavement, and they crossed the road together, and by the time they reached the social club, Katherine Cooper-Bunting was laughing again.

My stomach fluttered wildly, and I knew I wouldn't be able to live if I couldn't make her look at me that way at least once before today was over.

I imagined Grace sitting in the lunch circle with us.

She'd hated premade sandwiches because she hated mayo, and according to her, mayo lurked in every premade sandwich, and so she'd be having a crisp sandwich. She'd eat it and pretend it wasn't way too dry, and she'd probably look at me now and say something like: "Just let them be, Tills. They're cute together."

"Those two are like chalk and cheese," Olivia said IRL. "I honestly don't know what people see in Cooper-Bunting."

I brushed sandwich crust crumbs off my legs, wondered who these "people" were, and then I imagined her naked.

Scene 5

Our opening number was a song called "Seasons of Love" from a show called *Rent*, even though the main story isn't about people renting, but about the AIDS crisis in America in the 1980s.

Brian was like: "I was alive and young and gay during that time, okay, and, let me tell you, it absolutely devastated our community and our families. Maybe people will finally emotionally connect with it now that they've been through something similar."

"There will be a vaccine for HIV," Miroslaw said.

"And it's all thanks to the research that went into the COVID vaccine—you know that, don't you?" Brian replied.

"All these vaccines are getting out of hand," the Phantom's wife contributed. "I'm sorry, but I'm convinced it's the government trying to control us."

"I wish they'd develop a vaccine against stupidity, innit," Olivia said.

Brian quickly clapped his hands three times, and divided the group up into eight smaller groups, as "Seasons of Love" was originally sung by eight people.

Teddy and Miroslaw were in the same group, Olivia was on her own, as was Maeve, which made sense, because they were strong singers. Katherine Cooper-Bunting was teamed up with the Phantom's wife, and I could see from Olivia's face that she was loving that.

I obviously wasn't in it, and neither was Robin, so I sat down next to them, and we watched a video of the original cast of *Rent* on YouTube.

All the people in it were, like, in their twenties and really good-looking.

I looked at the stage and everyone there looked like this random group of rejects the toothless cat dragged in.

Apart from Olivia and Katherine Cooper-Bunting, of course. As everyone else was creeping farther and farther away from the front of the stage, those two kept pushing forward.

Olivia then looked at Robin and me, took a confident step to her left, maneuvering Katherine Cooper-Bunting off center stage, flicked her ponytail back, opened her mouth, closed her eyes, and belted out the first line, adding an extravagant little riff at the end that went on forever.

Everyone looked at her with their mouths hanging open, and she looked straight at Katherine Cooper-Bunting and went: "What?"

I bit my lip and looked back at Robin's phone, and Robin whispered: "She's so savage."

Since we were still without the piano, no actual singing

happened, but Brian had made copies of the sheet music, which he made me hand out, and which proved a complete waste of time and paper, because only Olivia, Katherine Cooper-Bunting, Teddy, and Charles knew how to read music, and in the end Brian just went: "Oh, why do I bother?" and posted a link to the YouTube video of the song on WhatsApp.

He then decided he would start rehearsing Maeve and Miroslaw's *A Midsummer Night's Dream*, which basically is about Miroslaw's character turning into a donkey, and Maeve's character falling in love with him because she doesn't realize he's turned into a donkey, because she's been drugged.

I wasn't needed since it was more of a read-through, because obviously no one knew their lines so far, and Brian didn't want to start directing yet, "daaaarling," and so I just sat next to Robin, who was looking up production pictures of *A Midsummer Night's Dream* and drawing costume ideas in their notebook.

"Ohmigod," I said, looking at one of them. "Do you think we'll be able to get a donkey head for Miroslaw?"

"I seriously doubt it. Stuff like that is so expensive. Unless you know someone at, like, the National or maybe the Victoria and Albert Museum who'll nick it for us. Or we could nick it. Do you fancy a heist?"

"My dad works at the Royal Opera House," I said, and Robin took my hand and went: "You're literally my new favorite person. Please, please, pleeeeease tell me he works in the costume department."

"Sorry, no, he's a conductor."

"That's so boring."

"He'd disagree."

"But he knows the people in the costume department, right?"

"I'm not sure that he does."

"But maybe he can give me a tour on which we happen to end up in the costume department?"

"I don't know."

"Tilly, please, you need to be on board with my storytelling here."

"Okay, sorry, yes, of course. He can totally take you on a tour and accidentally on purpose end up in the costume department."

"Where he'll distract the wardrobe mistress so I can remove a donkey head."

"How will you get it out of the building?"

"Under my top."

"It's huge."

"Then I'll wear it. No one would notice."

"I once saw a man with a tandoor on wheels on the Metropolitan line."

"That's so strange."

"Right?"

"Well, it's London. Please will you ask your dad?"

"I will."

"Thank you so much. And I wouldn't actually take anything if he gave me a tour."

"I'll let him know."

When rehearsal was over, I remembered I hadn't told Brian I'd be late tomorrow.

He was like: "Tilly, to be honest—"

"I have to take my grandfather to this thing," I said, because I'm obviously great with words, and of course Brian looked at me like I was just making that up, which TBH made me a bit cross, because I literally wouldn't lie about that.

Anyway, that whole interaction left me feeling all wrong and misjudged, and when I looked around, everyone apart from Charles and Maeve had left, and I was super annoyed because I'd really wanted to see Katherine Cooper-Bunting.

I went into the toilet, all huffy and hating Brian, and my parents, and basically everyone, and there she was.

"Hi," she said, and started washing her hands.

"Hi," I said, but there was nothing else in my brain, and then I was like, *Matilda Taylor, get a grip. Say something!*

Katherine Cooper-Bunting smiled but didn't say anything and reached for a handful of paper towels.

"Is it true that you're one of ten?" I asked, and I swear I didn't know I was going to ask it until I'd asked it.

"Olivia told you that, didn't she?" Katherine Cooper-Bunting asked back, and actually laughed. "Just because my dad's a priest. She literally needs to get over it. And, no, I'm one of five."

"Wow. That's a lot, isn't it?"

"Have you got any brothers or sisters?"

"I've got an older sister, but she lives in Scotland."

"I'm the oldest, and the youngest is four."

"Do you have your own room?"

"No, I share with my sister Stella. She's fourteen."

"Isn't that annoying?"

Katherine Cooper-Bunting shrugged and rummaged through her bag. "I've always shared. We don't really talk much when we're in our room, you know. We respect each other's privacy. It's okay."

"You don't fight?"

"We do." She pulled an almost-squeezed-out tube of hand cream from her bag and moisturized her hands. "Want some?"

"No thanks. But where do you practice, like, your monologues and all that?" I asked, and I don't know why, but maybe because I was watching her hands, I then wondered where she masturbates, but I obviously wasn't going to ask about that.

"I often sneak into the church," she said, and you can imagine the scenes in my head, because I was still well in Masturbationville. "I sometimes go into one of the small side chapels," she continued, and I was like: *Please, actually stop talking.*

I cleared my throat. "That must be so weird. Being alone

in a church. Isn't it haunted?" I asked, and she looked at me, grinning.

"I'm not sure Jesus has got a burning desire to come back again and give me tips on my acting."

"Do you actually, like, believe in all that?" I asked.

Her eyes danced over my face.

"I mean Jesus and . . . I don't know, Mary, I guess," I said, because I had to interrupt her silence. I knew nothing about the Bible.

"Of course I do," Katherine Cooper-Bunting said, and quickly checked herself out in the mirror. Then looked at me like neither our brief encounter as horses nor the finger-touching had ever happened and whispered as she walked past me: "After all, I'm a priest's daughter," way too close to my ear, and disappeared out of the door before I could even take a new breath.

By the time I went outside, she was already walking down Battersea Rise.

"Hurry the fuck up," Teddy shouted at me from the bus stop.

"Fuck off, I'm coming," I shouted back, wondering if I'd have to spend the rest of my life feeling both aroused and miserable.

Scene 6

I slept late the next morning because I couldn't sleep that night.

When I got downstairs, Grandad was still eating his breakfast, but Mum and Dad had already left for work.

"Cuppa?" Grandad asked.

"I can do it," I said, and put the kettle on.

"Do you think I should dress up for the games afternoon?" he asked.

"I don't really think it matters. Besides, you always look smart."

"And I imagine a lot of them won't remember me by next week, or even tomorrow, so I suppose it really doesn't matter."

"Did Dad write down the address for you? I only know it's in Wandsworth."

"No."

"These people make me so crazy," I mumbled, getting out my phone and messaging Dad.

"I know it's called something with Ericcson. I remember because I thought it sounded Swedish," Grandad said. "Your grandmother and I spent a whole month driving up and down the coast near Gothenburg one summer. I think she would have stayed forever. She loved it. Fresh seafood, sunshine. She swam naked every day."

"Ew."

"She was a very beautiful woman."

"Grandad!"

"She was," he said, and laughed, and then I laughed, too, and the kettle finished boiling.

I googled "Ericcson" and "dementia" and "board games" and "Wandsworth," and three seconds later, I'd found it.

"Ericcson Close," I said to Grandad.

"Oh good, because I wouldn't want to miss it for the world."

"Grandad, you don't have to go to this thing."

"It's all right, Tilly," he said, and reached for my hand, which was unusual, because he wasn't really the touchy-feely type. None of us were. I squeezed his briefly.

"Can you lend me some cash?" he asked.

"I don't think you need to pay for anything," I said.

"I was hoping there may be poker in the back room," Grandad said. "The risk of losing money may be enough incentive for my brain to not deteriorate at the rate they're predicting."

I watched as he picked up his spoon with a shaking hand and ate his Frosted Flakes.

I looked at my phone.

"Maybe you'll make friends," I suggested, but I think we both knew I was just saying it.

Imagine making new friends who all have dementia or

Alzheimer's, because, chances are, they won't know you the next time you see them.

Imagine every room you walk into being full of strangers.

Terrifying.

Anyway, Grandad got dressed in his usual attire, suit trousers, a crisp white shirt, and one of his many colorful cravats. Today's was pink.

When we got off the bus in Wandsworth, I had to get out my phone to check where we were going because I hadn't been to Wandsworth in, like, five years, and it looked nothing like I remembered.

The community center was down some side street toward Putney, and it looked like a run-down old school.

It was also used by the NHS for other things, like, there were signs for diabetes eye tests everywhere, and there were posters plastered on the walls reminding people to book their free flu and COVID and shingles vaccines.

"This looks like the set of a Stephen King film," Grandad said, and I was absolutely mortified that a) Mum thought this was a good idea and b) that he was going along with it. "Maybe they'll harvest my organs. And they'd get away with it, too, because I won't remember."

I laughed out loud but stopped myself straight away.

"Go on, you can laugh," Grandad said. "It's funny because it's true."

We got to a set of double doors, and I pushed them open,

and on the other side was what looked like a school dining room, and there were loads of old people sitting around tables, and nurses were pouring drinks into plastic beakers, and for some bizarre reason, it made me think of how Teddy always called them "plastic glasses" when we were little, which used to make me crazy, because how can it be a glass when it's plastic?

Two old ladies were playing cards, one lady was being fed cake, and an old man sat all alone at a table on the far side, rocking in his chair, staring at a tower of dominoes.

Only the pork-chop incident had stirred me that deeply on an emotional level since Grace and, well, obviously apart from certain stirrings caused by Katherine Cooper-Bunting, but standing there, looking at the scene in front of me, moved me to the point where I wanted to scream and vom simultaneously, which I don't think is physically possible.

And I knew, like, I KNEW in that moment that Emilin had been right, that I had to take charge of Grandad, because no one else would, and I knew that there was no way in a million years I could leave him to be part of this horror show. And not only because Grandma would come back and haunt me, but because Grandad's soul deserved so much better. Everyone's soul deserved better.

I watched a nurse making her way over to us, and I stepped in front of Grandad and was just like: *No.*

"Good afternoon," she said. "I'm Helen. Welcome."

"We're not actually staying," I said, then turned round,

grabbed Grandad's hand, and pushed through the double doors again.

"Sarah," Grandad said, but I walked even faster, dragging him behind me, his stiff and shiny leather shoes clickety-clacking on the faded lino floor, echoing in the sterile and empty hallway.

The posters on the walls were suddenly completely in my face, all DIABETES, COVID, OLD AGE, DEATH, and I dragged Grandad along until we were pretty much running.

Outside, it was warm again, and everything smelled familiar, of heat and traffic and KFC and dog roses.

I paused at a nearby wall and let go of his hand.

"You can't go to that thing," I said to him, my lungs scream-ing for air with sunshine in it instead of despair.

Grandad stood there, also gasping, and looking completely lost and out of place and friendless on a hot pavement in Wandsworth, and I was just like: "Grandad, you can't go to that. It was horrible."

He pulled out a hanky and wiped his sweaty forehead, and I realized I hadn't made him wear a hat, and he was probably getting sunburned.

"I don't think they had poker," he said, and smiled at me.

"No, I don't think they did."

We looked at each other for a moment, and then I was like: "Do you want to come to rehearsal with me? I think you'll like that much better. And it's cool in the social club. We'll get the bus now. Or we can go home, I don't mind. I'm really sorry we made you come here. It was a stupid idea."

"It's all right, Tilly," he said, and wiped his brow again. "I can spend the afternoon with you at your rehearsal. If I'm not intruding."

"No," I said. "You wouldn't be intruding at all, I promise. But just so you know, we're not professionals, but everyone's really nice."

"Sounds good," he said, and patted his pockets. "Only I seem to have misplaced my car keys."

"No, Grandad, it's fine. We took the bus. Don't worry."

"Oh, that's good, then, isn't it?" he said, and smiled at me.

"Come, it's this way."

"Buses in London are quite reliable, aren't they?" he asked, and I felt so much sadness at his attempt to make small talk despite—or maybe because of—everything that was going on with his illness, and so I linked arms with him, and we walked to the bus stop together.

We didn't say a word on the way over to Clapham Junction.

As the bus went up the hill, I watched an old person walk up it slowly, and I thought, you know, most people don't know how they're going to die, right?

But when you have something like Alzheimer's, you can look at people who are further down the road, and you know that's going to be you in the not-so-distant future, and really, how absolutely fucking terrifying is that?

Knowing you're going to be the person who's rocking in the corner, staring at a stack of dominoes. Or knowing that one day you'll be fed cake because you neither know you're hungry nor how to feed yourself.

And it wasn't, like, the other people's fault, or the nurse's fault, obviously, it was the fault of the Alzheimer's, and Wandsworth still being a shithole even though they've finally got a fancy shopping center.

We got to Clapham just after the warm-up, so, to be perfectly honest, Brian shouldn't have made such a meal out of me telling him I'd be late, because I don't need the warm-up, because all I have to do is sit down and read the words the people on the stage are saying and write down where he wants them to sit/stand/look.

Everyone was just chatting and getting situated.

Katherine Cooper-Bunting and Teddy were standing really close together and reading their scene, and her eyes and body language were all like: *Come hither*, and I hated it.

I watched Teddy laugh, and as he looked up, he saw Grandad and me standing in the doorway.

He let go of the script they were holding together and bounced over to us.

"Hi, Mr. Taylor," Teddy said, and held out his hand to Grandad. "I'm Teddy. We met many years ago at Christmas."

"Hello, Teddy," Grandad said, like he wasn't sure.

"Oh, I'm your neighbor."

"Yes, I remember," Grandad said. "You've grown tall."

"Thanks," Teddy said, and pulled on his earlobe.

"Teddy owns Rachmaninoff," I told Grandad.

"He's a lovely cat."

"He's a grumpy bastard," Teddy said.

"He's very musical."

"Chip off the old block, as they say," Teddy said, and shrugged. "Unlike me. I sometimes think my parents got me from a shelter and not the cat. If you know what I mean."

Not sure Grandad did, but he smiled anyway.

"Let me introduce you to Brian," I said, and quickly stole a glance at Katherine Cooper-Bunting, who was watching us. "Brian played Mr. Toad in *The Wind in the Willows*."

Grandad didn't look impressed but followed me to the front.

"Brian," I said, and Brian turned around. "This is my grandad, Douglas. Is it okay if he watches today? He was going to go to this thing, but now he's not."

"It was a games afternoon for people with dementia and Alzheimer's," Grandad said, and shook Brian's hand. "But it appears I still have a lot more marbles to lose before I'll enjoy that sort of soirée."

"Oh," Brian said. "I see. Well, of course, the more the merrier. Are you an actor, Douglas?"

"Afraid not," Grandad said.

"Grandad's a musician," I said.

"Do you play the piano?" Brian asked, and then laughed at what he obviously thought was a joke, but Grandad was like: "I do, as a matter of fact," at which point Brian looked like a miracle had occurred, and he grabbed Grandad's hand and whispered: "But then you *must* play for us."

Grandad looked unsure.

"You see, Douglas, our pianist is, sadly, deceased, and if I don't replace him soon, I'm going to have a riot on my hands."

"Oh, I don't know," Grandad said, and pulled his hand from Brian's eager grasp.

"No, no, no, you absoluuuuutely must," Brian boomed. "Douglas, daaaarling. And it's all for a good cause. Acting for Others, you see? Have you got any other commitments this summer? Do say yes to us, I implore you."

And then he actually got down on one knee in front of my grandad and folded his hands in prayer.

Everyone was looking now.

"Stop making a spectacle of yourself, Brian!" Maeve shouted from behind the bar where she was drying mugs, and Brian clumsily heaved himself back up.

Grandad suddenly looked confused, which made me feel a bit hot and panicky, and I remembered I should probably ask him if he needed the toilet.

"Let's sit a minute," I said, and made Grandad sit down on one of the plastic chairs.

I got a bottle of water out of my backpack and gave it to him.

"Here, you have to have a drink—it's really hot today. I'm sorry, I should have offered you this on the bus."

"Thank you, Sarah," he said, and gently cupped my cheek for a moment.

"That's okay."

"Maeve," Brian said, "make Douglas a cuppa, will ya?" And then he was like: "You don't have to decide anything now, fella. You're welcome just to be here, okay?"

"Thank you," I told him, and sat down next to my grandad.

"Right, everyone," Brian said, and clapped his hands. "We're continuing where we left off yesterday—"

"I'm up, bitches," Olivia said, and strode onto the stage.

"That you are, darling," Brian replied, and shook his head.

"Due to the lack of a pianist, I'll be singin' a cappella, though, innit. Not that I mind," she said, flicking her hair over her shoulder.

"I said I'm working on it," Brian said, but kind of under his breath, and looking at his notes. "Right. You're familiar with the song, I trust?"

"Yeah, mate. We've discussed this. It's Nancy's love song to a guy who's a creep and a bully and a domestic abuser. Totally romantic."

I know, *I* cringed.

"Yes, well, it's an audience favorite."

"That's all you need to know about the average voter, innit?"

"You're just going to have to dig real deep for it, then, won't you," Brian said.

"I'd say," Olivia said. She cleared her throat and went straight into the song, but five seconds later, Brian clapped his hands for her to stop and went: "This isn't *Dreamgirls*."

I was so engrossed in what was going on onstage that I didn't see Katherine Cooper-Bunting approaching me, and when she was suddenly right there, I literally flinched.

She knelt down next to me, put her hand on my actual knee, and held a cup of tea up to my grandad.

"Hi, I'm Katherine," she said, and I swear her hand spread a bit, like touching my knee was something she'd been doing for a long time. "Maeve over there's made you a cup of tea. Do you take sugar?"

"Two please," Grandad said. "Thank you."

"I'll be right back," she said, and her hand was gone, and my skin felt as if it was having some sort of emergency due to the loss of her touch.

She was back ten seconds later with the sugared tea.

"There's Hobnobs, too. Would you like one?" Katherine Cooper-Bunting asked, and gave him two on a napkin.

"I would," I said.

She turned to me and smiled; I could see the pulse in her neck, which made me lick my lips.

"Get your own," she whispered. "You're not a guest here."

"Is there a piano on the premises?" Grandad asked. He took a bite of his Hobnob and looked around.

"Right under Winston Churchill there," I said, and pointed to the corner. "But don't worry about that, Grandad. I'm sure he'll find someone."

"I can play the goddamn piano, Tilly," Grandad said, and blew on his tea before taking a careful sip.

"I know, but you don't have to do this now."

"Excuse me, Brian," he said, then put down his cup of tea and walked over to Brian's table. "Have you got the sheet music? Since I'm here, I might as well accompany the young lady."

Brian took a deep breath in, held it, opened his arms and his mouth, ended up not saying anything, but picked a folder from his pile, got out the score for *Oliver!* and gave it to my grandad.

Five minutes later the company had a pianist, and Olivia sang with such vigor that I thought the shabby roof would lift off the building.

Everyone was super giddy at break, and they all introduced themselves to Grandad.

Out of the corner of my eye, I saw that Katherine Cooper-

Bunting was behind the bar, alone, making a cup of tea, which made me need one, too, and with utmost urgency.

I looked around to find Teddy, but I couldn't see him.

It's an odd thing how quickly courage can appear and decency goes out of the window when you really, really want something.

She was leaning against the counter, looking into her still empty mug, and I sneaked up right behind her, and put my left hand on her hip.

"Excuse me," I said, and then casually reached up to grab a mug from the shelf above.

"You know, I would have got you one down," she said, and turned her head so I could feel her breath on my face.

She was a little bit too close, and I momentarily feared I'd gone cross-eyed, but our nearness felt too exhilarating to walk away. Or even move a millimeter.

"Where'd be the fun in that?" I asked. And I didn't quite whisper it, but almost.

Then I looked at the cutest of all the freckles on her nose.

She looked at my mouth.

My phone started ringing, and I swear I almost hit the deck from the shock of it.

I jumped away from her, and she giggled.

It was Mum.

"What?" I asked.

"Darling, we forgot about Grandad's games afternoon. Where are you?"

"No, *we* didn't forget, *you* forgot. We went, but we didn't stay. But now we're at rehearsal."

The kettle finished boiling, and Katherine Cooper-Bunting poured water into our mugs.

"Darling, I'm so sorry. I completely forgot to message you the address. What do you mean, you didn't stay?"

"What do you mean, what do I mean?" I asked, because honestly . . .

I stirred the tea bag around a few times, took it out, and dumped it on the plate with all the other soggy tea bags.

"Pardon?" Mum asked, and I was just like: *What is the matter with you people?*

"We went to the thing," I explained slowly, "and it was horrible, and so Grandad's not going back, but is going to play the piano for our cabaret thing instead."

Katherine Cooper-Bunting gave me an evil smirk and mouthed: "Cabaret thing?"

I shrugged and reached for the Hobnobs, but she grabbed them before I could take one and took them with her.

"Tilly, I think we need to discu—"

"Mum, I can't talk now, I've got rehearsal," I said, and before she could say anything else, I went: "I'll see you tonight, good-bye." And hung up.

Brian clapped to let us know the break was over, and so I made my way back to where I'd been sitting.

Teddy, Robin, Miroslaw, and Olivia walked in, and I realized they'd been to the shop. Teddy pulled a bottle of banana Yazoo out of his shorts pocket and gave it to me.

Then he pulled two bottles of water out of the massive side pocket on the other side. He gave one to my grandad, who was like: "Thank you very much for that, young man," and he gave one to Katherine Cooper-Bunting, who looked at him like it was the best gift she'd ever received.

My heart felt achy, and the dull pain spread through the rest of my body until I wondered if I could ever get out of the shitty chair, but then, half an hour later, on her way to the stage, Katherine Cooper-Bunting walked past me and casually put a Hobnob on my leg.

Then she ignored me for the rest of the afternoon.

I felt like I'd been pulled from the ocean, like I hadn't been drowning at all.

Scene 7

When Grandad and I got home, Mum, of course, was question central, but I told her straight up and in not so many words that, basically, Grandad was never going back to play board games in death's waiting room in Wandsworth, and that, in fact, I was never ever going to go back to Wandsworth for anything, and that we'd have to either serve Grandad an early brunch every day now or make him a sandwich, because he'd basically run away with the circus and joined a crap amateur dramatics society for whom he now played the piano.

Mum was on her phone straightaway and probably all like: "Dear Siri, should I allow my eighty-year-old father-in-law to take on unpaid work even though he's in the early stages of Alzheimer's?"

Siri apparently said: "Yes, Suzanne, that is a great idea," because half an hour later, Mum was like: "Douglas, I think it's a great idea," and I wondered what it must feel like to be treated like a child, by my mother of all people, when you've lived successfully and for, like, almost seventy years as an adult.

When Grandad went upstairs to have his bath, Mum was all over me like: "I'm just nervous that there aren't any medical professionals at your rehearsal. He needs regular water, he needs regular food, he needs to make sure he goes to the toilet."

I was like: "We all need to make sure we do those things, Mum. It's not rocket science."

She looked at me, and then she was like: "Well, by all means, if you think you know everything."

I don't think I know everything, but when we were at that awful place in Wandsworth I did know that you don't just ship someone off to a sterile day center where, yes, where there are nurses, but where life has already stopped.

I left Mum standing in the kitchen, where she was scheduled to teach a Zoom ballet lesson at eight, and went to my room.

The interesting thing about Mum is that it's so obvious now that she never really liked being a mother.

Emilin and I were always at Teddy's, like, after school, and to eat dinner, and obviously on weekends, and over Christmas when Amanda wasn't teaching, and all the other parents were performing *The Nutcracker* three hundred times a day.

And then during our school holidays we were always in Scotland with Grandma and Grandad. Or we'd go away with them, because Grandma didn't mind having us around even when Grandad was working.

She didn't mind traveling with us, either, whereas Mum was so inconvenienced by our presence that she literally tried to never take us anywhere.

And if Mum was rubbish, Dad was worse.

I mean, he could do nothing but think about himself.

Which was also 100 percent why I hadn't seen him since Grandad arrived. Which made no sense at all, because why if he was so sorry about Grandma dying alone was he basically going to let the same thing happen with Grandad? Because sharing a house with others didn't automatically mean someone wasn't feeling lonely and alone. Like, I knew all about that.

I sat down in front of my mirror and started to pluck my eyebrows, but the project quickly became too overwhelming.

I started getting proper pissed off with Mum, who was downstairs all: "We'll have a demi-plié, port de bras, and a lovely grand plié," like it was important.

I got out my phone and decided to update Emilin with the status quo, then my door was pushed open and Rachmaninoff stuck his giant head inside my room.

"Fuck off," I said to him. "This is my room."

He left, sat down in front of Grandad's door, shouted, and looked at the doorknob expectantly.

"I hate you," I whispered, and got off the floor.

I went to Grandad's door and knocked.

"Rachmaninoff's here," I said. "But you don't have to let him into your room. He doesn't live here."

A few seconds later, the door opened a crack.

"Thank you, Sarah," Grandad said, and the cat let out a roar of joy.

I went back into my room and collapsed onto my bed.

What a day.

My phone vibrated, and I hoped it was a WhatsApp from Katherine Cooper-Bunting, which I realized even then was a dumbass thing to want because it wasn't like we were BFFs or anything, and just because we'd had a bit of a game involving Hobnobs didn't mean she was going to message me.

It was Emilin.

Bravo! she wrote, but what did that even mean?

I looked at the ceiling and shook my head. "Why is everyone incapable?" I asked, but of course, there was no answer.

I wondered if I should speak to Katherine Cooper-Bunting about that.

The godly silence, that is, not Emilin.

Then I wondered how I was ever going to eat another Hobnob without thinking about her.

I went on IG to see if she'd posted anything, but she hadn't.

Robin had updated their story with sketches of costumes. One was for the scene that Teddy had with Katherine Cooper-Bunting. The girl character is called Rosalind, and the boy Orlando, and Robin had drawn a love heart between their faces.

I commented on the story by writing: Too cute! and sending lots of heart-eye faces, which made me feel both like an adult and desperately resentful at the same time.

Robin was online, and they liked my message straightaway.

Then they replied to me about the donkey head, and I

suggested we should try to get hold of the front part of a pantomime horse, and instead of being like: That's hilarious, but let's not, they went: That's hilarious, let's.

And then they were like: Isn't there that party shop by Clapham Junction? And I was like: Yes, and then they were like: We need to go during break tomorrow and check it out, and I was like: I can't wait.

And then I was thinking, *I wonder if they have pantomime horses in Poland*, and I really hoped they did, because imagine unpacking all that . . .

I checked Amazon, but they were all a bit expensive for how shit they looked, plus we obviously only needed the front bit anyway, and besides, you should always try to shop local, even if it's for a pantomime horse.

I was still lying there when Dad got home, and I was just about to switch off my lights when someone knocked on my door.

For a moment I was like, *I'll ignore it and pretend I'm asleep*, but then I thought that whoever was knocking could probably see the light coming from under my door and know that I was actually still awake and ignoring them, and I didn't want things in this house to get even more awkward than they already were.

"Yes," I said, and it was Dad.

"Hi," he said, looking completely out of place, still in his conducting suit. "I'm so sorry about the mix-up with the address for Dad's games afternoon."

Mix-up? Interesting choice of words.

"Your mum texted me about him having taken on a job, though."

"It's not actually a job. Like, no one's getting paid."

"I was trying to be funny."

"Oh. Sorry. Ha ha."

"And I think it's great."

"Okay."

"Yeah, that's all."

And then he stood there and kind of just looked at my room like he'd never been in there, which, when I thought about it a bit later, I wasn't sure he had.

"Night?" I said, because I was like: *Please go away, I hate awkward*, and he was like: "Yes, good night. Don't stay up too late."

And then he kind of walked backward in the strangest way and closed the door behind him.

I picked up my phone again, and the moment I opened IG, I saw that Katherine Cooper-Bunting had posted a picture of the book *As You Like It*, and she wrote: Looking forward to rehearsing this super-cute scene with @TheOdOreBOOker tomorrow for #CupidsRevenge @CriterionTheatre in aid of #TheActorsFund. Link for tickets in bio.

Teddy had liked it already and had sent her a heart in the comments section, which she had liked, and you know when a romance is unfolding in front of you, and it's really cute and you want them to be together, because you need them to be together, but your heart is shouting NOOOOOOOO, because it feels like it's being ripped from your chest?

"Why?" I asked. "Just why?"

Why everything?

Why me?

Why Katherine Cooper-Bunting?

Why did he have to fancy her?

Or, more importantly, why did *I* have to fancy her?

I put my phone away, and ages later, when I was just drifting off to sleep, there was scratching at my door, and then a low, gargly growl.

I kicked my sheets away, suddenly super resentful, and then my feet got all tangled up in them and getting out of bed became this awful full-body effort, and I was just like: *What is life at the moment?*

Rachmaninoff sat in the dark hallway just outside my door.

"What?" I hissed.

He hopped toward the stairs.

I switched on the lights and followed him down.

He proceeded to the back door which, of course, had been locked by my ever-aware parents.

I opened it, and Rachmaninoff growled at me one more time before leaving the house.

"Get to fuck," I told him.

Scene 8

The next day was the day Teddy and Katherine Cooper-Bunting got to rehearse their scene from *As You Like It* for the first time.

They started with a read-through, and Katherine Cooper-Bunting already gave it all that, and Teddy was stumbling over every other weird word, and TBH, I couldn't blame him, because it's all like "thou," "thee," "thy," "thine."

Also, despite Brian talking them through what was supposed to be going on, because you obviously would never know it from just reading the text, I still didn't really get it, which was a problem since I was the assistant director, and then I was wondering, you know, those people who watch Shakespeare and are all like: "Ya, ya, ya," are they actually getting it, or are they just pretentiously nodding along?

Anyway, the scene plays out as follows: Rosalind (Katherine Cooper-Bunting) loves Orlando (Theodore Booker), and Orlando loves Rosalind, but they don't know this about each other. She's dressed herself as a man to disguise her true identity for a reason I've already forgotten about again but isn't really important for the scene, and she then sneakily asks Orlando, who happens to be in the same forest as she (#coincidence and possibly the original version of the #therewasonlyonebed trope), about this girl called Rosalind, whose name has been carved into all the trees in some kind of testosterone-driven stupor. At that point Orlando, not realizing it's Rosalind, tells her that he's the fool who's done the carving because he's in love, and instead of going, this is great, let's kiss, Rosalind keeps pretending she's a boy, makes him call her Rosalind (which *is* her name . . .) and tell her all the things he wants to say to his Rosalind. In other words, she's fishing for compliments. Are you still awake?

TBH, I'm not sure anyone's going to get this at all. I mean, they'll be seeing it out of the context of the play, which doesn't help, and I bet everyone's going to be like: *Why is that girl dressed as a boy, and who is this Rosalind they're talking about, and why did we spend fifteen pounds to be confused?*

The Phantom of the Opera and his wife looked completely exhausted just watching, Miroslaw was doodling on a pad, and Maeve wasn't really paying attention either, and just kept making cups of tea for everyone and washing mugs in the tiny sink behind the bar.

Grandad was now BFFs with "Some Enchanted Evening"—Charles—and they were sitting in the back corner by the door and looking at a great big notebook Charles carried around with him.

I know Grandad had kind of told Brian, but I hadn't told anyone about Grandad's Alzheimer's, but he'd sort of mentioned it when he told Charles, "The old mind isn't what it used to be," and pointed at his head. "The tragic thing is that I still know it's happening. But I suppose the disease will get easier overnight one day."

Charles was just like: "I understand, old boy, just too well. Now, sit down next to me."

I'm not sure how well Charles understood, because Alzheimer's isn't the same as becoming casually forgetful, and so I made a mental note to regularly check in with Grandad and tell him to go to the toilet.

"This is literally the cutest thing ever," Robin said, aahhh-hing and looking at the stage, where Brian was repositioning Teddy and Katherine Cooper-Bunting to sit next to each other on two plastic chairs that were supposed to represent a fallen tree trunk.

"You think so?" I asked, and quickly wrote down the props we were using and how Teds and Katherine Cooper-Bunting were sitting.

"He's so cute—look at his adorable face. And his ears have gone all red. He's the perfect Orlando."

"Yeah," I said, even though I didn't know the first thing about Orlando. "He's perfect."

"And," Robin said, leaning away from Olivia and in to me: "Cooper-Bunting's always really good, so I think this'll be epic."

"I heard that, biatch," Olivia mumbled, but didn't look up from her phone.

"You know you're not supposed to be on that," Robin said.

"Mate, I'm organizing an extra shift at Waterloo tomorrow. I ain't got the luxury to just sit here and do fuck all and watch those two idiots. And is it hot today or what?"

"You can learn a lot by observing," Robin said. "Yeah, it's clammy."

"Such a gross word, innit? Clammy. It's gonna rain, though— check it out," Olivia said, and shoved her phone in our faces.

"I thought you were organizing work," Robin asked.

"I'm multitaskin'," Olivia said, and looked up at the stage where Katherine Cooper-Bunting, a.k.a. Rosalind, was now smiling at Teddy, a.k.a. Orlando, with laughter literally pouring out of her eyes.

"Get a room," Olivia muttered. She stuck her finger to the back of her throat and made a gagging noise. "Cooper-Bunting's gross. Bet she's never been kissed."

"What makes you say that?" I asked, and I tried to say it so it sounded like I'd definitely been kissed and was judgmental about those who hadn't been.

"You know, all that no-sex-before-marriage kind of stuff."

"Is that still a thing?" I asked.

"You'll have to ask Cooper-Bunting—she's the church person."

I looked at her on the stage.

As did Olivia.

Katherine Cooper-Bunting was now right in Teddy's face, making proverbial love to his eyes.

"She's such a flirt," Olivia mumbled. "Which is literally wrong when you're not going to do anything with it."

"Well, maybe she is," I said, hating what I was suggesting.

"She was going round with this boy at Stagecoach, yeah," Olivia whispered. "And he was clearly in love with her, but nothing ever happened, and I reckon he's the real reason she's here this summer, because she doesn't want to run into anyone at Stagecoach because she knows she behaved like a proper cocktease. Because she was too much in love with the way he was in love with her to tell him no. His name's Alfie."

"Poor Alfie," Robin said, and shoved their bottom lip outward.

"And, mate, he was, like, the only straight guy, too."

"What happened to him?" I asked.

"Got into RADA, mate. Reckon he'll be the next big thing. I bet she's regretting it so much. Ha! In your face, Cooper-Bunting."

I got out my phone to search for Alfie in her friends list, but I didn't even get past my lock screen because Brian caught my eye and shook his head at me.

I rolled my eyes and reluctantly put it away.

"Cooper-Bunting's going to look so cute dressed as a boy," Robin said, and I watched them draw a little mustache on their sketch of her, which made me let out an accidental hiccup sort of thing, and Robin was just like: "What was that?" and then we laughed, and when I looked back, Katherine Cooper-Bunting was looking at me, and she was smiling. And then I wondered if that was the way she used to look at Alfie.

When Teddy and Katherine Cooper-Bunting were done, we had a five-minute break before it was Maeve's turn to rehearse a song called "Send in the Clowns" from a show called *A Little Night Music*, which meant that Grandad had to accompany her.

I got up to get him and ask him if he needed to go to the toilet, but Charles had beaten me to it.

"He's just in the gents," Charles said to me.

"I need to check in with him, you know," I said to Charles, and he was like: "I understand," and we stood a bit awkwardly in the doorway to the toilets.

"It's gonna rain," I said.

"We need it," Charles replied, and I could already hear the first pitter-patter on the low roof.

When Grandad was done, I walked him to the piano and opened the sheet music for him.

"A bit of Sondheim for you, Douglas," Brian said, and patted Grandad's shoulder. "To keep you on your toes."

"Appreciate that," Grandad said, and I could hear thunder in the distance.

"Ah, mate, I ain't got my brolly," Olivia complained loud enough for everybody to hear.

"In England you must always have an umbrella," Miroslaw called across the room at us.

"Immigrants," Olivia said. "Coming here, giving good advice."

"Just take one from the lost-and-found box and return it," Maeve said from the stage.

Then she started getting herself into position and character by walking in circles almost in slow motion. She'd brought a large scarf as a prop that she started dragging behind herself, and thus inflating it like a giant polka-dotted parachute.

"She thinks she's Judi Dench," Olivia whispered, and watched, her face scrunched up in horror.

Robin just giggled and started sketching her.

I wasn't sure what the song was about, but clowns it was not, and Maeve performed it really different from her *Sweeney Todd* bad pie song, where she was all shrill and aggressive. Now she was breathy, half talking, half singing, and between her being all dramatic and Grandad playing the song with his eyes shut and not even looking at the sheet music anymore, and only every once in a while looking at her, I found the whole thing really difficult to watch, actually.

The fact that there was a thunderstorm approaching made it even eerier, and the rain was getting heavier, and I don't know, the whole thing made me feel really sad.

Teddy and Katherine Cooper-Bunting were sitting together over to my right, and their friendly banter had gone, their gazes fixated on Maeve.

Robin apparently wasn't affected in the same way, because they were watching and sketching away at a hundred miles per hour, and by the time the song was over, Robin's drawing of Maeve looked nothing like Maeve, or even Judi Dench, but exactly like Cruella de Vil.

I looked at Robin, and they looked guilty for a moment, and then went: "Yeah, soz about that. I think it's the Dalmatian-like scarf."

Olivia, who'd been humming along and looking up from her phone judgmentally every so often, now looked down at Robin's pad and went: "Mate!" before laughing hysterically, and then we all laughed and Brian had to tell us to be quiet, and I glanced across to Katherine Cooper-Bunting, who was looking at me, then at us, then at me again, and she wasn't laughing with us, but looked at us the way you look at people who are being really immature, like, in class, which made me feel like shit and like I had to somehow redeem myself.

Which is why, half an hour later, I followed her out of the room and found her by the open front door, watching the rain.

"Hi," I said.

"Hi."

A great big bolt of lightning snapped across the sky. I counted one, two, three, and then there came the thunder. "Did you know that light travels through the air about a million times faster than sound, which is why you always see lightning before you hear thunder?" I asked.

She looked at me. Crinkled her nose.

"That's why when you see the lightning, and then it

thunders almost at the same time, the storm is right where you are."

She shivered, and I watched goose bumps forming on her arms.

"You cold?" I asked.

"I'm always cold."

"Let's close the door, then."

"No. I like the rain."

There was another flash of lightning, and a low rumble of thunder in the west.

"Tilly," she said, and it was the first time I'd heard my name coming out of her mouth, and it made my heart beat faster than the torrential pitter-patter on the giant puddle on the other side of the door. "I was wondering if you wanted to come to mine tomorrow and pick up my dad's camera. He said it's fine for us to use it, and he's got time to show you it then."

I watched her watch my face.

"I know the performance isn't for a while, but maybe you want to practice beforehand?" she asked.

"I'd—yes, I mean, yes. Of course. I'd love to. I can do tomorrow. What time?"

"How about two?"

"Yes, fine, two is great. Of course. Give me your address, and I'll be there."

"I'll WhatsApp it you."

"Yes, cool, great—I mean, brilliant. Two o'clock."

And then I just left the conversation and walked into the toilet, pretending that was where I was going all along.

I washed my hands and imagined seeing Grace in the reflection, leaning against the radiator.

"You know you shouldn't," she said to me.

"I know."

"So, why?"

"Because I can't stop thinking about her."

"Can't or won't?" Grace asked, and then she was gone, and, well, I didn't know.

When I got back to the room, Teddy was sitting in my chair talking to Robin, and Olivia and Miroslaw were also there, looking at something on Robin's pad.

Katherine Cooper-Bunting was sitting at the opposite side of the room, reading her script.

I walked over to Teddy and everyone and peeked over Robin's shoulder at what they were all looking at.

Someone had drawn a Care Bear, but it had black crosses for eyes and a pierced ear and a pierced love-heart nose.

"Oh my God," I said.

"Mate, it's hilarious. Even I'd wear that on a T-shirt," Olivia said.

"There's a business idea for you, Robin," I said, and everyone looked at me, and Teddy went: "Actually, Miroslaw drew that. You know what they say about Eastern Europeans."

"They're a bit savage?" I asked, looking at the Care Bear's skull tattoo.

"No, they're really good at drawing," Teddy said, and we all laughed.

I looked at Katherine Cooper-Bunting across the room, and she was looking at us, and I realized that she hadn't touched me all day. And that I really wanted her to.

Then Teddy got up and made his way over to her to show her Miroslaw's drawing, and he was all beaming and bouncy and just a bit awkward and completely adorable, and I just thought: *I'm going to hell, aren't I?*

Scene 9

I looked up Alfie the moment I closed the door to my room that evening.

I didn't find him in Katherine Cooper-Bunting's friends list, but in Olivia's, and it absolutely pained me to see that he was incredibly good-looking. Even for a boy.

The fact that Katherine Cooper-Bunting and Alfie Lawrence were no longer following each other gave me all sorts of emotions, mainly bad ones, because you don't unfollow someone unless you had a serious falling-out, and you don't have a serious falling-out unless you meant something to each other. And then I lay there contemplating for ages why I was feeling jealous of a boy she was no longer speaking to.

I tried to go to bed early, but I couldn't get to sleep for ages. It must have been around four when I fell into a tossy-turny, dreamy non-sleep that had me imagining Katherine Cooper-Bunting lying naked in my bed and underneath an equally naked Alfie Lawrence, making all sorts of noises while rain was tap tap tapping on the window.

I woke up at six thinking: *Do I tell Teddy I'm going to her house?*

When I got up, Mum had "made" us breakfast before she'd left for work with a note saying *breakfast*, which was the weirdest thing in the world on so many levels, but mainly because she'd peeled an orange, but instead of just pulling it into its natural segments, she'd cut it into unnatural segments, which she then also cut in half again to make them into teeny tiny bite-size breakfast snacks, which she then placed in the center of a way-too-big serving platter, and by the time she was done with them, they looked like these really sad and saggy sacks of fruit skin.

Grandad and I made ourselves bowls of Frosted Flakes and pretended the fruit didn't exist.

I sat down on the sofa and started eating, and Grandad sat at the table.

I briefly wondered if the next time I'd be home alone would be when he'd die. I swallowed not-yet-soggy Frosted Flakes, and I liked that it hurt.

"You look very worried today, Tilly," Grandad said after a while.

"I'm okay," I said, thinking about Teddy again. "You know when you don't really know what to do? Like, when you have a difficult decision to make?"

"Oh, yes," he said.

"I don't know what to do about something. But it's not really important, actually."

"You should always make good choices," Grandad said.

"Yeah," I said. "It's not always easy."

"If it were easy, everyone'd be doing it," he said. "And nobody would ever die, say, bungee jumping. Or have you seen those silly videos when people lock people in portaloos and push them down hills?"

And I don't know what I found funnier, the idiots on telly or the fact that Grandad watched that sort of thing, but it really made me laugh, and then Grandad really laughed, too, and I felt better already.

Which is why I decided to make good choices and go with the truth. Well, sort of.

> Know how your GF's dad is going to provide the camera for the play and I'm going to be doing the filming? Her dad's got time to show it to me today, and so I'm going over there at two, and I was wondering if you wanted to come.

Deep breath.

The ticks went blue.

I waited one minute.

Two minutes.

Three.

Then he was typing.

> Why would I want to come?

Great.

> Because she's your girlfriend.

She's not. And I don't care if you pick up a camera from her house.

Really great.

What happened to your fierce love?

What's that have to do with anything?

And why are you making fun of me?

Am not.

Are too. Just get the stupid camera, Tills, I don't care.

I tried to come up with a witty reply, but I couldn't, and then it was time to go, because traffic on the weekend was always really bad and you could literally be on a bus for hours, and I wasn't even dressed. I ran upstairs and decided to wear the dress I wore that day we staged that completely cringeworthy scene at Teddy's.

As I was brushing my hair, I was like, *Shit, I can't take Grandad, can I?* and then I was like, *He's literally completely fine, and he even called me Tilly,* and so I was like: "Grandad, do you think you'll be okay for an hour or so, because I have to get the camera from Katherine's dad. You know, for *Cupid's Revenge.*"

"I'll be just fine," he said. "I'll read for a while, and I may have a nap."

And I believed him, because he was just fine.

I took the bus toward Clapham Junction and got off at Battersea Rise to walk up toward Clapham Common.

I could see the grass on the common was already yellow because we were having such a hot and dry summer; even the odd torrential rain shower couldn't salvage it now.

The midday heat was stifling, and the sounds that came from the people hanging out on the common seemed muffled by it. It smelled of barbecues and August sunshine, and the air flickered on the road.

When a church came into view, and the little dot on my phone kept moving me steadily in that direction, it occurred to me that she'd obviously already told me she lived in a church, or by a church, and that I'd had all those inappropriate thoughts about her masturbating in said church.

Sixty seconds later, I'd reached my destination and found myself in the car park of St. Barnabas, Clapham.

Its bell went *dong, dong,* making me jump.

I was right on time.

I tried to look casual, and kind of walked up and down a few times, wondering where exactly I was supposed to be going, because you don't just enter a church, do you. Besides, the door looked shut, kind of contradicting the CHURCH OPEN sign just to its right.

At five past I thought I was going to be perceived as either fashionably late or as one of those annoying people who can never be on time, and so I sent Katherine Cooper-Bunting a WhatsApp saying: I'm outside your church.

Thirty seconds later she appeared around the corner of

a huge lilac tree that probably had all its blossoms burned off during the crazy heat in May.

She looked as if she belonged here, but also didn't.

The way she carried herself and the way she was so beautiful and serious never quite matched the almost completely shapeless summer dresses she wore.

But today's was a cobalt blue, and the thought of what that color probably did to her eyes made me shudder.

As usual, her dress went to just below the knee. I'd obviously chosen to wear my short little floral number to show off my boobs and my legs, but instead of making me feel confident, it now made me feel a bit on the naked side.

"Hi," Katherine said, and when the sun caught her hair, it shone golden. Her eyes danced over my face in their usual playful way.

"Hi," I said.

"Did you get here all right?"

"Obviously."

"Sorry, that's such a stupid question." She laughed and looked at her feet, then back at me.

"No, I'm sorry, it was a stupid answer. Yes. Thank you."

"Okay," she said, and she looked like she was trying to blink the sun out of her eyes. "My dad's in the back."

She led me to the heavy main doors of the church and pushed one of them open.

Cool air that smelled of wax came rushing out.

When the door fell shut behind me, all the outside noise vanished with the closing swish, like when you seal something with those machines that suck the oxygen out.

I could hear the gentle patting of Katherine Cooper-Bunting's footsteps as she rushed down the center aisle.

I stopped and looked up, and you know when you're on a school trip to, like, Westminster Abbey or St. Paul's, and there are, like, fifty other kids there and a gazillion tourists, and everyone is whispering really loudly, and the teachers keep making shushing noises?

I don't think I'd ever been in a church that was so quiet, and it was, I don't know, magical somehow.

But not, like, Disney magical—like magic on steroids—but actual magical.

"You all right?" Katherine Cooper-Bunting asked, her voice echoing in the large space, too loud for it all somehow.

She was standing by the altar, and it was odd to think that someone could grow up in a place like this and would therefore stop seeing it for what it was.

"It's so quiet," I said.

She listened.

"It is, I guess. Well, if you like it, the church is open for private prayer daily. Feel free to stop by. All welcome." She giggled and turned toward the door to the left.

I followed her, glancing up at the altar in passing and kind of nodding at Jesus, out into a courtyard where a man was assembling garden furniture.

He turned around when he heard us.

"Dad, this is Tilly," Katherine Cooper-Bunting said, and I swear it had never occurred to me until that moment that priests would wear anything but that black dress thing with the white collar, even though we used to watch *The Vicar of Dibley* with Grandma, like, all the time.

The vicar of Clapham wiped his hands on his jeans and rearranged his Doors T-shirt.

"Hello," he said, and did an awkward little dance holding out first his hand, then his elbow, then his hand again, and in the end, we went for an elbow bump, and I think Katherine Cooper-Bunting was already mortified, which made her look completely delicious.

"I'm Nick," Mr. Cooper-Bunting said, and I was obviously not ever going to call him just Nick. "Let's go inside. Let me wash my hands, and I'll give you the camera. It's really straightforward, to be honest with you."

I looked at all the folded-up benches and the tables, still stacked on top of one another.

"Do you want help with these?" I asked.

"It's all right, I think I got it," he said, and wiped sweat from his forehead. "I always end up with the jobs that are no fun."

"I know all about that."

"Everyone else is inside, cooking and baking. We've got our parish summer fête tomorrow. Always a lot to do. Come along if you like. All welcome," he said.

"So I've heard." I smiled at Katherine Cooper-Bunting, who shrugged her shoulders.

"Let me help with this," I said, gesturing at all the furniture. "As a thank you for the camera. On behalf of all the actory types. And myself. And because I'm a good person."

Why I felt like I had to point that out I had no idea. Except, of course, I did.

Mr. Cooper-Bunting scratched his head.

"You not one of the actory types, then?" he asked.

"No. I'll be the filming type. I'm only there because my best friend didn't want to go to the audition by himself. And you know how things escalate."

"Tilly is Teddy's best friend," Katherine Cooper-Bunting explained, and I was like, *wow*, because my parents would not in a million years be able to retain this kind of information about a person I was working with/at school with. And they only have two children.

"That's very good of you," Mr. Cooper-Bunting said.

"I obviously don't mind being involved," I said. "And I really don't mind helping with this. I'm, you know, free," I lied (to a priest), because the truth was that I should be at home with Grandad.

"Well, if you're sure," he said. "But be careful. The catch under the tables is, well, very catching."

"Dad!" Katherine Cooper-Bunting groaned.

"Watch your fingers is all I'm saying."

I put my backpack down.

"Let me give you a hand with this one," he said to me, and together we lifted a long table off the stack of more long tables and laid it down in the grass, and I watched him snap one of the leg parts into place.

"I see," I said, and I felt obliged to pretend it was a difficult operation. Parents are odd like that, aren't they? Always explaining the obvious. Like: "Careful, it's hot." Yes, obviously, since it's just been in the microwave for five minutes.

I snapped the other leg into place, and we turned the table around.

"Here, Katie, take over," he said, and gestured for Katherine Cooper-Bunting to take his place.

She quickly wiped her hands on her dress, and we slid another table off the stack and snapped the legs into place.

"Katie?" I asked.

"It's Katherine," she whispered.

"Is it, though?"

She gave me a death stare.

"You know, I call you Cooper-Bunting in my head," I lied, just to see her reaction.

"You think about me often?" she shot back, and I quickly looked round to see if her dad had heard her, which seemed to amuse her, because her eyes lit up, and my heart did another hiccupy thing.

"So, Tilly, apart from being the filming type, what other type are you?" Mr. Cooper-Bunting asked from the stack of benches he was now putting up.

"I'm the generally noncreative type," I said. "But as you can see, I'm very good with garden furniture."

"Yes, I can see that."

"My family are all super creative. Musicians, mostly," I told him. "But I literally can't play the recorder."

"Everyone can play the recorder," Katherine Cooper-Bunting said.

"Everyone in your life, maybe."

"Everyone can play the recorder," she said again, and put her hands on her hips, which made her look all kinds of authoritative, and I realized this was something I was into. And then I felt guilty immediately for having these thoughts about a priest's daughter in his garden in his very presence.

"I'm not exactly musical, either," Mr. Cooper-Bunting said. "But I can hold a tune." And then he started singing: "And did those feeeet in ancient tiiiime—"

"Dad's been doing a lot of funerals," Katherine Cooper-Bunting explained.

We grabbed another bench and assembled it.

"And was Jeruuuuusalem builded here," sang Mr. Cooper-Bunting.

————

"Thank you for helping us with this," he said.

It only took us about twenty minutes to put up all the furniture in the end, and when we were done, we were all hot and sweaty, and Mr. Cooper-Bunting told us to go into the house to cool off and have some water.

I love getting to look into other people's houses, and so when we walked in, my eyes were all like, hello, but there was no subtle exploration of space, because the Cooper-Bunting family home was mayhem.

There were children everywhere.

And you know when someone has a go at you about cleaning your room, and they're like: "It looks like a bomb has gone off in here," even though the only thing on your floor is a pair of knickers?

Well, it looked like a bomb had gone off in the Cooper-Bunting kitchen for real.

The sink was overflowing, there were bowls and utensils and ingredients everywhere, and mixing machines of all varieties were in operation.

A small person was standing on a step so they could reach the counter, and they were cutting strawberries in half. It was impossible to tell if their little fingers and hands were covered with blood or strawberry juice, but no one seemed to care, which was absolutely wild.

Katherine Cooper-Bunting stole a strawberry from the bowl, shoved it into her mouth, and the child shouted: "Mum! Kaykay is taking my strawberries."

A woman with short blond hair that was shaved at the sides just above her ears came into the kitchen, looked at the child, and went: "Why are you telling me? Tell Kaykay."

"It's not fair," the child protested, and Katherine Cooper-Bunting laughed and kissed their head.

"I love you, Mattie. Your strawberries are the best." And then she took another two, ate one, and before I had time to even understand what was happening, she'd pushed one into my mouth.

"Mum!" screamed Mattie.

Jesus! screamed my insides.

I watched Katherine Cooper-Bunting lick her lips and smile, and then I followed her out of the kitchen, down the hallway, and into one of the rooms in the front of the house, where her dad was taking the camera out of its bag.

The racket from the kitchen echoed through the whole house, but no one seemed to care.

"Right, here it is. The only thing I'd say is, make sure it's actually recording," Mr. Cooper-Bunting said, and pointed at the red dot at the bottom of the display screen. "When this comes on, it only means it's ready. Press it again, and you'll see a red circle appear, like this, and that's when it's on."

"Apparently Dad talked to himself for a whole twenty minutes one Sunday," Katherine Cooper-Bunting said, and laughed.

"And my delivery was exceptional, too, so it's a real shame no one heard it. Do you need a cable to charge it?"

"No, thank you. I've got cables at home."

"All right, it's all yours."

"Thank you."

"Thank you, Dad."

"Play with it for a few minutes, and if you have any questions, come get me. I'll be outside," he told us, and left the room.

Katherine Cooper-Bunting looked at me and smiled, and I knew that I needed to get home, but that I also needed to stay.

"Where do you want to go?" she asked, and I didn't have a clue about anything, suddenly, because I hadn't actively imagined myself past this moment in time.

"I don't know," I said. I could barely think, with her being the only other person in the room.

"Let's go back into the church. It's nice and cool in there. We'll go through the front. The kitchen is dangerous," she said, but she laughed, and I realized that laughter was something we didn't really do at my house at all.

I mean, apart from Teddy and me, of course.

But even we'd been doing it less since Grace died.

Back inside the church, Katherine Cooper-Bunting reached

for my hand like it was nothing and led the way down the narrow aisle immediately to the right.

"Come," she said. "This little corner's my favorite."

My head was spinning again, and when I regained my equilibrium, we were standing underneath a statue of the Virgin Mary.

"I always liked her dress when I was little," Katherine Cooper-Bunting said, nodding at Mary. "It's so pretty with the yellow, isn't it? And we always put fresh flowers around her, too. Well, in the summer, anyway."

I looked at Mary, but instead of her face, I saw Grace's, and she looked back at me like she knew all my secrets, and I was like, *What*?

"I played Mary in the Nativity," Katherine Cooper-Bunting said, and laughed, then pulled me down to sit on one of the benches next to her.

She let go of my hand.

"Oh yeah?" I asked, and I decided I couldn't just pretend the hand-holding didn't happen, and so I took hers back in mine and kind of kept entwining our fingers. "Is that why you want to become an actor?" I asked.

"I *am* an actor, daaaarling," she said, and then giggled, and I wondered if she'd taken Alfie to church, let him play with her hand, and told him this story once upon a time.

I let go of her and started unpacking the camera.

"I guess that was the beginning of it," she said. "I know it sounds arrogant, but I really loved the attention. You know, when everyone is silent, waiting for you to speak, and they've actually come to listen to you."

"I get it," I said. "My parents are the same. You're basically on a huge power trip."

"Basically." She laughed, completely not bothered by my questionable comparison and/or analysis. "I guess I'm like my dad. I want people to listen and learn, and want to do good, but not through Jesus, but through the stories of normal people."

"I thought Jesus was normal," I teased. "As in, he was a man."

"He turned water into wine," she said, eyeing up Mary again. "That's not normal."

"What's your party trick?" I asked, and I was immediately like, *Shut up, shut up*, and I quickly went: "Do you, I mean, do you think he actually did that, though?"

She smiled at me, wrinkled her cute nose, looked at me through half-closed eyes, brought her face way too close to mine, and whispered, "Yes," across my lips.

I didn't reply, and I didn't back down from the way she looked at me, and we sat like that for what felt like ten minutes, but was probably just a couple of seconds.

I finally shook myself free and flapped down the display screen of the camera.

Then I pressed the red button twice.

"I think we're in business," I said.

"I'm not going to do a scene," she said.

"You can just talk."

"About what?"

"Talk some more about your friend Mary here if you want. You're the actor, Cooper-Bunting."

"Really? You don't call me Katherine in your head?" she asked, and looked straight at the camera, and thus me.

"Everyone calls you Cooper-Bunting," I said.

"Olivia calls me Cooper-Bunting."

"And Robin."

"Robin only does it because Olivia does it."

"I'm sorry."

"No, it's fine. It's just that, you know, I'm called Katherine."

"It actually appears you're called Katie," I said, and watched the corners of her mouth twitch.

"Everyone calls me Katherine," she insisted, which made her look cute.

"Everyone apart from your family," I teased.

"And those who call me Cooper-Bunting," she said, and now actually smirked a little bit.

"Well, all right, I'll make more of an effort."

"I don't want you to have to make an effort," she said.

"Let me zoom in on your nose."

"No, don't do that."

"Why not? Your nose is cute."

"You think so?"

"Extremely cute," I said, and because I was talking to her through the camera, I found it super easy to tell her this.

"There's a freckle I like," I said, and I watched her skin redden underneath. "You're blushing."

"It's warm in here," she said, and I focused on her lips.

"No, it's not," I said.

"All right, it's not," she admitted.

I put the camera down, and we looked at each other for a few seconds, and I felt this invisible force literally pulling me toward her, and I thought: *Pleeeease tell me I'm not the only one feeling this.*

"Tell me about yourself," she said, and I snapped back into my original position that was still way too close to her to think clearly.

"My dad's a musician, my mum is a classical dancer turned teacher—"

"I know all that."

"Oh yeah?"

"Theodore told me. And FYI, I *do* know that no one calls him that. What about you?"

"Teddy's trying to be more manly," I said to her, and looked at her mouth. "And I don't really know what to tell you. Why don't we talk about you?"

"Because we already have."

"But what do you want to know?" I asked.

"So much," she said, and my brain was like: *GglrghhharghCHHHHHH!* Like when you put a roll of Mentos into a bottle of Coke.

My phone beeped, and I was like, *shit*, because shit, and because I knew it was Mum.

I got it out of my backpack, and when I saw I'd been correct in my assumption, I didn't even read the message.

"I left my grandad on his own," I said to Katherine Cooper-Bunting.

"Do you have to go?" she asked, and I hated it, but I did.

She picked up the camera, and I opened the case for her to put it in before zipping it up.

Our fingers touched and lingered.

We looked at each other briefly and got up.

"I—"

"You like girls, don't you?" she asked, and in a moment of frenzy, I pushed her against the wall underneath the Virgin Mary and kissed her.

And the thing was, I'd never kissed anyone before.

Like, never.

And it was weird, because I always thought it would be a bit odd, and that I might not know what to do, but I knew exactly.

I opened my mouth, and she did the same, and then we were properly kissing with tongues and everything, and I thought how she tasted of strawberries, and that I hadn't been that physically hot in all my life. Like, my skin was on fire. And I wanted to get inside her, like, deeper and deeper, and she seemed to want the same, because she was pulling me closer and closer and closer, and I thought my head would explode. Or I would faint. Or just die.

I tried to open my eyes to look at her but couldn't, and so I kissed her harder again and again and again, and then I became aware of her body—her boobs pressed against mine, and I had to, absolutely had to stop.

I put my hands on her hips and took a step back.

"I have to go," I said, and the whole world felt like it had changed.

"Okay," she said. Her face was flushed, her eyes a deep blue.

My lips were tingling.

She was smiling.

"See you Monday," I said. I put on my backpack and picked up the camera case.

"See you," she said, still leaning against the wall underneath Mary.

I don't know how I managed to walk out of that church.

The moment I was in the car park, I started running.

I ran all the way down the hill to the bus stop and chased the 219 up the other end of Battersea Rise.

Once on the bus, I collapsed onto the seat behind the driver.

I touched my lips with my fingertips.

What kind of insatiable beast was desire?

Scene 10

The moment I put my keys in the door, I heard Mum's tippedy-tappedy footsteps, and I was essentially paralyzed by dread.

"Where the hell have you been?" Mum whispered in a super passive-aggressive way.

"I'm so sorry," I said, and I was sorry, but mostly not. "My phone died," I lied. "I had to pick up the camera from Katherine's house, and because they're having a barbecue at her dad's church tomorrow, I helped them put together a couple of bits of furniture. I was only going to be an hour tops, but there was a sinkhole on Windmill Road. It took me two hours to get home from Clapham Common."

"I can walk from here to central London and back in two hours, Matilda," Mum said, all ragey.

"But you're, like, really fit," I said under my breath, and I swear she looked as if she was going to actually murder me. "I'm sorry, Mum. I won't do it again."

I went to go upstairs, but she grabbed me by the arm and was like: "This conversation is not over, Tilly."

"Oh my God, Mum, I said I'm sorry—what else do you want me to say?"

"I want you to appreciate that your grandad is a vulnerable person who cannot be left alone for long periods of time. I thought you understood that."

"Was he fine when you got home?" I asked.

"Yes, but he might not have been."

"He said he was going to nap."

"You can't leave people just because they're napping."

I literally laughed in her face then, and I was like: "You always left us."

"We never—"

"Yes, you did. I remember Emilin and me staying in a hotel room somewhere when we were little, and you ordered us room service and put the telly on, and then you and Dad disappeared for the night. I bet you could have gone to jail for that. Also, if you were so worried about Grandad, you would've adjusted your work schedule instead of expecting other people to look after him twenty-four seven, but have you done it? No, you haven't."

"I think you need to cool off, madam," Mum said, still whispering in that way that makes me want to scream. "And maybe we need to come to a better understanding of what it means to look after your grandad. Because this clearly isn't working."

"Grandad is fine," I said again. "He's never just wandered off, and apart from calling me Sarah all the time and getting a bit disoriented, he's still mostly together. And I think the reason why his Alzheimer's got so bad back home is because of the shock of Grandma dying, and then he never had anything to do anymore, or anyone interesting to talk to. How would you like it if you could only ever talk to the nurse who comes twice a day? And he couldn't even go to the theater, or to a bar, either, because of the plague. I reckon he'll actually get better now. Being here with us, being able to go out, doing things."

"That's not how Alzheimer's works, Tilly, and you know that. Just because you want him to be better doesn't mean he is. And please can you message Teddy and tell him you're back, because I went round there looking for you."

"Who did you speak to? Amanda?"

"I spoke to Teddy. Hence me asking you to message him. Are you feeling okay?" Mum asked. She shook her head at me and pressed the back of her ice-cold, bony hand against my forehead.

"Get off me—I'm fine. I told you I had to get this camera, and it took me forever to get back. I'm probably dehydrated from being on that hot bus for so long. And FYI, Teddy knew where I was, so I don't know why he didn't say anything. Can I go upstairs now? I have to message him."

She let me pass, and I took two steps at a time.

My room was lovely and cool because I hadn't opened the curtains, and I let myself fall onto the bed.

I hugged my pillow, and my head was wonderfully woozy from kissing Katherine Cooper-Bunting.

I got out my phone to see if she'd messaged me.

But apart from Mum's calls and one message all in capital letters screaming WHERE ARE YOU and a bunch of exclamation marks even though that's a question, there was nothing.

Why did you tell Mum you didn't know where I was? I wrote to Teddy, and the two ticks turned blue straightaway.

> ?

> You knew I was at your GF's house to pick up the camera.

> You said you were going at two, and your mum came around after four, so I figured picking up a camera didn't take you that long, and you must have gone somewhere else after. Sorry.

> Whatever

Teddy never responded, even though he stayed online for ages, and you know when you think you'll feel great after having had the last word?

Well, it didn't feel good at all.

Also, I'd kissed her.

I'd gone to her house, and I'd kissed her under the watchful eye of the Virgin Mary.

And kisses like that—I don't know, but they meant something, didn't they?

Act III

Scene 1

I fell head over heels in lust with Katherine Cooper-Bunting that night.

And it was literally the worst.

I felt like I was on fire.

And when I didn't feel like I was on fire, I felt like throwing up.

I had absolutely no idea what to do with myself after that kiss, and so I tried to lie on my bed and keep calm, but every single part of me was in absolute turmoil.

In addition, I felt awful because I'd been horrible to Teddy. I mean, never mind kissing his GF (okay, she wasn't, but . . .), but then getting all cross with him when in fact it was definitely I who was being the absolute dick.

And to make things even worse, I believed with all my heart that I wouldn't be able to live if I couldn't kiss her again.

Like, how insane does that sound?

I must have fallen asleep sometime around five, but was woken up at seven fifteen, when Dad slammed the front door so loudly that the whole house shook.

I was like WTAF, and wondered if something terrible had

happened, but then I heard the unmistakable sounds of *The Lark Ascending*.

I hugged my pillow and thought of Katherine.

I imagined us waking up together.

All I'd have to do would be to reach across and touch her.

Everywhere.

"I hate that song!" I shouted.

And because sleep was now definitely over, I went downstairs to make a cup of tea.

Mum was in the garden, all barefoot and stretching and breathing and whatnot.

"Was that you shouting?" she asked, without really looking at me.

"I thought I heard an explosion."

"Your father has gone for a walk," she said, and as the ascending lark reached its soaring heights, Grandad appeared.

"Who was shouting? Oh, I adore *The Lark Ascending*," he said. "Is that coming from next door?"

"Yes," Mum and I answered at the same time.

"It's magnificent."

"It's noise pollution," I said, and sipped my tea.

"I think your father is going to lose his mind if David keeps that up," Mum said, and went full-on downward dog. "You know the only thing that annoys him more than the song itself is when the public vote for it as their favorite in Classic FM's annual Hall of Fame."

"I think it's rather magnificent," Grandad said, and rose on his tiptoes to peek over the fence.

"I don't particularly care for it, but it doesn't make me psychotic," Mum declared, and her voice sounded all weird because she was still upside down. "To be honest, I forget it's there after a while. It's quite sameish, isn't it? Like actual birds. I don't really care for them, either."

"You know, I should introduce you to Teddy's dad," I said to Grandad, who was still peeking over the fence. "You'd get on."

"Tilly, maybe let's wait with introductions until those two have sorted it out."

"Teddy's dad used to work with Dad," I explained to Grandad. "At Covent Garden. But he wasn't rehired. You know, budget cuts and all that."

"Damn shame what's happened to musicians," Grandad said. "Bloody government's not giving a toss about the arts. Bastards."

"We'll raise some money with the play, though, won't we?"

"It'll barely make a dent. And how is it being advertised? We need the theater to be packed. How many seats are in the Criterion?"

"I have no idea."

The music stopped.

Mum rolled herself up into a standing position.

"I believe the lark has ascended," she said, and looked at Grandad like she was waiting for him to laugh at her music joke.

He didn't.

He just stood in the garden, looking at the fence, then the house, then me and Mum.

"Grandad, do you want breakfast?" I asked.

He looked at me.

"Do you want Frosties? Or toast? Or I can boil you an egg if you like. I may make myself soldiers—do you want soldiers?"

He took a few steps toward me, and he looked around like he'd never been in our garden.

"Thank you, Sarah," he said, and I saw Mum's head turn toward him.

"Tilly, I think we—"

"I'm all over it." I cut her off. Her inability was once again making me rise to the occasion. "Here, Grandad, let's go into the house and eat breakfast together."

He let me lead him inside by his elbow, and it made me so sad I literally felt my heart breaking just a little bit, which was almost worse than a full-on emotional catastrophe.

I sat him down in the kitchen, boiled water, and was just putting the eggs in when suddenly Teddy appeared in the back door.

"Good morning, friends," he said, and my breaking heart from moments ago was replaced by a wrecking ball that slammed into my chest full force.

I kissed her, I thought, and couldn't look at him.

"How did you get here?" I asked, even though I obviously knew exactly how he got here.

"Yeah, that's a really funny story. I've already told your mother, but the back of the fence seems to have come loose," he said, and tugged at his earlobe.

"That was our secret," I said, and watched the water in the pan.

"It's still our secret. Or do you think she's going to investigate it? Or try to fix it? Or that she's going to use it as a through-route to go to ours?"

"That's not the point."

"What's the point?"

"Why are you here?" I asked, and I don't know why it came out super aggressive, but you know how they say you project the vile feelings you have about yourself onto those you love the most?

Teddy went to the fridge, got out a carton of juice, and poured himself a glass.

"Mr. Taylor, are you having juice?" he asked Grandad, who was looking at the crossword puzzle in yesterday's *Times* someone bought or found on the tube.

"No, thank you, young man."

"And how are you today?" Teddy asked, and sat down next to Grandad.

"I'm terrific. How about you, young man?"

"Grandad, that's Teddy."

Grandad looked at me and shook his head. "I know that's Teddy. Plays Orlando. Funny scene, too."

"Oh yeah, you think so?" Teddy asked, and scooted closer to Grandad.

"Teds, do you want toast?" I asked, and I had an image of Grace casually leaning against the counter next to me going: "You realize he can never know about that kiss."

"I'll have toast. Why not," Teddy said. "And I've come to ask if you wanted to come out with Robin and me. We're going to look around charity shops in Clapham for costumes and then go to the costume shop for a pantomime horse. Apparently, you already talked to them about it."

"Oh yeah, we were going to go the other day. We forgot."

"Come today," Teddy said, and smiled at me.

"Your girlfriend's having a church fête in Clapham; you should say hi," I said, because dropping her into the conversation as soon and as casually as possible seemed to be a good idea.

"Oh yeah?"

"I helped put up furniture for it yesterday. Apparently everyone's welcome."

"I'll message Robin," Teddy said, and got out his phone. "Do you want to come, though?"

Yes, I thought. *Yes, yes, yes.*

"No," I said. "I have to stay in today," I lied, and kind of looked at Grandad, who wasn't looking at me, and Teddy kind of nodded to say he understood.

Teddy's phone vibrated.

"Robin says they're not a fan of the church because they reckon it promotes constitutional homophobia and transphobia among other things, but that we should pop by if there's free food."

"So, basically, they don't approve of churchy people, but they're happy to eat their food?" I asked.

"To be fair, Jesus ate with his enemies," Teddy suggested.

"Judas," Grandad said, and I felt seen.

"Whatever happened to Judas?" I wondered, my throat suddenly dry, my voice croaky.

"I bet no one knows," Teddy said.

"He hanged himself," Grandad said.

Oh . . .

Teddy was now leaning over the crossword puzzle with my grandad.

"Received ten commandments," Teddy read, and looked up at me.

I shrugged, because I didn't know what that meant.

"That was Moses," Grandad said, and Teddy looked around for a pen.

"Here," I said, and gave him a blunt pencil that lived on the pad that was the shopping list.

"Katherine doesn't bang on about all that, but I probably should read up on Jesus and Co.," Teddy said.

"Why?" I asked, and gently lowered another egg into the boiling water. The shell cracked anyway.

"Because I figure Jesus is a big part of Katherine's life. And in order to understand people, you have to understand where they come from."

"Clapham Common," I said, looking at the eggs jiggling about in the pan.

"I feel like you're in a foul mood this morning, Matilda," he said.

"I'm fine," I lied.

"Capital of Senegal starting with a *D*," Teddy said.

"Dakar," Grandad said.

"You're on fire, Mr. Taylor. We should go to a quiz night," Teddy said, and wrote into the squares.

I looked at the eggs again, then set the timer on my phone and watched it count down from five minutes.

"I think your girlfriend will like you even if you're not BFFs with Jesus," I said to him when there were three minutes and fifty-eight seconds remaining.

I could still feel her lips on mine.

"She's not my girlfriend," he said, getting up and putting two slices of bread in the toaster. "But I'd like her to be. Sorry about the thing with your mum yesterday. Love makes me stupid. And I've thought about it all in great detail overnight, and I was jealous," he admitted like the brave person he was. "And the thing is, I'm obviously glad you get on with Katherine, and if you tell me you're not interested in her, then I believe you."

I was silently choking.

"And the thing is," Teddy continued. "I want you to be friends with her, obviously. Because then it'll be almost like having Grace back."

"Teddy—"

"I'm not trying to replace her or anything, but—"

"You are," I said. "But you can't. You know that, don't you? It's not the same, it can't be the same, because Katherine isn't Grace, and I don't want her to be Grace, and if you want her to be Grace, then—"

"Tills, chill," Teddy said, and shook his head. "I didn't mean it literally. It's just I always had fun going round in our little group. I don't want Katherine to be Grace either. Grace was Grace, and she was an absolute one-off."

"She was great," I said.

And then I smiled at him, and he smiled back, and there was so much between us that meant everything to me.

After breakfast Teddy got ready for his day out, Grandad sat down with his book, and I went back up to my room and watched the video I'd made of Katherine, her nose, her freckle, and her mouth for another twenty times, which made me feel absolutely miserable.

I picked up my phone, because you know when you just can't leave something alone?

> I hope you're having a great summer fête today.

> I'm chilling at home with Grandad

I wanted to say something clever about the kiss, but I didn't know what, and so I left it at that.

Then I watched the two gray ticks for an hour, but they never changed color.

I imagined Katherine with her brothers and sisters, surrounded by people I didn't know. I imagined Teddy and Robin popping by, sitting on the garden furniture I'd assembled, eating the things that were being made in the chaotic kitchen, the strawberry cake.

I imagined being there, too, and Katherine looking at me through all the hustle and bustle.

I imagined flirting with her, taking her by the hand and us sneaking off into the church together, right underneath that statue of the Virgin Mary. I imagined her wearing the dress she'd worn yesterday, me kissing her neck right where she'd nuzzled mine that day we were horses, and then I imagined running my hand up the inside of her naked thigh. And up and up, and a little bit farther up.

Scene 2

#friendstolovers #churchsex #firsttimesex #lesbiansex

That afternoon I felt like one of those racehorses you see on telly that's too shocked about the starting barriers coming away to run, and so it just stands there and kind of horsey marches on the spot in a bit of a panic.

My body felt jittery, my brain had become a sluggish cloud of real-life fan fiction, and meanwhile my friends had an afternoon that was an IG dream.

A dream I watched on my phone.

It looked like Teddy and Robin made it to the church fête sooner rather than later and weren't shy about joining in the activities.

Teddy even bought a raffle ticket, which hilariously had the number 666. So, of course, he and Robin sneaked into the church and positioned it in all sorts of places, including the statue of the Virgin Mary where the unspeakable had happened and the memory of which made me physically melt to the floor temporarily.

Forgive me, Teddy, for I have sinned, I thought, but was literally salivating at the thought of Katherine and the way I could still feel her breasts push against mine through our clothing.

She was in a couple of the story posts, too.

In one, she had her arms around Teddy and Robin, and Teddy wrote: *Love spending time with my pals.*

Because I had nothing to do and nowhere to be, and because I'd already been awake and in my bedroom all night, I finally decided to go downstairs again, where the back door was wide open.

Dad had returned after his hissy fit about *The Lark Ascending,* and he was in the garden inspecting the fence.

Mum stood a few meters back, arms crossed, talking.

Grandad was playing the piano, and Rachmaninoff was asleep on the bench next to him.

"What are you playing?" I asked Grandad.

"*Camelot.*"

"What's *Camelot*?"

"The musical is called *Camelot.* Charles is singing one of the numbers from it in the show. It's magnificent. Julie Andrews, Richard Burton, and Robert Goulet were in it when it was on Broadway."

"Goulet is a weird name."

"Oh, everyone was in love with Robert Goulet."

"What's the show about?" I asked.

He looked at me. "Camelot."

I looked at him.

"King Arthur, Tilly. Honestly, what do you talk about at

202

school all day?" he asked. He plinkety-plonked the intro on the piano again, and then he sang the whole song for me, and I learned that Grandad had a really lovely voice.

I hummed along and googled *Camelot* on my phone, and yes, of course I knew the story of King Arthur, but I don't think I ever quite knew just how much his wife was into her knight. Or how much he was into her. As in, he was literally inside her regularly, which led me to the unsurprising conclusion that they don't ever teach you the good stuff at school, which really is a shame. Because if I'd known about Guenevere having a hot affair with a man who wasn't her husband, which was obviously a complete scandal, but that her husband may or may not have also had the hots for him, I may have been a bit more invested in the legend.

"How much money do you think we need to raise with *Cupid's Revenge* to make a difference, Grandad?" I asked.

"Millions," he said. "And those Tory bastards should get none of it."

"Yeah, but realistically?"

"Well," he said, and stopped playing, "let's see. How many people does the Criterion hold?"

I shrugged.

"Look it up, then. You're already on your phone. There must be a seating plan or something online."

I googled it. "Five hundred and eighty-eight."

"Okay, so let's say five hundred and eighty, and multiply that by how much a ticket costs. That's the maximum you can earn, so that's what we should aim for. And I tell you what, we should also do a collection on the night."

"But no one has cash anymore."

"They've got these machines—I've seen them. You just tell it how much you want to donate, and you pay by card. *Big Issue* sellers have them, too. It's rather handy."

"We need to get hold of them."

"I'll speak to Brian," Grandad said.

"Five hundred and eighty times fifteen is eight thousand, seven hundred pounds. Wow. That's a lot."

"Not really, Tilly, if you think about how much people have to pay in rent and bills. That'll help one family for a little while."

"So I say we should aim for ten grand. Why not."

"Bravo!"

"But how?"

"I'll think about it," he said, and started playing again. "But you should think about it, too. Because you've got the better brain."

"Sorry about that," I said.

"Don't get too excited," Grandad said. "Because, you know, genes."

And it was brutal but funny, and I really laughed, and I completely understood why Grandma had kept him around.

———

Just before I went to bed at ten thirty, Teddy added another post to his story of him and Robin on Clapham Common. They were in the little fake pond that usually has water in it, but because of the drought, it was dry, and they were skating up and down it, and Robin was doing stunts, and Teddy looked like he'd never been on a skateboard.

I still hadn't heard back from Katherine, and I can honestly say I'd never been more miserable in my life.

Because did the kiss not mean anything to her?

And if not, how?

Because how can one person feel so much and the other person nothing?

Was anything in life more unfair?

I lay there in complete anguish, thinking about Katherine Cooper-Bunting as Guenevere, and me as Lancelot, sneaking into her bed and doing all sorts of things.

Then I googled "King Arthur fan fiction" and let me just say that I'm not the first person to have fantasized about this.

When I closed my eyes to go to sleep that night, I was out like a light.

Scene 3

On Monday, everyone was super friendly at rehearsal after their Sunday get-together.

Olivia was annoyed she hadn't been there because she had been working, and Miroslaw was like: "Why did no one tell me?" and we were all like: "Because we really suck." Then we promised to never do it again.

My heart was absolutely pounding from the moment I woke up, because I had no idea what would happen when I saw Katherine.

She was talking to Maeve when we walked in, and when she saw me she smiled, and I felt the adrenaline rush through my body, and my heart was like: *Yay*, but then she went back to her conversation and blowing at her cup of tea, leaving me dizzy and wanting.

She came to stand/lie next to me during the warm-up, but there was no touching, which made my whole body ache for it, from my fingertips to the inside of my belly button.

She ran lines with Teddy when Brian and I were setting up for the first scene, which was Miroslaw and Maeve's *A Midsummer Night's Dream*, and I watched them out of the corner of my eye, wondering if I'd actually kissed her or if I'd somehow imagined it, like the way I imagined Grace sometimes.

Or maybe it was something she did regularly. Kiss people.

Because it wasn't that *she* said she liked girls, she only confirmed *I* liked girls. However, she then fully accepted that we launched ourselves at each other (#consent).

I watched her laugh at something Teddy said.

She was entirely beautiful, and I couldn't imagine not wanting her.

"Daaaaaarlings!" Brian interrupted the general chatter and clapped his hands three times. "Let's get to work, okay?"

I picked up the script of *A Midsummer Night's Dream* and sharpened my pencil.

Brian looked at me, and I nodded to say I was ready.

I'd seen a ballet of *A Midsummer Night's Dream* when I was little, which was partly beautiful with lots of tiny fairylike dancers being flown in from the rafters, but mostly disturbing because the main love pas de deux is the woman dancing with a man who is wearing a massive donkey head. And because he obviously had no facial expressions, the fact that his cock and balls were entirely visible through his tights kind of made me see little else.

I know the title suggests it's a dream, and I appreciate that you dream weird shit that doesn't seem to make any sense at all, and sometimes when you see people, it's not actually them (but it is), but to be completely honest, I found the ballet resembling not a dream exactly, but more like someone's drug-induced delirium. With giant penises. Not that I actually knew about either of those things.

No wonder I was completely surprised when I found Maeve and Miroslaw's scene not only accessible, but also hilarious.

Maeve was outrageous as the main lady, Titania, who is the queen of the fairies, and Miroslaw was completely hilarious, too, as a man who doesn't know he's a donkey, and they were almost off the book already, and twice when they got stuck I was late giving them their lines because I'd been too engrossed in the goings-on onstage.

I could feel Katherine Cooper-Bunting's eyes on me, but I decided to remain professional and not even look at her at all.

The first time I got to speak to her was during break.

"Hi," she said.

"Hi," I replied. "How was the fête?"

"Sorry for not replying to your message, but I didn't have my phone on me," she said. "And then it was late, and I thought maybe you'd gone to bed."

"I only wanted to say have a good day, anyway," I lied, because what I'd actually wanted was to flirt with her via WhatsApp.

"I thought maybe you'd come, too," she said. "You could have brought your grandad, you know."

"I kind of needed a day to myself."

"I see," she said, and started playing with one of the buttons on the front of my top.

"Did you want me to come?" I asked, watching her face.

"Daaaarlings!" Brian hollered, and we jumped apart. "It's less than two weeks until we're on staaage, and two weeks in show business is nothing, so I'm asking you to really stay on the ball, okay? At the end of this week, at the very latest, I expect you all to be off book. That means you will know your lines and your songs by heart, and your stage directions, okay? If you have any questions, remember, Tilly and I are here to support you. And on Monday, a week from today, we shall attempt a full run-through."

Charles lifted his hand and was like: "I won't be able to make it on Monday, Brian, I'm afraid."

Brian looked as if he was going to throw a tantrum, and I felt Katherine Cooper-Bunting go all tense.

"You see, the one hundred thousandth Eurostar service will arrive at St. Pancras that day, and we're all going to document it."

Brian didn't move, and I don't think I did either, and before I could ask, Brian was just like: "All right. We'll do it Tuesday. I wouldn't want you to miss the Eurostar."

I obviously needed the whole story, so I sought out Maeve behind the bar, and she told me that Charles was one of those people who stand at the end of station platforms with enormous cameras and photograph trains for no apparent reason, and then write notes about them that mean nothing to normal people, in tiny little notebooks.

How weird are train people?

And who knew they just walked among us?

Anyway, after the break we rehearsed "Seasons of Love," and

it turned out that no one apart from Olivia and Katherine had learned the words off by heart or knew how to read them off the sheets they were holding, and at the crucial point where they have to sing this great big list of things by which you could measure time, they sounded like they were collectively and uncommittedly just mumbling made-up words.

"It's bad," Robin whispered directly into my ear.

"It's so bad."

Teddy, who was standing next to Katherine, kept looking at her mouth as if to lip-read, and she was blushing, and the thought of anyone but me making her blush like that made me so lovesick I wanted to die.

I looked down at the sheet music and wondered if I should shout out the correct lyrics, but the whole thing sounded like such a hot mess already that I reckoned if I started contributing, Brian's head would probably explode.

I looked back at Katherine.

She was still flushed.

It crossed my mind that it could be an embarrassed blush because maybe she knew they sounded like a bunch of tone-deaf tourists doing karaoke.

In the end it was Grandad who ended the horror show by hitting a billion wrong notes on the piano. Everyone stopped singing, at which point he started playing something super dramatic, like *dadadadaaaaaaaaa, dadadadaaaaaaaaaa*, and everyone looked at him with their mouths hanging open.

"That was rubbish, wasn't it?" Grandad said.

Olivia snorted, because, yeah, it was funny, but I was also like: *Is he having one of his aggressive episodes?*

He got up from the piano, looked at everyone on the stage, and went: "Why are you all here when you don't care?"

"Sorry, but I care," Oliva said, stepping forward and raising her arm.

"I care," Katherine said, somewhat predictably, and stepped out of formation, too.

Teddy pulled on his earlobe.

"You want people to give you their money, and you don't want to work for it? You think when you go to the theater on a Saturday night, the people onstage can be lazy? Or fool around? Or not know their lines? They've done that same show seven times that week already. And had rehearsal. And had voice lessons and warm-ups and costume fittings. And they still deliver."

Everyone looked sheepish, apart from Olivia and Katherine.

"Everyone gets something wrong sometimes, but then you get on with it. I know you're not professionals, but that shouldn't matter. Brian just told you to stay on the ball. And you can't even be bothered to look at your sheet and read your lyrics? Shame on you."

It went super quiet then with people just standing and slightly fidgeting, and then an ambulance drove past, blaring its siren, and people finally moved.

"Right, people, take five minutes to gather yourselves," Brian said, "and then we'll do this again."

Everybody dispersed quietly, except for Olivia, who gave us another demonstration of her vocal capabilities by singing the opening lines of "Seasons of Love" full volume and then some on her way to the toilet. We could still hear every word she was singing even after the door had shut behind her.

"She'd be great at initiating a flash mob," I said, and laughed, and then I was like, *Wait a minute*, and I turned to Robin and grabbed their arm, because: "That's exactly what we should do. A flash mob. That'll get so much attention. I could film it and put it online, and then people will come and see us at the Criterion, and we can make five hundred twenty-five thousand six hundred pounds. We can post a link to the Acting for Others Fund for people to donate. Oh my God, this is the best idea I've ever had."

Robin looked at me, clapped their hands, but then ended their excitement prematurely mid-clap.

"Where would we do it? Down at Clapham Junction? That's a bit shit. Also, there's only, like, fifteen of us. And that includes you and me."

"That doesn't matter since we've got Olivia. She's so loud."

"And I feel like Teddy could try harder. He doesn't have a bad voice—he's just lacking confidence," they said.

"I mean, I obviously can sing along, too. I mean, I'm not a singer, but—"

"Hey, why should everything be about whether or not you're good at something? Sometimes it should be enough if you want to do it," Robin said.

And you know what? I'd literally never thought of it that way, and I wish I had because I think there could have been a lot more joy in my life up to now.

"Well, maybe not, like, brain surgery," Robin added. "Or piloting a commercial aircraft."

I googled "how do you organize a flash mob," and I caught Katherine's eye purely by accident as she walked past us, carrying two cups of tea. She smiled, and I watched her make her way over to the piano. She sat on the bench next to Grandad and put their cups on the top of the piano.

She talked to him, and he nodded and smiled at her.

"I don't know why Olivia hates her guts," I said.

Robin followed my eyeline, then looked at me and said: "And I don't understand why everyone's in love with her."

"Everyone who?" I asked.

"Everyone you," they said, and I got hot hot hot.

"Oh, no, it's literally not like that."

"Keep telling yourself that."

Katherine and Grandad started playing "The Entertainer" on the piano.

And you know when a song is such a predictable choice, and also basically shit, but it makes you laugh anyway?

I looked back at my phone and had another stroke of genius.

"Oh my God!" I said, and jumped up and sat immediately back down again, because, you know, dizziness, but then I got up again and was like: "I know where we'll have the flash mob. And I know how it can be bigger."

I got my feet all tangled in the strap of my backpack, and I kind of stumbled along our row of plastic chairs.

I walked over to the piano and knelt down next to Katherine.

"I need your help," I said, and she stopped playing.

"Are you okay?" she asked, and moved to sit sideways on the bench to face me.

No, I thought, because I was on my knees and looking up at her, and I'd read that sort of fan fiction only last night.

"Yes," I said. "You need to convince the people at Stagecoach to help us with a flash mob."

She looked at me like we didn't speak the same language.

"We're going to stage a flash mob at St. Pancras station when that Eurostar arrives, and I'm going to film it, and we'll put it online, and then loads of people are going to want to come and see *Cupid's Revenge*, and that way we'll raise loads of money. And you and Olivia can be famous."

She still looked at me.

"Please."

"I don't actually want to be famous."

"Lies."

She tried not to smile, but couldn't quite stop her mouth from doing it.

"Okay, fine, maybe I do."

"Olivia said your mum is one of the main people at

Stagecoach. You need to convince her to get all the Stagecoach mums involved, and I bet they'd totally go for it. If not, just show them, like, really good flash mobs on YouTube or something, and I bet they'll change their minds, like, straightaway."

"But that's on Monday already."

"Yeah, a whole week away. I thought they had rehearsal every day, like us."

"Yes, but they've got their own show to rehearse for. They're doing *Thoroughly Modern Millie*."

"Please," I said, and then I made the monumental error of taking her hand, but I only did that because we were being super friendly, and it felt natural.

Well, for a second it felt natural.

She kind of looked down at our hands, and back up at me, and then our fingers went wandering, and entwining, and in fan fiction I would have just buried my face between her legs because, you know, that's how #friendstolovers happens. Not necessarily in front of other people, though.

"It could be fun," I said, watching her watch our hands. "We'll rehearse together, like, on Friday or maybe Saturday or something, because they're only up the road at your church, aren't they? And then we'll go to St. Pancras Monday morning."

"I can't promise anything," she said.

"Obviously."

"But I'll ask Mum."

"Thank you," I said, and got up, and my right foot had gone

to sleep because I'd been crouching all awkwardly. I went to turn away from her, but she didn't let go of my hand.

"Tilly," she said, and pulled me back.

"Yes?"

"I've got two standing tickets to see *As You Like It* at the Globe this Sunday. Will you go with me?"

"You should really go with Teddy," I said, my heart pounding. I looked around to see where he was.

He was behind the bar sipping a cup of tea, talking to Miroslaw.

"I mean, you're doing a scene from exactly that play."

"But I don't want him to get the wrong idea."

"What do you mean?" I asked, even though I knew exactly what she meant.

"He likes me, doesn't he?" she whispered, and looked past me, probably at him. "But I don't feel that way."

And my heart felt like a person in one of those shark movies, where they get attacked, and the shark is taking great big chunks out of them, but the person is still trying to get away even though they already no longer have legs and are bleeding out.

"Teddy is literally the nicest person," I said to her.

"I know. I just ... It wouldn't be fair. Please don't say anything."

"Okay," I said, and she finally let go of my hand, and the loss of her touch made me pause, and the anticipation of what could be made me speechless.

Scene 4

What do you do when you know that the person your best friend is in love with isn't in love with them? And you've kissed the object of their desire and have since fallen into a lustful stupor?

Well, it's easy, right? You confess; of course, you confess, else you wouldn't be their best friend but a liar and also a cheat.

I obviously couldn't do the first thing, and there was no way I was going to tell him about the second thing, never mind the third, and so I pretended Katherine Cooper-Bunting had never said anything to me about him, and that I had no idea what it felt like to have my tongue in her mouth.

On the bus the next morning, Teddy and I ran lines, and he was literally stumbling over every other word.

"You need to get it together," I said to him. "I realize you're in love and all that, but these aren't hard."

"No, Tilly, they're actually very hard, and I'm not convinced a lot of them even mean anything. Nor do they rhyme."

"Of course they don't rhyme. It's not, like, 'Humpty Dumpty.' These are people who are having an actual conversation."

He looked at the text.

Then at me.

"Why are you suddenly on William's side?"

"I'm on Orlando's side."

"Tilly, you don't understand. Acting is literally the hardest thing I've ever done."

"How?" I asked. "You said these people were parrots. Explain to me why you suddenly think it's hard. Look, Teddy, you don't have to think beyond what's on the page. Honestly, it's not like you have to come up with anything new and/or interesting. These words have been said millions of times by millions of people. The effort is minimal—you need to just get on with it."

I looked at Grandad, who was sitting in front of us, but he was either not listening, or choosing not to react.

"Wow," Teddy said, and pulled his earlobe. "Have some compassion for a fellow human, Matilda."

I don't even know why I was so annoyed. Except, maybe I did. This exaggerated kind of artistic suffering that I knew so well from home really rubbed me up the wrong way. When apparently no mere mortal can ever comprehend how hard it is for them as creatives. You know, they struggle so absolutely even when they're just living and breathing.

And yes, I get that dancers and musicians kind of have to be masters of their bodies and instruments, but that whole "acting" thing is just bollocks, isn't it, because all you need to do is concentrate on what you're saying and know why you're saying it. Right?

And when you're not doing it right, then the director or the assistant director will tell you.

Teddy looked at his scene again and groaned.

"You know what they say about the road to hell, don't you?" he asked.

"Yes, it's called Cooper-Bunting," I replied in a staggering moment of clarity.

"I'm really glad my broken heart is providing you with so much entertainment."

"How is your heart broken?" I asked.

"I'm just not sure she likes me."

"I think she likes you just fine," I said, and I wasn't lying then, because she did like him.

"What do you think I should do?" he asked. "Because I've done all the basics. Like, I've gifted her chocolates, and I'm paying her compliments, and I'm asking her a lot of questions about herself and her family. And I remember things, like, the other day her sister Stella went to a party, and I asked how it went."

"Teds," I said. "Why don't you just be yourself and see what happens? You can't force these things."

"It's just, you know, I don't want to make the same mistake again."

"What mistake?"

"Like with Grace."

"But . . . Teds. You did nothing wrong."

"I should have told her that I liked her. I shouldn't have

waited, hoping she'd look at me one day and feel the same. I never got to tell her, you know."

"Teds . . ."

"I think she died not knowing that I loved her."

"She knew."

"Not that I was in love with her."

"Love is love," I said. My lamest moment yet.

"You'd want to know if someone's in love with you, wouldn't you?" he asked, and I honestly didn't know the answer. I mean, the thing is, of course I'd want to know, but only if I was in love with them, too. Because if not, it would be forever awkward, and every time that person hugged me a bit too long, I'd feel a bit gross.

"You'll find someone wonderful," I promised him, because he would. "Just be yourself."

"I'm being a bit of an idiot around Katherine, aren't I?" Teddy asked, and I laughed.

"I wouldn't say idiot—"

"Oh no, but you would, Matilda."

"You're perfectly relaxed with Robin and Olivia and Miroslaw, so just be like that with her."

"These things are easier said than done."

"I'm just saying don't force it."

"If I were a Care Bear, would I be Desperation Bear?" he asked, and I LOLed, but I didn't answer him, and in retrospect I probably should have done, because you know when people don't say anything in those situations it usually means they agree with the thing you want them to not agree with.

"Now," I said, "Robin and I are going to Wimbledon after rehearsal this afternoon to check out the charity shops for a donkey head. Because you didn't find one on Sunday."

"We weren't looking very hard, to be honest," Teddy said. Then he pointed at Grandad and looked at me inquisitively.

"Grandad is going trainspotting with Charles, and then they're taking the train to Wimbledon, where Charles lives, and I am collecting Grandad from the station, and we're taking the bus home."

"You know, Matilda, you should consider a career in operations."

"You know, Theodore, just because I'm not a total idiot when it comes to arranging an afternoon and people other than myself traveling on public transport, this doesn't mean I need to make a career out of it."

"I may come," he said. "Unless Katherine wants to run lines. I think she's starting to get fed up with me, because I literally forget everything all the time. But how am I supposed to remember things when she's right there?" he asked, and gestured ridiculously.

"Just . . ." I said, and what I really wanted to do was to scream, because why her? Why? Whyyyyy? Besides, it was all Grace's fault. If she hadn't died, Teddy and she could be one of those cute couples who get together super young and stay together forever, and I

221

could kiss Cooper-Bunting all day long without feeling this crippling guilt. "Look. Orlando's in love with Rosalind, and she's in love with him. So, really, all you have to do is say the words, because you, Teddy, are also in love with Katherine."

"I've already explained to you that I'm not sure she's in love with me," he said, and I rolled up the printout of his scene and whacked him on the head with it.

"Well, Orlando isn't sure either, so just bloody channel that. Honestly, why is this my life? And how are actors even worse than musicians?"

"Don't compare me to our parents," he said, and whacked me back. "Do you really think you'll be able to find a donkey's head in Wimbledon?"

"Fuck knows," I said, and Grandad turned round.

"Sorry," Teddy and I said simultaneously.

———————

Katherine didn't want to come to Wimbledon, and Olivia was working a late shift, but Miroslaw was up for it, and so he, Teddy, Robin, and I went.

"Where is the tennis?" Miroslaw asked when we got off the bus in the center.

"Oh, that's actually not here. That's by Wimbledon Park," Robin explained. "When it's on, there are special buses that take you."

"Is it good?" Miroslaw asked.

"If you're into tennis, I guess," Robin said. "I've never been to see it."

"I'm into Rafa Nadal. He's so sexy."

"Ew," Robin said. "He's old. That's dirty."

"That's sexy," Miroslaw said, and smacked his lips, and we were all like: "EW!"

According to Robin, who was a charity-shop pro, the charity shops in Wimbledon weren't as good as those in Chiswick or around Notting Hill, for example, but you were still able to find really good stuff sometimes.

Apart from the donkey head, we also needed to find breeches for Katherine, some sort of cowboy outfits for the Phantom and his wife, and a massive, gown-like dress for Maeve's scene from *Sweeney Todd*. She said she could provide her own knives and pies and even blood, but Brian said he was concerned about her getting arrested if she got caught by British Transport Police on her way to the Criterion Theatre carrying an actual cleaver. Also, when she mentioned the blood, he gagged so hard that he got tears in his eyes, which was a bit LOL.

Anyway, first we went to Subway to get a giant sandwich each, because we were literally starving, and Robin made us all get the vegan cheese instead of the regular one, because they were like: "You'll never want actual cheese again," but everyone was like: "No, you're actually wrong."

Miroslaw got a meal deal again, because he was obsessed,

and as we were walking down the main road, he kept going: "It's only one more pound for a drink and crisps," every two seconds.

Anyway, we didn't find anything in the first charity shop.

In the second one we found an ancient men's nightshirt, and Robin said they'd transform that into an actual shirt for Teddy. We kept walking down the Broadway, past the Starbucks and the pet shop, and then we literally stopped in our tracks, because in the window of this charity shop was an Eeyore onesie.

"No," Miroslaw said.

"Yes," Robin said.

"I'll go back to Poland."

"No, you won't—you're ours now," they said, and linked arms with him. "Let's just ask how much it is."

"No way," Miroslaw said, but Robin was already opening the door, and we all piled into the shop.

"Maybe you can cut off the hood," I suggested.

"Excuse me," Robin said to the man behind the till. "How much is the Eeyore onesie in the window?"

"The Eeyore onesie in the window is ten pounds," he said.

"Is there any way we can get a reduction on it? We're doing a charity concert and are in need of costumes."

"No," the man said, but smiled.

"I see," Robin said, and looked around. "You see, the thing is just that we're raising money for charity."

"This is a charity shop," the man said. "We're raising money for cancer research."

"I understand that, and it's a really good cause, but maybe we could make a deal or something. We could write in the program that we got our clothes here, for example."

"Kate, customer!" the man suddenly hollered, and we all flinched.

"Let's just go," I said to Robin, and went to leave.

"No, w—"

"You all right, Alex?" A Scottish woman interrupted us. "How can I help?"

The man, Alex, looked at us, Robin looked at him, then at the woman, Kate.

"Hi. I'm Robin. This is Tilly, that's Teddy, and this is Miroslaw. We're doing a charity concert for a charity called Acting for Others, which is a theater charity, and we need a donkey head, but it's really hard to find a donkey head—"

"Have ye thought of getting the front bit of a pantomime horse?" the woman, who apparently had zero problem following our story about needing a donkey head, asked.

"Well, yes, but we don't want to get anything off Amazon if we can get it at charity shops and, also, we literally have no budget, and we'd rather get a donkey anyway. I mean the head."

"You should call New Wimbledon Theatre, pet," Kate said. "I bet they've got all sorts of nonsense lying around."

"The thing is, it's kind of not this Sunday but the Sunday after, and I'm in charge of costumes, and I was wondering if maybe you could reduce the onesie in the window for us."

She scrunched up her whole face, took a deep breath, and went: "I hope it's a comedy, pet, because whoever you're going to put in that suit is going to look ridiculous."

"I'm wearing the suit," Miroslaw said, and raised his hand.

"Oh, pet."

"It's *A Midsummer Night's Dream*," he then told Kate, who looked at us like: *Why are you being horrible to the nice Polish boy?*

"You can have it for a fiver," she finally said.

Alex clearly didn't agree with the reduction.

As he was putting it through the till, Kate undressed the mannequin in the window.

Before Robin went to pay, Alex went: "Can I interest you in a stick-on mustache collection for three pounds?" and Robin went: "You absolutely can."

They held it up for the rest of us to see and went: "These are for Cooper-Bunting."

Teddy stared at them for a moment, and you literally could see his brain working, and then he went: "I bet she's hot with a mustache."

"You two need to get a room," Robin mumbled.

Alex chuckled.

I got all trembly at the image of her with a mustache, because, well, lust was this weird thing that just grabbed you and shook you, even when you were just standing at the till of a shitty charity shop.

Scene 5

The next day during break, Robin was teaching Teddy to jump off the low wall in front of the social club on their skateboard, and Olivia was inside singing Malcolm's song "Being Alive," because apparently, she was "properly obsessed with it, mate," and wanted to add it to her repertoire.

Since we hadn't actually met Malcolm himself, we'd never heard it before, I mean, I hadn't heard it before, but all the theater types said they knew it, even though I wasn't sure they were being truthful, because, you know, people want to sound important/knowledgeable, and so they go: "Oooooh! Yes!" when they actually mean: "I have no idea what you're talking about."

Grandad was accompanying Olivia and kept playing cute little flourishes. He only ever did those when he was working with her, and sometimes with Charles, but only when Charles had his hearing aid switched on. Once he'd tried it with the Phantom of the Opera and his wife, and they almost lost their minds about it and sang all the wrong notes and words, and it was basically a complete catastrophe.

Katherine and I were outside, sitting under the big tree just across the road.

She was reading her Shakespeare, and I was finally getting a closer look at the mustaches, which we'd gifted her earlier, and I could hear Olivia giving it all the "Being aliiiiiiive."

"She sounds incredible, doesn't she?" I asked, trying to break into the plastic.

Katherine gave me a look.

"What?" I asked. "She does. She's great. Get over it."

She passed me her sheets. "Run lines with me," she said.

"Anything for you, Cooper-Bunting," I said, and she blushed. "You know you're going to have to wear one of these, don't you?" I asked, and held up a ridiculous, enormous ginger mustache to her face.

She slapped my hand away.

"In your dreams."

"Why not?" I asked, sticking a thin black one on me. I leaned back against the tree and closed my eyes. "And I don't need the script. Photographic memory, remember? At least sort of."

"Fine," she said. "There is a man haunts the forest that abuses our young plants with carving Rosalind on their barks—"

I literally LOLed, because she said it at a million miles per hour.

"What?"

"Once more with feeling, maybe?" I asked.

"We're just running lines."

"Doesn't mean you have to sound like Alexa on speed."

"Fine. There is a man haunts the forest that abuses our young plants with carving Rosalind on their barks," she said, and I heard her slapping her hand against the tree we were sitting under.

When it was my turn, I looked up into the sky and proper exaggerated the emotion.

"I am heeeeee that is so love-shaked!" I said to Katherine and reached for her hand. "I pray you, tell me your remedy."

She looked at me, as Rosalind, then smiled as Katherine, and started laughing.

"You look really cute as a boy," she said.

"I look really cute as a girl," I told her, and she blushed some more. "Have you asked your mum about the flash mob?"

"Yes, and she's talking to the parents today."

"That's great, thank you."

"She's actually totally into it," she said, drawing small circles on the back of my hand with her thumb. I shifted slightly so no one could see it from across the road. "She says if we put it on YouTube, she could add a link on the Stagecoach home page, too."

"What if it all goes really wrong?"

"It's not going to go really wrong. Your girl Olivia will save the day, no doubt."

I looked at her, and I was like: *I think you're jealous—please be jealous.* Even though I know that's, like, totally immature.

"All I said was that she's good. And she is," I said.

Katherine let go of my hand, picked up her pen, and scribbled some notes onto the page.

"Why don't you like her?" I asked.

"Why do you love her?" she asked back.

"I don't."

"Have you decided about coming to the play with me?"

"I—"

There was a high-pitched yelp, a skateboard clanked, a car came to a screeching halt, and "Being Alive" stopped.

I jumped up.

Teddy had failed at his stunt and was lying in the middle of the car park like a human beetle, arms and legs flailing in the air, and the skateboard was in the middle of the road, under a car.

I completely froze.

I registered Robin apologizing to the driver, saying it was their fault, and it wouldn't happen again, and then I looked over to where Teddy was still lying on the ground, but everything looked like I was seeing it through a lens and with a yellow filter.

"Tilly?" Katherine Cooper-Bunting asked me, but I couldn't drag my eyes away from the car, and Robin, who was retrieving the skateboard from underneath it.

"Tilly," she said again, and took my hand, which spooked me completely and pulled me right out of my trance.

I ran across the road, jumped over the low wall, and raced over to Teddy, who was trying to get up.

I grabbed his arm and pulled at it.

"Are you stupid?" I shouted. "Get the fuck off the ground, you asshole."

"I'm fine, Tilly," he said, and reached for my other hand, and I pulled him up.

"Why are you stupid?" I asked again, and slapped his arm. "Or are you trying to kill yourself?"

"I'm fine. Stop shouting. It was an accident."

"Yes, I know all about accidents," I yelled at him. "The fuck, Teddy!"

Olivia approached us carefully.

"Mate, I'm first-aid trained. Let's get him in the recovery position."

"Let's not," Teddy protested when she was trying to push him back down onto the hot concrete. "I'm fine. I'm just really clumsy."

He looked from me to Katherine, who was now standing behind me, and his face went from stupid to full-dimpled grinning, and I swear I wanted to slap him all over again.

"And when I say I'm clumsy, I mean I'm still growing into my limbs. But I'm mostly grown. I'm definitely grown in other areas. Like, you know what I mean? Fully grown."

"Shut up, you idiot," I said. I slapped his arm again and gawked into his eyes to check for brain damage or something. His pupils looked blown, but they always looked that blown when he was in close proximity to Katherine, and so I just shook my head at him.

"Mate, you feelin' okay?" Olivia asked, and inspected his dangly arms and hands.

"My pride is hurt," he declared, and brushed himself off. "But I'm fully functioning. Like, everything is in perfect working order," he added, looking at Katherine and Olivia, and then he did that unbearable thing of wiggling his eyebrows, and I decided it would be the kindest course of action for me to physically remove him from the most cringeworthy scene of his life thus far. But I was still absolutely livid.

"Everyone all right?" Brian asked, standing in the entrance.

"Fine," I said, and pushed past him, Teddy in tow.

"Fine," Olivia said. "Just a man being a man."

"She called me a man," Teddy whispered to me, and I pushed him down onto a plastic chair.

"I think maybe you should take your stunts to the skate park," I said.

"Then I can embarrass myself in front of people my own age. Brilliant," Teddy replied.

Robin appeared and handed him a glass of water.

"Would you rather be embarrassed or dead?" I asked.

"Would you be offended if I told you I'd have to think about that?" Teddy mumbled.

"Fuck off, Teds," I said, because that's such a stupid thing to say.

I imagined Grace sitting on the bar, shrugging at me, and I was just like: *Even the dead are making fun of being dead now? What is this?*

"I'm glad you're okay," said Katherine Cooper-Bunting, who

had appeared out of thin air and, honestly, you should have seen Teddy's face, and I thought: *Isn't love just the absolute pits?*

I went to the bar to boil the kettle, but Maeve was already all over it.

"It's so nice being around young people," she said to me.

"I'm finding us exhausting," I said, but she just laughed.

"At least you still know how to have fun. We're all miserable old bastards." And then she shouted: "Aren't we, Brian? We're miserable old bastards."

Brian looked at her and went: "What are you on about, you crazy old woman?" and then Maeve laughed again, but this time it was a full-on cackle.

Brian told them all to gather so they could have another crack at "Seasons of Love," and it appeared Grandad's telling off on Monday had had an effect on them, because they all knew their words, and the Phantom's wife seemed to be proper into it, despite the song being about all the things she clearly regards with utter contempt: gays, drugs, and HIV.

Brian was pleased, and after two successful run-throughs, he was like: "Let's leave it there for today, everybody. Well done."

When we left, there was an ice-cream van parked on the exact spot Teddy had fallen off the skateboard.

"Mr. Whippy, anyone?" Robin asked.

A man was sitting in the driver's seat, window rolled down, reading, but when he heard us, he lifted his hand and waved.

We all waved back and then we were like: *Why are we waving at the random man in the ice-cream van?*

"Mate, this is creepy," Olivia said.

"This is my dad," Miroslaw told us.

"I'm sorry, what?"

"My dad got an ice-cream truck from Clacton-on-Sea. It's a good truck, no?"

"We call it a van," I said, and we all went closer.

"Why did you get a van, mate?" Olivia asked, and looked inside it through the hatch window.

"My dad is an entrepreneur. Ice-cream vans are a good tradition in England. He got all the papers and hygiene certificates now."

"I can show you good routes," Olivia said. "I know this part of town better than anyone. And I can tell you the shitty little roads no ice-cream van'll ever go to, and people there want ice cream, mate, so I'm not being funny, but I think that I'm your gal."

The door opened, and Miroslaw's dad got out and was like: "Hello."

"This is my dad," Miroslaw said, and everyone was like: "Hello, Miroslaw's dad."

"Can we have ice cream?" Robin asked, and Miroslaw's dad was like: "Sorry, no ice cream yet. First the truck, then the ice cream. I only picked it up today from Clacton-on-Sea."

"Olivia will show us where it's good for selling," Miroslaw said to his dad, and it struck me that they probably never actually spoke English to each other.

"Mr. Lewandowski, if you give me a lift home, I'll show you a good route right now," Olivia said, and blinked at him through her enormously long lashes.

Miroslaw's dad did a comedy curtsy, opened the passenger door for Olivia, and gestured for her to hop in by wildly flailing his arm around. Olivia did a funny little full-body shake, and climbed in the van.

"Sorry we can only take one," Miroslaw said to the rest of us. "Road safety is very important. And Dad only just got his British driving license back from the DVLA."

He got in next to Olivia, and it was literally the cutest thing, with her sitting between them and waving at us like the Queen.

"Sarah, let me get you an ice cream," Grandad hollered, coming out of the social club and power walking toward us. When he got to me, he smiled, took my hand, squeezed it, and then got out his wallet.

Everyone was looking at me.

"They don't have any ice cream yet, Grandad," I said.

"Oh. Just as well because I don't have any cash on me. Or maybe they take card? Everyone takes card these days. Remember the toilets in the station in Paris? Even they took card. One euro to pee. Bloody rip-off. Bloody French."

I didn't say anything, but linked my arm into his.

Katherine smiled at me, and it felt so overwhelmingly personal that I had to take an actual step away from her.

Miroslaw's dad honked the horn, and then he put the music

on, and the van started playing a crackly rendition of "The Teddy Bears' Picnic" as they reversed out of the car park.

————

On the bus I sat next to Grandad, and Teddy sat behind us.

At one point his head appeared right next to my face, and he said: "I'm sorry I was an idiot."

"Just—" I looked at him. "Be careful. You promised."

"I know. I'm sorry."

"Okay."

When we got home, I had a wee and washed my hands, and when I looked at myself in the mirror, I realized I was still wearing that mustache.

I'd spent the whole afternoon wearing a fake mustache.

I'd had an emotional come-apart about Teddy, wearing a fake mustache.

I'd met a parent, wearing a fake mustache.

Grandad mistook me for his wife when I was wearing a fake mustache.

"At least I'm cute with one," I said to my reflection before winking at myself and then pulling off the mustache in one swift movement.

"Ouch!"

I imagined Grace sitting on the floor next to me. "You're such a dick, Matilda," she said, and rolled her eyes.

Not three seconds later, the whole area where the mustache had been started to itch, and an hour later, I'd developed a blistery fake-mustache rash. And instead of going: "My poor child, what happened to your sweet face?" Mum just went: "There's steroid cream in the medicine box."

At dinner, Grandad told us the story about Rachmaninoff having no teeth for the twentieth time, and then he kept calling me Sarah, and Mum kept going: "That's not Sarah, Douglas, that's Tilly," and I was so exhausted from just being in the same room with them that I went to my room at, like, seven, to go to bed.

Olivia had posted an IG story about her trip in the ice-cream van, which was hilarious and made me think that if she had her own TV show, I'd watch. Like, I wouldn't even care what it was about. She's literally so entertaining.

Teddy messaged me at nine.

> Do you think Katherine thinks I'm an idiot?

> You are an idiot! I'm still cross with you.

> Soz, but seriously.

> I think she thinks you're great.

And you know when you say things to make other people feel good, and it's the right thing to do, but at the same time it's also the wrong thing to do?

Scene 6

> Stagecoach is on board and ready and willing to rehearse with us on Saturday morning.

> They want to know if we need permission for a flash mob.

> Because they don't want to get arrested.

I let my head fall back onto my pillow.

It was only six thirty in the morning.

I'd been willing to ignore one beep, but not three, and Katherine had clearly decided three messages were necessary to deliver this news.

> Why are you awake, Cooper-Bunting?

> We pray at sunrise.

> Joking.

> Good news re: Stagecoach. I'll find out about legal issue.

I saw that she was typing, but then she wasn't, and she went offline.

I would've given anything to know what she typed but then decided not to say.

I sat up in bed and looked around my room.

Who do you call to ask permission for a flash mob? And wasn't the point of them that they were a surprise?

"Why does everything have to be so complicated?" I asked no one, and as I moved my lips, my mustache rash felt like it had a pulse.

I googled "do you need permission for a flash mob," and the internet said no, but to let security know, and I decided this was easy enough as there were always loads of security people at stations. I also took a screenshot of the page in case anyone asked about it on the day. But who would arrest a bunch of stage-school kids and geriatrics singing a song about seasons of love?

Having said that, though, this might be exactly the sort of thing people would get arrested for these days.

Then I googled "what gets rid of mustache rash" and the internet was like: "Do you mean beard burn?" And I was like: "Kind of," and then the internet was like: "Put on the cream your mother told you to put on yesterday," and I was like: "Fine!"

I lay back down, but I couldn't go back to sleep, and half an hour later I messaged Katherine to say that you didn't need permission for a flash mob, but that we'd have to tell the people at St. Pancras station.

When I got to rehearsal at twelve, Katherine had already

spoken to Brian, who had already contacted Mrs. Cooper-Bunting's boss at Stagecoach, whose name was Nora; Nora had said that she was going to find someone in charge at St. Pancras, because we needed to know where to plug in the electric piano, the location of the "facilities," etc., etc.

Also, first aiders had been appointed, Olivia being one of them.

"I see you don't need my help at all," I said to Katherine.

"The early bird catches the worm and all that," she said, and then made a ridiculously cute little chirping noise.

"I thought we were horses," I whispered, which made her really laugh, which delighted me to no end.

"I feel like we never got adequately acquainted as horses," she said.

"No, we got adequately acquainted at church," I said, and checked her pupils for a reaction, then her nose, and her cheeks, which blushed right on cue. "Also, you were scary as a horse."

"I was not," she said, and she looked cute when she was pretending to be outraged.

"You were biting me," I said. "I was so relieved when you left my territory."

"I was never biting you. Horses mutually groom one another as a sign of care and attention."

"You were going for my jugular."

"Was not."

"You so were, Cooper-Bunting," I said, and then she blushed full-on, and I can honestly say that I'd never felt quite that sense of satisfaction from anything I'd ever done. I mean, apart from having my tongue actually in her mouth. I was just about to say something about vampiric horses when, out of the corner of my eye, I saw Teddy, who was making the sign for tea in my direction, and so I shook myself off like a horse that had just rolled in dirt, nodded yes, and took a big horsey step away from her.

"Tilly," Katherine said, and stepped too close to me again, and I wanted to run, but I wanted to stay, and her lips were moving, but I was like: "What?"

"About Sunday. Will you come to the Globe?"

And I was once again at that point in life where I knew I should have just left it and walked away, but I didn't because I couldn't, and so I just looked at her, my heart racing, my body temperature suddenly way above normal, and I was like: "I'd love to." And then I allowed myself to smile, and she smiled back at me, and it was the best feeling in the world.

———

For the rest of the day, I felt like I was a person in a TV series who's having an affair, and at the same time I was the audience watching me. Like, I wanted nothing more than to spend time with Katherine, but I was like: *Nooooo, don't spend time with*

Katherine, because there's only one way this is going to end, and that's in tears, so why are you going there?

I was trying to concentrate on my job, but ended up just staring into space, and at one point Robin was like: "What is wrong with you today?" and I was like: "I was up at six," and they were like: "Anything on your mind?" And I was like: "Not really," and when I scratched my mustache rash, they were like: "You have to stop touching it," but I ignored them and scratched it some more.

On the way home, Grandad asked me a million things about the flash mob and flash mobs in general, and I ended up showing him one where a full orchestra and choir invaded a town square and sang that song by Beethoven that's in German, and all these German people in sandals and mustaches were taking pictures on actual cameras.

I spent the evening figuring out how to start a YouTube channel, which FYI isn't difficult, just a bit of a faff.

At nine my phone beeped.

It was a WhatsApp from Katherine, and of course I felt like I was going into complete cardiac arrest even before I'd opened the message, which was a picture of two beige horses nuzzling each other.

I flopped down on my bed and buried my head under my pillow.

Half an hour later I'd finally decided how to reply: That's a good picture of us.

I watched the ticks go blue straightaway and, I don't know, but her not responding was somehow perfect.

I looked at myself in the mirror, and I was grinning, and then I imagined Grace-face, reclining on my bed, filing her nails, singing: "Tills and Katherine sitting in a tree—"

"Stop it!" I said to my reflection.

Scene 7

The day after was Friday, and Brian had messaged the group and asked everyone to bring in the costumes they thought they wanted to wear for the performance, and OMG!

Eeyore's detached head from the five-pound onesie was now a bonnet, and when Robin put it on Miroslaw, who was, as usual, in a black pair of super-skinny jeans and a cutoff black T-shirt that was almost long enough to be a dress, Brian was just like: "Darling, this isn't Eurovision."

Robin took my hand and was like: "Please will you ask your dad to ask at his work if they have a donkey head? Because this is my first official gig and, I mean, look at Miroslaw."

Miroslaw pointed at his head and was like: "It's not my fault," and Robin was like: "I know, babe. It's my fault, because that thing's bullshit and we need a donkey head."

"I'll ask my dad," I said.

"I'm such a twat," Robin said, and looked at Miroslaw. "That Kate woman was right—he looks completely ridiculous."

"I look sexy," Miroslaw said, and stuck his bum out and slapped himself, and I LOLed, but then I was like: Wait, because maybe he's actually into that.

"I'm messaging Dad right now," I said, and scratched my mustache rash.

"You have to stop touching it," Robin said, and I was just like: "I'm not touching it," and Robin was like: "You're touching it," and I was like: "You're not my mum," and then Robin looked at me and we burst out laughing.

Robin was like: "Luckily we didn't stick one on Cooper-Bunting's angelic face."

I didn't say anything, but looked over to where Katherine was rehearsing with Teddy and got out my phone to message my dad.

I watched the ticks go blue, but he didn't reply.

Katherine was laughing, and Robin and I both looked up.

"Teddy's so funny," Robin said.

"He's hilarious."

"Do you think if you were straight, you'd fancy him?"

"That's—"

"Yeah, a completely stupid question. I just listened to myself say it. Sorry."

"No, it's not even that. But you know he's like my brother, right?"

"In *Game of Thrones* there was a lot of brother-on-sister action."

"Ew, no. In the Taylor and Booker households, there'll be exactly zero brother-on-sister action. I can't even imagine him having sex. Ew! Stop it, don't make me imagine it."

"I reckon he's a giver," Robin said, and I was just like: "EW!" And everyone turned to look at us, and Robin cackled at my distress, and then they were like: "Cooper-Bunting's a lucky woman."

"She is," I mumbled, and if Robin was imagining Teddy with his face between Katherine Cooper-Bunting's legs, well, I was imagining my face between her legs.

And then I thought, you know, it was absolutely feasible that I was just horny, and maybe if Katherine and I actually had full-on #friendstolovers #oralsex, it would be out of our system. Because surely, once the anticipation is over, you can live like a normal person again, rather than be forever caught up in this hormonal stew of stupidity.

And then, maybe, we could be just friends without this sexual tension, and we'd be much happier, and not every look and every conversation would need to be analyzed.

Because, you know how when someone says something to you, you're like: *Oh, okay*, but then when someone you fancy says something to you, you're like: *What do they actually mean?*

Like, come on!

I swallowed really hard and tried not to think about Sunday.

During break, Grandad, who'd made it his business to regularly check the ticket sales for *Cupid's Revenge*, announced we'd only sold fifty-three tickets, and he was like: "You realize that's only seven hundred and ninety-five pounds, and the average rent down here in London is one thousand seven hundred pounds per month. So this really isn't going to help a lot of people, ladies and gentlemen, so we need to impress with our flash mob and start selling those tickets."

His little announcement made me laugh, especially when he said "flash mob," because to me it's always a bit hilarious when old people say words that didn't exist when they were young.

I asked Grandad if he needed to go to the toilet, and we walked there together, and then I was like, *Oh well, when in Rome*, and I went into the ladies', where I found myself once again face-to-face with Katherine, and I was just like: *Does no one else ever have to wee?*

Katherine was like: "We can take the bus to Waterloo and walk along the river to the Globe if you like."

"I can meet you at the Northcote Road bus stop?"

"Play starts at two thirty, so let's say twelve? Just in case?"

"Just in case," I said, and we sort of just gravitated toward each other, and the next thing I knew was me being pressed against the sink right next to the out-of-order hand dryer, and she was kissing me.

"Sorry," she whispered against my lips. "I've been wanting to do that for ages."

"Keep doing it," I said, and she did.

"Have you, erm, have you told anyone about this?" I whispered. "I mean, not this, but Sunday?"

Katherine Cooper-Bunting stepped away from me, and I

was like: *Why did I even have to say anything? We could still be snogging.*

"I got the tickets for my birthday, so Mum and Dad obviously know I'm going," she said.

"No, I don't mean your family. People here," I said, and put my hand under the out-of-order dryer for no apparent reason.

"I'm not exactly besties with Robin and Olivia," she said.

"Do you mind, like, not telling Teddy?"

"Why would I tell him?" she asked. "I told you I don't want to hurt his feelings, so I'm obviously not going to say anything."

"Okay, great, because I don't want him to be, you know, sad."

"I'll see you tomorrow," she said.

I wanted her to say something else, preferably in relation to the snogging, but all she said was: "For the flash mob rehearsal. We're starting at ten—don't be late."

"When have I ever been late?" I asked, suddenly super irritated.

She didn't even look at me again. She just opened the door, walked out, and left me standing there, and I was like: *What just happened?*

————

At dinner I decided to bring up the donkey head to Mum, because Dad never messaged me back, and of course Mum was all like: "I don't know if your father has time for that sort of thing at the moment."

"Mum, all he has to do is speak to the wardrobe person and say: 'Do you have a donkey head?'"

"I'm sure everyone's really busy."

"Suzanne," Grandad said, and sat up in his chair. "To be honest with you, I can't see how it's a chore to ask about a costume. I'd do it, but I don't know anyone at Covent Garden anymore. Hell, you could do it—you worked there long enough. It would be for a good cause, and no one can say anything about that, can they? Especially when it's people like us in need. These kids are working hard to make a difference."

Mum pushed the peas on her plate into a neat square, and then started eating them row by row. She didn't say anything else about it.

I was getting ready for bed when there was a knock on my door, and I thought it was Dad, because I'd heard him get in half an hour earlier, and I assumed he'd come to tell me about the donkey head.

"Come in."

"It's me," Teddy said, and stuck his head inside.

"Oh, hi. Your cat's probably next door."

"I hate that cat," he said, and took his shoes off. "I've come to spend the night."

"Excuse me?"

"Yeah, like we used to."

"When we were ten."

"Yeah."

"No, you're not."

"I've already brushed my teeth, and I'm in my pj's."

"No. What's wrong with your own bed?"

"My bed is fine, it's my home that's become unmanageable."

I looked at him.

"Mum has taken on two new students."

"At ten o'clock in the evening?"

"Yes, and also no."

"What are you even saying?"

"She's teaching via Zoom, and they're in New Zealand, so it's actually Saturday morning there, but it's ten o'clock here, and I can't sleep with that going on, because Mum thinks she has to speak and play extra loudly, you know, like Zoom is this crazy abyss you have to shout into or something. Why are old people so clueless when it comes to technology?"

"I think that's just our parents," I said.

"It's not. The Phantom of the Opera just messaged to wish me and my lovely wife a very happy fortieth wedding anniversary."

"Okay, fine, you can stay, but if you snore you can fuck off."

"When have I ever snored?"

"Well, you haven't yet, but as I was saying, the last time we did this we were ten."

"I think Grace was here, too," Teddy said.

"Yes, and she slept in the bed with me, and you slept on the floor."

"Please, don't make me sleep on the floor," he pleaded, and plopped himself down on the bed. Then he picked up the one-eyed teddy I'd had since birth and went: "Barnaby, mate, Tilly's so cruel."

"Give me that," I said, and took Barnaby, and Teddy made a snoring noise. "Teddy!"

"Just hold my nose shut when I snore. But I don't snore."

"Apparently, all men snore, and it obviously has to start at one point, so I'm guessing puberty, and since you're so full of puberty at the moment, I'm probably correct in assuming that the snoring has commenced."

"That's why you're a lesbian, right?" Teddy asked.

"That's exactly why I'm a lesbian."

It was too hot for a duvet, and so we just lay on our respective sides, and I switched off my bedside lamp.

There was a light breeze, and apart from cool air and scales on the piano, it also carried the all too familiar tune of *The Lark Ascending*.

"You realize this is musical warfare, don't you?" I asked.

"We should move out asap."

"Together?" I asked. "Because I thought you and Katherine Cooper-Bunting were going to live happily ever after."

"I don't think she likes me," he said after a pause that had me wondering why I had to bring it up in the first place. "You know, like that."

"I'm sorry, Teddy," I said.

"So, you're not even going to lie to me and tell me I'm wrong?"

I imagined Grace lying on my other side. She was a thumbsucker, and she was doing it now. "Tell him the truth, Tilly," she whispered at me.

"I can't look inside her head, what do you want from me?" I asked Teddy.

There was another silence, apart from *The Lark Ascending*.

"Yeah," he said, sighed, and rolled to lie on his back. "Do you remember when I fancied Ramona Hutchison?"

"No."

"Yes, you do. She ended up going out with Simon Hughes?"

"Oh, yes."

"And he turned out to be the dumbest kid ever."

I giggled. "He was pretty stupid, wasn't he?"

"I learned back then that that's literally the only thing that will ever help you get over heartbreak. The person you thought was everything suddenly dating someone who's literally a total knob."

"Or ugly AF."

"I hope that if Katherine rejects me, she at least has the decency to start dating someone really dumb and really ugly."

"Me too," I said ever so quietly, and wondered when exactly lying had become so easy.

Scene 8

"I'm going to go over there right now and beat him to death with his violin, I swear by all that is ho—"

"Good morning," Teddy interrupted Dad, who was raging in the kitchen.

"I didn't see you come in," Dad said, and Teddy was like, "I actually spent the night, Roger, because the humble lark isn't exactly in my top ten, either."

Dad looked at him, then at me.

I shrugged.

"Is Grandad up yet?" I asked. "I'll make some breakfast, because we've got to go in half an hour."

"It's Saturday," Dad said.

"We're collaborating with Stagecoach today."

"Doing what?"

"Something secret."

"Nothing illegal, I hope."

"Dad. It's Stagecoach. They're, like, Brownies, but singing and dancing."

"Brownies on speed. All tits and teeth," Teddy said, and Dad looked worried.

"I'll check on Grandad and then I'll make tea," I said.

Only halfway up the stairs did it occur to me that I hadn't heard anything from his room, and I was like, OMG, what if he's dead, but instead of thinking: *That would be horrendous, because I don't want him to die*, I thought: *That would be inconvenient because we've got rehearsal.*

I knocked really loudly, you know, loud enough to literally wake the dead, and I can't tell you my relief when I heard footsteps.

"What do you want?" Grandad asked, and I took a step back. He was wearing literally nothing but one of those white undershirts old men wear on telly.

"We were just wondering if you're almost ready."

"What are you doing at my house?"

"Grandad?"

"What do you want?"

"I . . . Grandad, it's Tilly."

"Get out of my house!" he shouted, and charged at me, and I got such a fright that I ran down the stairs.

Mum and Dad, who'd heard the shouting, were already at the bottom and coming up toward me, and Grandad was behind me, still shouting for me to "Piss off, you!"

It was horrible.

Like someone had suddenly removed all filters and gone: Welcome to dementia.

Mum let me go past her, and Teddy took my hand and

pulled me toward him, and Dad went up toward Grandad, like someone who didn't want to spook a horse.

"Get out of my house! Get the hell off my property!" Grandad kept shouting, and I pushed Teddy away and ran into the garden.

"Douglas, calm down," I heard Mum say, and then there were a couple of huge thuds, and Mum shrieked, and then I heard someone groaning, and then Dad went: "Teddy, give me a hand."

I tiptoed to the back door and peeked inside.

"Roger, we should call an ambulance," Mum said.

All I could see were everyone's legs and feet, and Grandad sitting on the bottom step with his bottom half literally exposed, and I can't tell you how much I wished none of that was my life.

"He's fine, Suzanne," Dad said. "He just slid down a few steps. Does anything hurt, Dad? Does your back hurt?"

Slowly I walked back inside.

Grandad looked at Dad and went: "Of course my bloody back hurts. I fell down the bloody stairs, didn't I?"

And then he shrugged off Dad and Teddy and started for the kitchen and went: "I need a cup of tea. Sarah!"

When he saw me, he stopped and asked: "Can't a man get a bloody cup of tea around here?"

"I'll make you one," I said.

"I think you should finish getting dressed first," Dad said, and kind of gestured for Grandad to go back up the stairs.

Grandad looked around, but didn't move.

He looked at me again, and I said: "Go on, I'll have your tea ready when you come back down," and then Dad touched his arm, and Grandad shrugged him off and kind of growled, but he did let Dad walk him up the stairs, and then Grandad went: "Stop rushing me, Dad."

We stood there in complete silence for a few seconds, and then Mum stated the obvious by going: "Tilly, I don't think he's well enough today to come with you."

"I'll stay at home," I said. "I don't need to go to the thing. I'm not even really in it."

"I'll stay with you," Teddy said.

"I'm going to cancel my lesson," Mum said, and looked at her phone, her bony little hand shaking.

"It's fine, really. I can manage," I said, and put the kettle on. "I'll be fine."

"I'll stay, Suzanne," Teddy said. "Honestly, I'm a terrible singer, anyway. They'll probably get on a lot better without me."

"I'm going to pop next door to speak to your parents," Mum said to Teddy, and picked up her keys and disappeared out of the front door like a woman on the run.

"Can you call Brian?" I asked Teddy, and he nodded. "And maybe Katherine?"

"Yeah, cool, I'll do that. Let me quickly go next door, too, and get my charger and all that."

"Thank you," I said, and sat down at the kitchen table.

When Teddy came back, I still hadn't made tea.

Mum and Dad went to work, Teddy and I sat on the sofa and watched the first season of *Chilling Adventures of Sabrina*, and Grandad stayed upstairs in his room.

Rachmaninoff wandered in at one point, and Teddy took him up to visit Grandad.

We made sandwiches at two, because we were finally getting hungry, and then the doorbell rang.

I thought it was the postperson or something, but when I answered, Robin and Katherine were standing outside.

"Surprise!" Robin said.

"Hi," Katherine said, and my heart was so happy that I wanted to cry.

"What are you doing here?" I asked.

"Teddy told us you were having a crisis, and so we thought we'd come by and report on the great success that was the Stagecoach rehearsal," Robin said.

I looked at Katherine.

Who looked at me.

My whole body was trembling, and I wanted her to hold me.

"We're just making lunch. Do you want a sandwich?" I asked them.

"Sure," Robin said, and Katherine said nothing, and I was like: *Okay, maybe I should stop looking at her and actually let these people into my house.*

I opened the door all the way and led them into the kitchen.

"What are you all doing here?" Teddy asked, looking up from grating cheese.

"Look at you being all domestic," Robin said, and walked over to give him a hug. "Cheese and pickle for me, please."

"What do you want?" I asked Katherine.

"Just cheese, thank you."

"Boring," Robin said.

"It's not boring—it's just cheese."

"How about I make us all a Theodore Booker Special," Teddy asked.

"What's that?" Katherine looked at me.

"I don't know," I said. "He never makes me sandwiches."

"That is such a lie, Matilda. I make you sandwiches all the time. But maybe I've simply never offered you my special."

"You've definitely never offered it to me."

"It's cheese," Teddy said, and placed grated cheddar on the bread. "And crisps . . ." He grabbed a pack of barbecue beef crisps and put a handful on top of the cheese. "And ketchup."

And you know when ketchup makes that disgusting squelching sound?

Everyone went: "EW!" And then laughed.

Teddy put the other slice of bread on top and squeezed down. Some ketchup trickled out from the side.

"That's . . . amazing," Robin said.

"That's disgusting," I said.

"You haven't even tried it," Teddy complained, and made another one.

Robin grated the rest of the cheese, and when Teddy had made four Theodore Booker Specials, we all went to the garden and pulled the table and chairs into the shade by the fence which, surprising to no one, was still broken.

"All the Stagecoach kids are psyched about Monday," Robin said. "I think one step up from being onstage is the prospect of being on camera, and I bet everyone's getting their hair and nails done as we speak. Also, they literally all have super-pushy parents—failed actors, if you know what I mean—which means that there's no way they won't know the words on Monday. So even if our lot suck ass, the others'll pull us through." Robin took a huge bite out of their sandwich. Crisp crumbs rained down onto the plate. "This is delicious," they added, mid-chew.

"Nora, who is really nice, by the way, played the piano for us, so it'll be okay if your grandad can't come on Monday," Katherine said to me, and I wondered if I could ever look at her and not want her.

A moment later her leg made contact with mine, and everything felt right again.

"The plan is for everyone to arrive in smallish groups," Robin explained. "Luckily, there's a public piano at St. Pancras, so we don't have to bring the electric one. Nora's already spoken to an actual person at the station, and someone's going to make sure it's ready and COVID-cleaned for us. Nora, or your grandad, is going to just be randomly playing the song, and then the smallest people are going to start singing, which is going to attract a crowd—"

"Obviously," Teddy said, his mouth full of sandwich.

"Oh, I know. I don't even get it. I mean, who actually wants to hear children singing? But, anyway, then we'll all join in group by group, and then Olivia is going to really give us the great big finale, and at that point we're hoping that all the Eurostar people will have come off the train and made it through the customs bit."

"And you came up with all that in, what, a couple of hours?" I asked, and licked ketchup off my hand.

"Well," Robin said, and looked at Katherine. "Her mum's one of the pushy people."

"A failed actor," Katherine said, and nodded.

"Oh, whoops," Robin said, but Katherine waved them off.

"No, it's true. Mum always says she would have liked to have been an actor, but you know, life."

"That sucks," I said.

"Yeah," Robin said. "Imagine you can't be who or what you are."

"I think she's all right, actually," Katherine said. "She really likes being a mother. And she loves running her Stagecoach franchise."

"And now she's able to live vicariously through you," Robin said, and it actually didn't sound bitchy.

"It's great, actually," Katherine said. "Because, you know, some people have a really hard time convincing their parents that doing something creative is a good idea."

"Tilly and I have spent all our lives trying to convince our parents that doing something noncreative is a good idea," Teddy said.

"Speaking of your 'rents," Robin said, and reached for my arm. "Any news on the donkey head? I mean, you obviously have bigger fish to fry at the moment, but it's kind of urgent. Like, in a very privileged way."

"I'll speak to my dad again. I didn't have a chance with all the drama."

"No, no, I totally get it. Are you really okay, by the wa—"

"What are you all doing here?" Grandad asked, and I actually flinched.

He stepped out into the garden, and I was like, *Thank God he's put clothes on this time*. Rachmaninoff was right behind him, cheerfully hopping along on his three legs.

"Grandad, this is Teddy and Robin and—"

"I know who everyone is, Tilly. I'm just asking what they're all doing here?"

"We're just eating lunch, Mr. Taylor. Would you like me to make you a sandwich?" Teddy asked.

"Cheese and pickle, please, young man," Grandad said, and when Teddy opened his mouth, I was like: "Cheese and pickle, Teds."

Everyone smirked.

"Your cat is adorable," Robin said, and walked over to him. They knelt down to pick him up, but he swatted their hand away and growled.

"I literally love him," Robin said, but retreated.

Robin and Katherine stayed until after five, and you should've seen Mum's face when she got in and we were all sitting in her garden.

Like, it's obvious she thinks Teddy and I have become incapable of forming friendships since we lost Grace, and to suddenly walk in on a group of us having fun in the garden made her physically twitch a bit, and I was just like: "Mum, this is Robin, they are the costume person at our show, and this is Katherine, and she's an actor."

Everyone went: "Hi, Mrs. Taylor," and because it sounded like they were literally five years old, we all laughed, and Mum was just like: "Hello."

Then she looked over to where Grandad had fallen asleep in the chair with Rachmaninoff curled up on his lap, and they were both snoring.

"He's fine," I said. "He was with it through lunch, he had his pills, and now he's napping."

"We should be off," Robin said, and looked at Katherine, who was like: "Yes, definitely. I have to be home for dinner."

Teddy and I walked them to the door, and when I looked at

Katherine, there was suddenly this huge proverbial elephant in the room, because of our theater date the next day, and because we hadn't been alone since snogging in the toilets.

I could see that she was thinking about it, and I was obviously thinking about it, but she wasn't going to say anything, and I wasn't going to say anything either, and in the hallway our fingers brushed, and then we just kind of stood there, and did the whole "bye, see you Monday" thing, and all the while the air was getting thinner and thinner, at least in my opinion, and hotter and hotter.

Just before she stepped out of the house, she turned to me, traced my mustache rash with one finger, and said: "I feel bad for saying it, but I'm so glad it was you rather than me who tried that thing on."

"As humans our greatest accomplishments come through observing other people's failures," I said.

"At least she looks good with a mustache," Teddy said, interrupting whatever looks Katherine and I were giving each other.

"That's exactly what I said," Katherine said, then left and, unlike Robin, once again didn't turn back round to wave at us.

But she did message me later.

I was already in bed, trying to go to sleep, but everything that had happened that day plus everything that didn't happen, and everything that might or might not be happening in the future, a.k.a. at the Globe the next day, was going round and round in my head.

> If you can't come tomorrow, I understand. Just let me know. You don't have to feel bad about it. I get that family comes first.

And so then, of course, I was like: *Does she really mean it, or is she giving me an out? And maybe she doesn't want to go with me anymore, but why? Did she not like kissing me? Is this goodbye? It feels like goodbye.*

I don't know about you, but for me everything is worse in the dark, and so I was having a proper episode about it all, and I had to literally make myself breathe in and out a couple of times to get a grip.

"Why is this the worst thing ever?" I asked no one, and I was just going to lie there and suffer in silence, but then I decided to message her back.

> My mum and dad are home all day tomorrow, so I don't have to worry about Grandad. I'm looking forward to seeing the play.

I read it three hundred times before I decided it was kind, yet noncommittal, and then I pressed send.

I put my phone away, rolled over, and closed my eyes.

A minute later it vibrated.

> I'm looking forward to the play, too.

And it wasn't at all what I wanted to hear.

Scene 9

What do you wear to the Globe?

I tried on my favorite summer dress, but because it's red, it looked ridiculous with my red-raw mustache. But I couldn't wear jeans because I'd melt, because the Globe's literally outside, and I obviously couldn't wear the dress I wore when we kissed in church, and then I was like why is even something as basic as getting dressed suddenly this completely stressful thing?

I decided I really like my red dress, and in order to break the ice in regards to the rash, I messaged Katherine to tell her that I knew it was there and that it looked bad.

You could barely see it yesterday, she messaged back, and I was just like: Says the woman who had to poke it.

I didn't mean to make fun of you.

Did too.

Did not!

When we met at the bus stop, she just looked at me and went: "It's actually fine," and then she gave me the quickest peck on the lips which made me forget all about my insecurities immediately.

Let me say just one thing about the Globe theater: It's so much more fun than indoor sit-down theaters, where you're forced to stay in your tiny seat all squashed up between other people who are squashed up in their tiny seats.

I mean, you can obviously also sit at the Globe, but you're still basically outside, and there are no seats but benches, but the whole standing thing was great.

Also, the actors used the groundling area (because that's who we were, "groundlings," i.e., lesser people/the poor) as part of the play, which made you feel like you were literally in the play.

To say Katherine was delighted would be the grossest of all understatements, because she was beaming.

When her and Teddy's scene came around, she grabbed my arm and didn't stop squeezing it until it was over.

It was interesting seeing other actors play it, because Teddy and Katherine do it really well, but it's mainly funny and a bit silly, probably because Teddy is both funny and silly, but the actors at the Globe played it more like: It's great to be in love, but at the same time it's the most awful and inconvenient thing in the world, and if you could go back and not fall in love, you probably would. Which obviously resonated with me.

So, the whole time I stood there wondering if Orlando and Rosalind, and all the other lovesick idiots in the play, as well as

Katherine Cooper-Bunting and I, just needed a good shag in order to move on with our lives, because you basically can't be that long-suffering forever without losing your actual mind.

And then I realized that Shakespeare was a bastard because he chose Rosalind to "cure" poor Orlando. Like, imagine real-life Katherine dressing up as a boy and tricking Teddy into helping him get over her by constantly declaring his undying love. That's, like, cruel. But as an audience, of course, we're laughing.

Anyway, I had a lot of interesting realizations that afternoon. Which I suppose is the point of theater. Apart from entertainment.

When the play was over, we whooped and cheered, especially at the woman who played Rosalind, because she was excellent, and she even turned to us and blew us a kiss, and Katherine was just like: "That really made my day. How brilliant of her to acknowledge us."

"Make sure you'll do it one day," I said, and she took a deep, deep breath, and I thought she was going to say something really actory and profound/wanky, but she just nodded.

South Bank was busy when we got out, and we walked back slowly, holding hands, and Katherine gave me a rundown of what we'd just seen.

I decided to not share my newly attained wisdom on the cruelty of love, and then we bought a 99 Flake just under Waterloo Bridge, where we stood in the shade by the booksellers, leaning on the wall and looking down into the river.

The tide was out and there were small, gentle waves lapping at the sandy shore.

"You know, I've literally never touched the river," I said, and ran my index finger down the inside of her arm from her elbow. "Your skin is so soft, by the way."

"We went swimming in it once," Katherine said. "Thank you. Somewhere near Richmond. But I didn't like it. It's so gross."

"It's not gross—look, there's nothing in it. Like, no weeds, no giant underwater plants, nothing."

"You don't know what washes in with the tide."

"Shoes, look," I said, and pointed to a washed-up one.

"Imagine a shoe touching you while you're swimming," Katherine said, and shook herself like a wet dog.

"I thought nothing could faze the Cooper-Bunting."

"Why would you say that?" she asked, and wiped ice cream from my nose with her thumb, then licked it off.

My knees turned to jelly.

"You just give that impression. You're calm and collected, and you know what you want and don't want."

"Like what?"

"Like, you want to go to drama school, so you're pursuing that, and you don't want to go out with Teddy, so you're not doing that."

"Do you want me to fancy Teddy?" she asked, and I decided to take an actual bite out of my soft-serve ice cream just so I could have my mouth full and think about an answer.

"Because I don't fancy him."

"You can't help who you fall in love with," I said, and then I was like, *OMG, why are you saying words like* love?

"No, you can't," she said, and her eyes seemed to be telling me she was definitely not falling in love with me, either. I wasn't sure she wanted to even snog me again, a thought I found impossible to deal with.

Which is why I sucked another huge bite of ice cream into my mouth that made the front of my brain feel so painful that I thought for a moment my body had decided to spontaneously reject my right eye.

"Why do you want me to fancy him?" she asked again after a moment.

I noticed that she had moved a couple of centimeters farther away from me.

"Because he fancies you," I said.

"And you don't?" she asked, and I decided to not answer the question.

I also decided to not look her in the eye.

I did, however, decide to be honest with her.

"We had a friend," I said. "Her name was Grace. She lived a couple of doors down, and we hung out together, like, all the time, and I guess Teddy really loved her. And one day she was out on her bike, and she was run over by a car. Just like that, you know. And Teddy, well, he never told her how he felt, and he thinks that she died never having known how much he loved her, because he never said it because, well, we always think we've got all the time in the world, don't we? And he wants it to be different with you. He wants to do all the right things. And he really wants a happy ending."

Katherine looked at her shoes.

"We all want a happy ending."

"I know."

"How long ago did this happen?"

I imagined sixteen-year-old Grace, leaning against the railing with us, eating a 99 Flake. "We were thirteen when she died. Three years ago."

"I'm sorry," she said.

"Thank you."

"And I'm sorry I don't fancy him."

"He'll get over it, I'm sure."

"Of course he will."

I turned back to face the river and watched the Thames Clipper sailing past.

Katherine stood next to me.

Our pinkie fingers touched.

"Are you ready to go?" I asked, and she nodded. Her little nose scrunched up, and I booped it, and she may or may not have blushed because of that, and she was starting to say something, but I decided that what I really wanted was to kiss her, and so I did, and she kissed me right back and made a little noise in the back of her throat that went right down to my reproductive organs, and I was like: *Mmm, bliss.*

My heart was beating wildly in my chest, and surrounded by the city and a warm evening breeze, with the river flowing alongside us, lust wasn't the only player in the game anymore, and I'd be lying if I said it wasn't completely terrifying.

Not only because I knew I'd have to tell Teddy, but because it felt like my heart was literally on a slab for Katherine Cooper-Bunting to do whatever she wanted with.

And who wants to be that vulnerable?

When we got to Waterloo, we'd just missed a bus, and because I was parched and we had time, we went into the station to buy a bottle of water.

We walked into WHSmith, where we proceeded to be really silly in the magazine aisle, because the cover model of *GQ* had a mustache like the one that had caused me my awful rash, and Katherine was holding up the magazine next to my face, and then I decided it was a great time to push the boat out—the love boat, to be precise—and I went: "Admit it, even though he's totally rocking that mustache, it looked a hundred times better on me," and she pretended to think about it for a minute, then went: "Maybe, maybe not," and I kind of launched myself at her, which made her shriek, and two seconds later Olivia was coming round the corner of the shelf going: "Mate, what's with the shouting?"

The moment she saw that it was us, she literally stopped in

her tracks, and we froze, and she was like: "Decided to come and visit me at work?"

And obviously that was not what had happened, and she definitely knew that already.

I was still holding the *GQ* magazine as well as a bottle of water, and I went: "I didn't actually know you worked here," and Olivia went: "So when I said I'm doing extra shifts at WHSmith Waterloo, you didn't think this would be the place?"

"I mean, no, I mean, yes, I mean, obviously. You know what I mean."

"Going anywhere nice?" Olivia asked, and looked at Katherine, and Katherine was just like: "We actually went to the Globe this afternoon. It was a birthday present from my parents."

"Happy birthday," Olivia said.

"Oh no, my birthday was in May."

"Belated."

"Thanks."

Olivia looked at me, and I have to admit I think I just stood there, looking like the idiot I was.

"Was it good?" she asked.

"Amazing," said Katherine.

"That's good then, innit. Do you want me to put that through?" she asked, pointing at the things I was holding.

I put the magazine back on the shelf.

"I can use the machine," I said.

"Good," said Olivia. "Because my KPIs are better that way."

"What's KPIs?" I asked.

"Key performance indicators. The goal is to have as many people as possible use the self-service checkout."

"They check how many people use the self-service checkout?" Katherine asked.

"Mate, have you never had a job? They check everything. And if people refuse to use them and I have to put it through the till, my manager has a fit."

"But that's not your fault."

"Well, bad things happen to good people," Olivia said, and rearranged a row of orange and green Tic Tacs.

"When do you finish?" I asked her.

"Nine."

"We won't wait for you, then," I said.

"What play did you see?" she asked.

"*As You Like It*," Katherine said.

"Should have taken Teddy, mate," Olivia said to Katherine. And if looks could kill . . . "But I guess you know that."

Katherine and I walked to the bus in complete silence.

Only when we sat down on the upper deck and I offered her a sip of water did she speak again.

"Do they know about Grace?" Katherine asked.

"I really don't know. I haven't told them."

"You can't go out with someone just because everyone thinks you should go out with them."

"No, of course you can't."

"Olivia clearly thinks I'm leading him on, and I'm not. I really like him, I mean, how can you not like him, but just because he likes me and he's a nice guy, doesn't mean I have to like him back. I mean, in a romantic way."

"No, of course it doesn't."

"And just because I'm nice to him doesn't mean I fancy him," she said, and took a swig of water. "What is wrong with wanting to be just friends, anyway?"

"Nothing," I said, and watched her throat as she swallowed. "But if one of you wants more, it won't work."

"Love's so stupid," she said, and shook her head, still not looking at me.

"It should definitely be avoided at all costs," I said, and watched her face.

I couldn't read her expression exactly, but she didn't seem to disagree.

Scene 10

The next day, the day of the flash mob, I didn't wake up until my alarm. I felt heavy and sluggish, and really wanted to stay in bed.

Nothing else had happened with Katherine Cooper-Bunting on our journey home the previous evening, except that, before she got off the bus, she gave me a rushed last-minute kiss that felt like goodbye for real that time. And then she never messaged me again, and I just lay on my bed all motionless and pathetic.

By the time I was getting dressed, I'd convinced myself that my brief affair with her was definitely over because it had been somehow consumed by the stifling shadows of a past lost love that was Teddy and Grace, and so, naturally, I spent half an hour trying on every single cute dress she hadn't seen me in. Because someone will definitely change their mind about a possible future together and fall desperately in love with you because of your outfit . . .

Did I say love again?

I went downstairs, poured Frosted Flakes into a bowl, and

sat down at the table with Grandad, who was humming. He poured milk over my cereal and went: "Matilda, I barely slept."

"Are you feeling okay?"

"Everything's fine. It's just—what does one wear to a flash mob?"

That made me laugh, and Grandad was like: "What?"

I shrugged, but then I said: "It's fun with you living here," and he didn't say anything, but he winked at me, and it was everything.

———

When we met Teddy, he promptly asked me if I'd had a good Sunday, which should have been the moment I said to him: *Actually, Katherine asked me to go to the Globe with her and I did, and by the way, we kissed*, but instead, I chose to not say anything about it, like the deceitful dick I was.

I sat next to him on the Northern Line in complete silence, reading the ARE YOU TIRED OF BEING TIRED? advert over and over again, and the picture of the woman yawning made me yawn; all the while Grandad, wearing a tux, kept humming "Seasons of Love."

I was finding this whole flash mob thing really stressful. I think it was even more stressful because Teddy and I didn't know the other people, because we hadn't been to the all-important rehearsal with the Stagecoach lot. And you know when you're going somewhere specific, and you're on the tube, and you're looking around, and you're wondering if all the other people are going to the same thing, too?

Every time I saw a child, I was like: *I bet they're part of us*, but of course it was the summer holiday, so they could have been anyone.

We'd been instructed to be at the piano at ten. The one hundred thousandth Eurostar from Paris was scheduled to arrive at ten thirty.

When we came up from the Underground, I could already see that the station was busy, and among the people rushing through and the people with bags and wheely suitcases, there were a lot of old white men with notepads and cameras.

The piano was situated under an escalator right opposite the Eurostar Arrivals, and as we approached, an old woman with enormously fluffed-up hair was standing next to it, speaking to a member of the maintenance staff.

"Good morning," I said to her. "We're here for the secret thing."

Her face cracked into an enormous grin.

"Good morning, I'm Nora. I'm in charge of Stagecoach Southwest. And you must be Douglas," she said to Grandad, and held out her hand in a flamboyant, actory way. "What a pleasure to meet you."

"Enchanté." Grandad took her hand and actually kissed it.

"You're a charmer," Nora said, and I swear she pressed her

hand farther up against his mouth, and then giggled. "I'm so glad you could make it. Because I'm not keen on playing in public. I'm a much better singer than I am a pianist."

"I'm sure you're only being modest," Grandad said, and I was like, *EW*, because have you ever seen old people flirting?

A man with four smallish children walked past, and the littlest one raised her hand to wave at Nora, and one of the bigger ones slapped it back down, which resulted in tears and them being dragged away toward the toilets.

"I assume they're with us, then," I said, and Nora laughed.

"Oh, this was such a wonderful idea, darling. It's always such a joy to perform together and for other people. I was delighted when we were approached. And for such a good cause, too."

"Indeed," Grandad said.

"Dear," Nora addressed the maintenance person, who was just finishing giving the piano a little polish. "Are we almost good to go?"

"I can't tell you if it's in tune, but it looks as good as new," they said.

"Swings and roundabouts." Grandad laughed, and sat down, and Nora giggled.

Grandad played a few scales, and Nora clapped, and I was just like: *OMG*.

I put the camera bag onto the piano and took the camera out.

I'd obviously film the actual event, which was then going on

YouTube, but I also wanted to film a few bits and bobs before and after for extras or outtakes, because people love that sort of stuff.

"Smile for the camera," I said to Teddy, and zoomed in on his face. "Why don't you introduce today for us?"

"Hi," he said. "Ladies and gentlemen, boys and girls, and all other fellow humans, we're here today to surprise a bunch of French people who are traveling to London on what is the Eurostar's one hundred thousandth journey from Paris."

"That's pretty cool," I said, prompting him.

"It's incredibly cool. Or as the French say, c'est incroyable . . . I think. Sorry, I'm not very good at French."

I smiled behind my camera. "And can you tell us who you are and a little bit about your involvement today?"

"Yeah, sure, my name is Theodore Booker, and I'm playing Orlando in *As You Like It* for a cabaret evening in aid of Acting for Others, and if *you* like it—see what I did there—you can book tickets for it via the link. Don't forget to put the link in, Tills."

"Obviously."

I finished the shot by swinging the camera round to the Eurostar Arrivals area, then switched it off.

"You're a natural, Teds," I said.

"Don't look now, but Katherine's over there by Fortnum and Mason with lots of children. Is that her mum? She's hot," he said.

I looked across.

It was her mum.

I didn't think she was hot.

Katherine Cooper-Bunting caught my eye.

She smiled.

My insides felt like they'd been flashed by a solar flare.

"It's weird how she always looks beautiful, isn't it?" Teddy asked. "Like, she doesn't look like she makes an effort, and yet she's the most beautiful woman in the room."

"We're not in a room, we're in a station," I said, and pressed a few random buttons on the camera.

Robin and Olivia walked by a couple of minutes later.

Olivia gave me a look, and let me just say it wasn't "hello," and Robin didn't look at me, so Olivia had obviously told them about Katherine and me going to the Globe, and I was just like, *Well, this is great.*

I mean, I didn't think I'd been wrong going to the theater with Katherine, but I obviously should've told Teddy.

I obviously should've told everyone.

"Douglas, can I get you a cup of tea?" Nora asked Grandad. "I'm going to check with the staff if the train is running on time, and then I'll pop into Le Pain Quotidien."

"Two sugars, please," Grandad said.

"Two sugars?" Nora asked. "Douglas, darling, you're sweet enough." And then she laughed so loudly that it echoed, and everyone looked.

When she returned, she confirmed what every person with average eyesight who knew how to read a monitor already knew: The Eurostar was running on time, which meant it was going to arrive in five, which meant we had to start in six.

I looked around to work out who else was on our team.

A few small and medium-size children were standing here and there, and too many of them were completely unsubtly looking our way, and I noticed Nora giving them the eye.

I spotted Brian, who was standing with Maeve, a man I'd never seen before, the Phantom of the Opera, and his wife, and they were looking at Charles, who was taking two steps at a time up the moving escalator, a camera with an enormous lens strapped around his neck, a notebook in hand.

Grandad took a sip of his tea, and then started playing some random musical gibberish.

Then it was 10:28, and all the train spotters who were still downstairs started running, and I pressed record and started filming Grandad.

He played a variation of the "Seasons of Love" theme, and already some people stopped to listen to him.

A few minutes later, Nora gave the sign, and the tiny girl who'd tried to wave earlier and was dragged off screaming came over and started singing.

At this point, of course, everyone came over, because, you know, an old man playing a piano, and a tiny little girl singing . . .

I got some great footage. I filmed people watching, people wandering over, people filming on their phones.

Enter the next group of children, and then the next, and suddenly there was a real flurry of activity, and you could literally feel the energy in the air.

People started coming out of the Eurostar area, and some people in suits rushed straight toward the exit, but loads actually stopped and listened to us.

Nora, who was still standing right next to Grandad, gave a sign for some of the adults from our group to join in, and the man I'd never seen before, who I noticed was wearing a three-piece suit, and Maeve, Brian, the Phantom of the Opera, and his wife started singing.

More and more people were coming over, some were filming from inside the shops as well, and I did one of those 360-degree shots round and round and round.

In true British fashion, everyone started clapping along in rhythm. Katherine and Robin and Miroslaw joined in next, and Teddy fought his way through the masses to stand and sing with them.

Sixty seconds later, the place was heaving, and Nora finally gave the sign for Olivia to come in.

Her voice kind of vibrated above everyone else's, and people were literally like: "Wow," and everyone started filming her, and then she did really funky riffs and started to proper show off.

Some little kids who had arrived, either on the Eurostar or another train, or were just passing, were dancing, and laughing, and when Nora gave the sign to finish, the whole crowd, including everyone who'd just been singing, erupted in thunderous applause.

I filmed all of it and pushed through the crowd to get close-ups on all the participants, as well as on some of the people who were watching and filming on their phones and all that.

I ended up by Teddy and Katherine and everyone, and I did a group walk-around of all of them, and then some close-ups.

Katherine grabbed the camera from me and tried to film me, but I kind of wrestled her to get it back.

"Spoilsport," she said, and fake pouted, which was adorable, and I hated that.

"Look, we all have our parts to play, and mine is behind the camera."

"I can't even see your mustache anymore," she said, and I clung to her teasing tone like a drowning person to some driftwood.

"I'd actually forgotten about the rash," I said, and boofed her away from me with my hip, taking the camera back and switching it off.

"Yesterday you were obsessed," she said, and laughed, and you know when you kind of just ignore when someone's said something, and hope everyone else is doing the same?

Well, apparently it only works when you say things that don't matter, because as soon as it's something actually important, literally two seconds later, someone, in this case Olivia, will be like: "Did you see each other yesterday?"

Everything kind of stopped then. I became completely unaware of all the people who were still milling around; I could no longer hear Brian making his announcement about our show at the Criterion, or Nora's high-pitched giggles from where she was sitting with Grandad. My ears were ringing, and all I saw was the way Teddy looked at me, then Katherine, then me again, his smile slowly fading, and his whole being growing distant from me.

"Wish I could go to the theater on a Sunday, but some of us have to work, innit?" Olivia enthusiastically babbled into the silence.

"I don't go to the theater every Sunday," Katherine said to her. "And I told you already that it was a birthday present from my parents, so just shut up about it now. What's it got to do with you, anyway?"

"Nothing, mate. Just wondering why it was all hush-hush."

"It wasn't hush-hush. We just didn't want it to be awkward, because I only had one spare ticket."

"All right. Sorry, then," Olivia said, but it didn't matter that she was sorry, because everything that shouldn't have been said had been said.

Teddy and Miroslaw just stood there, looking at us all puzzled and sweet and innocent, and Olivia and Robin looked like I'd personally inflicted pain on them, or inconvenienced them somehow, and then Katherine went: "Oh, for fuck's sake. Tilly and I saw a play at the Globe yesterday. Big fucking deal. Get over it, everyone—it's ancient history."

Teddy looked at his feet, then somewhere into the middle distance, and then Robin went: "Babe, do you want to come to South Bank and skate with me? I mean, since we're in town anyway?"

He looked at me, at Katherine, and then at Robin, cleared his throat, and went: "Yeah. I mean, yeah."

And then nobody spoke, and it was literally the most awkward I've ever felt in my entire life. And that includes the time Grandad was at the bottom of the stairs with his bits out.

"See you all tomorrow," Robin said, then kicked up their skateboard and walked off toward the tube with Teddy.

Olivia took a deep breath in and out.

"That went well, chumpsters," she said. Then she turned to Miroslaw and went: "You ready to go?"

"Ready to go," he said, and I wished so much that I was an immigrant who knew no one and hadn't done anything wrong in this place that was now home.

"You didn't have to say anything," I said to Olivia.

"Mate," she said, and addressed me specifically. "Why are you sneakin' around? If there's no reason to, then don't do it. And don't lie to your best friend. It's vile."

"I didn't lie."

"Whatever," she said. And then she, too, walked off toward the tube.

"I'm sorry," Katherine said.

I couldn't look at her.

"It's my fault," I replied. Because it was.

"It's not."

"It is."

"We haven't done anything wrong," she said.

"I know," I said, but I didn't actually believe it.

And then the most unexpected thing happened.

She took my hand, fingers interlacing and everything, and looked me straight in the eye and said nothing at all.

My vision went blurry, like I only saw our hands in pixels, and I'd forgotten how to read facial expressions, and then it felt as if I was looking at us from outside my body, and I thought: *What if it's love?*

"What are you doing for the rest of the day?" she asked finally, like she wasn't even holding my hand.

"I don't know."

"Do you want to run lines with me?"

"I have to take Grandad home."

"We can do it at yours."

"I can make us lunch," I said, all croaky-hoarse.

"That would be really nice," she said.

"Okay. Let's go and rescue Grandad from Nora, then."

"I think he likes her," Katherine suggested, and smiled at me.

"I like you," I said.

"I like you."

———

After lunch, which consisted of cheese sandwiches and eye contact and silence and Katherine's hand on my lower back every once in a while, and me touching her to maneuver her out of the way so I could open a drawer here, get to the kettle there, Grandad went upstairs to have a nap, and Katherine and I went to my room because Mum was in the garden doing all sorts of bizarre things on a tiny trampoline.

I had no idea what it would be like to be alone in my bedroom for the first time with a person who made me want to crawl out of my own skin in the most delicious way.

"Do you want t—"

She didn't let me finish, but kissed me.

We did some super-polite snogging for a minute, and then our teeth clocked together, which made us giggle.

The bed became the elephant in the room, but we eventually gravitated toward it and sat on the edge, still kissing, and ridiculously I was like: *I think this is a #friendstolovers situation*, and then I couldn't stop thinking *#friendstolovers, #friendstolovers, #friendstolovers*, and then I was like: *I'm not ready!* but at the same time I was like: *But I am!*

I gently pulled Katherine onto my bed with one hand, while pushing poor Barnaby in between the mattress and the headboard with the other.

Katherine's dress was all tangled, and her naked thighs were right there, which meant I got to actually live the fantasy I'd had ever since the Virgin Mary incident in church and touch them.

Halfway up her thigh, it occurred to me I should probably ask if this was okay, and so I whispered, "May I touch you?" across her pretty mouth, and she smiled, and nodded, and said: "Yes, please," which almost made me faint, because, how sexy is consent?

Then, of course, came that absolute terrifying moment seconds before my hand got to where it was going, and I don't know if she sensed my hesitation, but Katherine huffed a cute little laugh across my face and, in a bold move, she shifted, sat up, and proceeded to take off her underwear, pull her dress over her head, and undo her bra, at which moment I, of course, was too overwhelmed to look anywhere but into her eyes.

"Your turn," she said to me.

I got up, locked the door, and got completely naked in front of another person for the first time in my adult life.

We did a lot of kissing and touching, which felt just so good, and was kind of already #friendstolovers in my opinion.

The actual #friendstolovers sex was mostly terrifying because no matter how prepared you think you are for going down on someone, suddenly finding yourself down there is scary.

However, it's not as scary as being on the receiving end. In my opinion, anyway.

Let it be said that the fan fiction Teddy had pointed me toward was absolutely right about the #friendstolovers taking turns reaching their soaring heights of satisfaction, because a great big mutual #soulshatteringorgasm it really was not. And you know what? I'm not entirely sure that's even anything that could be achieved at the #friendstolovers stage of a relationship. And you know what else? That's absolutely fine.

Afterward, when we were cuddling, and kissing, and actually laughing about the whole thing, and Cooper-Bunting looked both pleased with herself and shagged, I wanted to never leave that moment.

"I've never had sex," I said, and I probably should have said it half an hour ago, but there you go.

"No, you just did," she teased, her eyes bright blue.

"You know what I mean. Before just now."

"Me neither," she said, and smiled at me. "I liked it. A lot. You okay?"

I nodded. "You're very beautiful."

"You're very beautiful, too," she said, and touched my lips with her fingertips. "I'm happy."

"Me too," I said.

"It's taken me a long time to get here."

"I thought it was quite bish bash bosh in the end."

"I mean the girl thing."

"Oh," I said, bursting with post-sex eloquence. "Because of, I don't know, Jesus?"

She giggled, and it was cute.

"No, not because of that. I guess everyone always assumed I was straight, and I kind of assumed it, too, and then there was this boy, and I really liked him, and everyone, including me I guess, thought I'd end up with him, but—"

"Alfie?" I asked, and she nodded and traced the edge of my belly button.

"But I didn't fancy him like that. And when I met you, I just knew. Like, I knew I fancied you."

"I'm really flattered."

She shrugged.

"I've always been a big lesbian," I told her, and she laughed, and it was the most beautiful thing I'd ever seen.

When I checked my phone what felt like hours later but wasn't, I had twelve missed calls and a voicemail from Robin.

They said that Teddy had come off the skateboard and they were at St. Thomas's A&E.

Katherine and I got dressed and ran to the tube.

Act IV

Scene 1

After Grace was hit by the car, they took her by ambulance to St. George's A&E, which isn't far from us. Maybe five minutes in the ambulance when people aren't being dicks, blocking intersections.

When we got there, Mum, Dad, Teddy, Amanda, David, and I, she was in surgery already, and we had to wait downstairs.

And here's the thing: People you actually know don't die in hospital, do they? I mean, you see people die in hospital on TV shows, and you know that lots of people die in hospitals all the time, but you don't know them.

And when you get to a hospital and the doctor is like: "Your friend is in surgery," you expect them to be okay, don't you?

Well, Grace wasn't okay.

I'll never forget when the doctor came to tell us.

Like, she didn't have to say anything—I knew straightaway.

Teddy's mum got up to speak to her, and when she turned around to us, Teddy knew, too, and the way he looked at me haunted me viciously for a really long time.

I don't really remember getting home, and I don't really remember the days after, or the weeks, because losing someone who's such an integral part of your every day is so big, and there was no way I could function.

Teddy didn't get out of bed for weeks. We didn't go to school, and no one made us, and one day we were in his room together, and we made each other promise to never die.

Which of course is stupid, because everyone dies, which is why, months later, we revised that to: I promise to never die in a road-traffic accident. Which, I suppose, was also stupid, because it wasn't that Grace wanted to be run over by a car.

I suppose Teddy hadn't had a road-traffic accident exactly, but I was so desperately worried and enraged that I couldn't wait to get to the hospital to inflict physical pain on him.

I'd missed another call from Robin when we were on the tube, but they left a message to say they were waiting for Teddy's parents to get there because he'd fractured his collarbone and needed surgery, at which point I wanted to absolutely vom.

"If anything happens to him, I'll never forgive myself," I said to Katherine as we ran out of Waterloo.

We got to St. Thomas's A&E just before seven.

Robin was sitting by the vending machine, playing on their phone.

"Robin," I said. "What's going on?"

"Teddy's shoulder's literally broken," they said, and hugged me and then Katherine, and I briefly wondered if they could tell we'd had sex. "He's all, like, at the wrong angle. I never should have let him be an idiot."

"It's not your fault," I said, and sat down. "I shouldn't have lied to him about the whole—" I gestured wildly between Katherine and me. *Sex thing*, I thought. "Theater thing," I said.

"It's not your fault, either," Robin said, but I knew they were only saying it to make me feel better.

Besides, I knew what Teddy was like. I knew he went to the skate park, clumsily mounted the highest ramp, and probably shouted: "I'm the king of the world!" before launching himself off.

Katherine sat opposite instead of next to me, and my whole insides tangled at that, like those necklaces at the very bottom of your jewelry box you'd forgotten about that literally have no hope of ever being separate again in this life.

"What's happening right now?" I asked Robin.

"His mum and dad are here, and I think they're waiting for him to go into surgery. Apparently it only takes, like, an hour to fix him. How cool is that, by the way, knowing how to mend a collarbone," Robin said, and touched theirs. "There's a lot going on in the shoulder section, isn't there?"

"I should have been here," I said.

"It wasn't pretty."

"Was he scared?"

"He was really brave until they had to cut off his Care Bears T-shirt."

We all went: "No!"

"Did he cry?" I asked.

Robin nodded, unzipped their backpack, and pulled it out.

The shirt was ruined, with zigzaggy scissor cuts down the front.

The fact that they'd cut right across Good Luck Bear's heart-shaped nose ended me.

"Hey," Robin said, and actually laughed a bit at my hysterical weeping. "He's fine. And I can fix this."

"No, you can't," I said, snot now joining the tears that were coming out of me. "It's all ruined."

"Tilly, it's just a T-shirt," Robin said, and leaned over to hug me.

"I'm going to call my mum to let her know where I am," Katherine said, and got up, and I'd never felt lonelier in my life, which made me cry harder.

The moment the automatic doors shut behind her, Robin let go of me and was like: "Hey, Tilly, what's really going on?"

"I'm really scared. And I just had sex with Cooper-Bunting," I said, and wiped my face with my trembling hand.

I didn't have a tissue, and so Robin rummaged around their backpack and found a Christmas napkin.

I blew my nose.

"And I think I really like her," I said, and it felt like the biggest tragedy.

Robin looked confused.

"I'm sorry," I said. "I know this isn't about me."

"No, it's about Cooper-Bunting being a lesbian."

"Please don't say anything. In case, you know, it's nothing."

"I'm really glad she's a lesbian, actually. It explains so much. I just wish she could have just said." Robin turned their whole body toward me.

"People shouldn't have to explain themselves like that," I said.

"No, of course not. It's just that we never got why she and Alfie never became a thing. I mean, they were literally besties, they did everything together, and we thought they totally fancied each other, and then, you know, nothing."

I wiped my eyes, hating Alfie.

"And the funny thing is everyone always expects the male BFF to be gay, but not the female one. Odd, right? I feel like we've got work to do on that front."

Robin cuddled Teddy's T-shirt.

I stared at a poster that said BLEEDING OVER BREATHING OVER BONES.

Grace had died of a massive bleed in her brain.

"How was the sex?" Robin whispered.

"Really nice," I told them.

"You're thinking about it right now, aren't you?"

I hadn't been, but then I was.

"Have you had sex?" I asked them.

"Yes, but it wasn't with anyone I really liked."

"I'm sorry."

"Oh, no, it's fine. I was curious. I feel like it wasn't worth the effort, though."

"I feel like I've discovered a fourth dimension," I mumbled.

"Ew. I hope you're not talking about Cooper-Bunting's vagina."

The automatic doors opened, and Katherine walked back in.

She looked at me, smiled a sad smile that looked once again like the end of everything, and sat down in her original seat.

"Do his parents know you're still here?" I asked Robin, and they nodded.

"I told them I wasn't moving until I know he's all right."

"Did you have to get an ambulance?" Katherine asked, and Robin shook their head.

"We walked. Well, it was more like I carried him here."

"He does feel pain more than the average person," I said. "Physically and emotionally."

I looked at Katherine staring at her feet.

"No, Tilly, it was nasty," Robin said in Teddy's defense.

"I should have been here," I said again, and I don't know what was worse, my regret, or the fact that Katherine was sitting all the way over there.

"I guess he's out of *Cupid's Revenge*," she said after a moment.

"Oh my God, Cooper-Bunting," Robin all but shouted. "Can you think about anything but yourself for one second? He's upstairs with a broken fucking collarbone he probably never would have broken if you hadn't led him on and then had sex with his best friend behind his back."

"That is *not* what happened," she said.

"But it *is* what happened, isn't it?"

Katherine shot out of her seat.

"What?" Robin asked. "You wanna have a punch-up in A&E?"

"You're vile," Katherine said, picked up her bag, looked at me like she hated me, too, and literally walked out.

"Wait," I said, and ran after her. "Wait, Katherine."

I followed her outside, but she was power walking, not turning around, and I only caught up with her when she was already on the pavement.

"Leave me alone, Tilly," she said, and she was actually crying, and I felt an avalanche of emotions I didn't understand come at me and bury me, and then I couldn't breathe, and I was terrified.

I grabbed her by the arm, but she pulled it away, and her bottom lip was trembling, and the most enormous tears rolled out of her eyes, and I was just like: *Please let me hold you*, but she flinched when I tried to touch her again, and walked away.

I think I would have gone after her, but having someone recoil from me in horror was new, and coming from a person I'd been naked with earlier that day, I don't think I'd ever felt that cruel kind of rejection.

I was breathing lungfuls of air, but I felt like I couldn't get enough oxygen into my body, and so I stood in the middle of the pavement, gasping.

And because it's London and being kind was so last year, I was unceremoniously shoved aside pretty much immediately, and I felt overwhelmed by everything and just stood there, leaning against a wall, wondering if anyone would help me if I passed out.

I watched a black cab pull up by the bus stop and a man in a suit get out, and I was just thinking: *Maybe he'd help me*, and then I realized it was my dad.

He shut the door and waved at the driver, and then he looked at me, did a double take, and was like: "Tilly?" and I properly ran over to him and hugged him, and I took a huge, gulpy in-breath that finally seemed to oxygenize me. But it also made me cry all over again.

Dad held me and kissed my head.

"It's okay, darling. Don't you worry. Everything will be okay, I promise," he said, and I remembered being told that when Grace was in surgery, and I proper sobbed.

We stood there for a while, and then he put his arm round me and walked us back to A&E, and when Robin saw us, they got up and rushed over.

"Sorry I shouted at Cooper-Bunting, but she really gets my goat," they said.

"I don't even know why I'm so upset," I lied, and Robin got me another Christmas napkin out of their backpack.

"He's in the best place, girls," Dad said, and I was like: "Robin's pronouns are they/them."

Dad looked confused for a second, but then offered Robin his hand and went: "Pleasure to meet you. I'm Roger."

"Oh my God, yes, Roger. It's a pleasure to meet you," Robin said, and shook Dad's hand with enthusiasm. "Nice suit, by the way. Do you happen to know if the Royal Opera House owns a donkey head they'll loan us for a scene from *A Midsummer Night's Dream*? I hope you're coming, by the way. It's on Sunday."

Surprising to no one, Dad went: "I still have to buy my tickets," but then he went: "But I'll be there."

I thought about *Cupid's Revenge*, and then I was like: "Shit, I haven't put the flash mob video online. I haven't done anything with it. It's literally at home, unworked-on, still on the camera." And Brian and all the stage-school kids were probably like: *WTF has she done with the video?*

"We can do that when we're done here," Robin said. "I'll help you if you want."

"Don't you have to go home?"

"One day, sure, but if I can stay at yours, we can do it tonight, and then we can go to rehearsal together tomorrow, and maybe when we get there at lunchtime, it will have gone viral."

"Make sure to tell your parents," Dad said. "I have to say, I'm very impressed by how invested you all are in this."

"It's for a good cause," Robin said. "Especially as no one seems to give a shit about the arts at the moment. Not like the

301

football. So we have to look after our own. Teddy says his parents have been arguing about money constantly since his dad was made redundant, and that just sucks."

Dad looked at me and smiled a quick smile, but he suddenly looked sad, too.

"You better get your tickets, Roger," Robin said. "Because this time tomorrow, they'll be sold out and then you'll have to buy them from someone dodgy or off a scammy website."

"You're a really good salesperson," Dad said.

"I'm really good at a lot of things," Robin told him, and Dad nodded in appreciation and got out his phone. "I better get on it asap."

"You're a wise man, Roger."

"Are you actually coming?" I asked.

"Why wouldn't we come?"

"Mum, too?"

"Of course."

"Because you really don't have to."

"Tilly," Dad said, looking at me all exasperated already. "We're coming. You look pale. Do you need a drink? Or a snack?"

"I'm not hungry."

"I'll have a Dr Pepper if you're offering," Robin said, and pointed to the vending machine.

Dad got Robin a Dr Pepper, me a chocolate Yazoo, because that was the only flavor they had, and himself a Lilt, and when he opened his drink, he was like: "Haven't had one of these in years. Oh, that brings back memories."

"Only good ones, I hope," Robin said, and I don't know why the thought of Dad doing anything other than wave his arms around to music made me physically cringe.

"Why are you here, by the way?" I asked, and he was like: "Your mother called to say you'd stormed out of the house because Teddy had come off his skateboard and that you were here."

"He actually came off my skateboard," Robin said.

"Apparently Amanda and David are upstairs, and Teddy needs surgery," I said.

"I already called David," Dad said. "They know we're here."

———

Maybe another hour later, Teddy's parents finally appeared.

Amanda looked like she'd had a really long day, but when she saw us, she smiled, and my heart beat the loudest beat yet.

She hugged me and held me.

"Everything went really well," she said, stroking my hair. "He's through surgery and in recovery already, but they're going to keep him overnight because it's so late and he's absolutely exhausted."

Then she hugged Dad and Robin, and then Dad hugged David, too, and I think it was the first time they'd even been in the same room in over a year.

Dad and Robin and I took off a few minutes later and walked to Waterloo to take the tube home.

I had no messages from Katherine, and I kept checking my phone every two seconds, and when we got to ours, and after eating Marmite toast at one in the morning and going up to my room to edit the video footage, Robin was like: "What happened to Cooper-Bunting?"

"Her name is Katherine," I said. "I think it's over. Whatever it was."

"Do you want to talk about it?"

"No."

"Why not?"

I looked at them. "Because I don't know how to talk about that sort of thing."

"Love or sex?"

"Being sad."

"I get it," Robin said. "Maybe try one day, though. I promise I'll listen."

I nodded, but I couldn't say anything because I felt like I was drowning all over again, and so I made us get on with editing the video.

Turned out I do my best work when heartbroken, and at around five in the morning, the video was done, and it was epic, and Robin and I finally fell asleep on Katherine's and my sex sheets, which was something I couldn't stop thinking about.

My phone beeped at five thirty.

It was Teddy.

> FYI, I had surgery because I fell off a skateboard, but I'm okay. FYI also, I know now that Grace wasn't scared, and never even knew she was dying, because you literally feel nothing at all when you're under.

> Love you, byeeeeeeeeeee. Xxxxxxx

"What is it?" Robin asked.

"Teddy."

"He okay?"

"Has he ever told you about our friend Grace?" I asked.

"Mm-hmm," Robin confirmed, and so I held the phone to their face.

"That's, I don't know, sweet?"

"It is, isn't it?"

"He's also high on morphine, right?" they whispered, and we chuckled. "By the way, I'm sorry I was awful to Cooper-Bunting—sorry, Katherine."

"It's fine."

"No, it's not. I don't actually think she meant to lead Teddy on. But she did."

I swallowed hard.

"I know it's not her fault he got hurt," Robin said.

"No, it's not."

"Do you actually love her?"

"I don't know," I said, but it was a lie, because I did.

And you know when people tell you that being in love is the best feeling in the world?

They lie, too.

Scene 2

While Robin and I were having breakfast just after ten, Teddy came strolling in through the back door.

He looked like a brand-new person, freshly showered and glowing, his arm in a sling, and when we gawped at him, he was like: "What?"

Robin was out of their seat first, and hugged him, and then apologized for hugging him and hugged him again, and then it was my turn.

"You don't look like someone who's had to have their collarbone manually rearranged from the inside not twelve hours ago," I said.

"Ah, the wonders of modern medicine," Teddy replied, and sat down. "I've just watched and shared the video of the flash mob," he said. "It's excellent."

"Thank you," Robin said. "We worked all night."

"I think it's already got over a hundred hits."

"I hope everyone buys tickets now."

"I think Olivia is going to be a star," he said. "She sounds so fierce."

"I think the whole thing sounds amazing," I said.

"And loads of people are reposting the video to IG stories and tagging each other in it, which is great," Teddy said.

"I bet you're going to have to extend your West End run," I said, and we laughed.

I made Teddy toast with extra jam, and he was like: "It really sucks when you're a teenager and in hospital, because they obviously don't want to put you with the children, but that means you're with old people, and some of them are literally dying, and everyone's, like, groaning and snoring and farting. I made friends with a nice chap called Barry. He fell over with a ladder. Broke his leg in three places."

"Ouch," Robin and I said simultaneously.

"Yeah, he wasn't happy."

"What about you?" I asked.

"I'm all right. Better now that everything is fixed. Tired." He took a big bite of toast, chewed, swallowed. "I'm going to have to tell Brian I'm out, though. I don't think I can concentrate on Shakespeare, to be honest."

"Cooper-Bunting's going to have a fit," Robin said, and I'm not sure they weren't a bit pleased about that.

"Really?" I asked Teddy. "You couldn't just sit onstage and say the words?"

He looked at me, and I was like: *I see.* Because it wasn't really about the shoulder. It was about his heart.

The bite of toast I swallowed felt dry enough to tear open my esophagus.

Robin looked at me, and I looked at my plate.

"She'll get over it," I said. "She's still got her Lady Macbeth, anyway."

And then I remembered that I literally watched her orgasm, and I felt like someone walked over my grave.

Teddy looked at me, and I felt guilty and aroused and embarrassed.

"You know, Tills, you could be me," he said.

"That's the best idea ever!" Robin said, and raised both their arms in triumph. "The whole play is about gender deception, so why not have a girl play a boy, and a girl play a girl who is playing a boy. OMG, this is the gayest of queer dreams ever. And I'm using gay in its original sense here, because how is this not sheer happiness? I'm messaging Brian right now. And also, Tilly will totally fit the clothes I've got for you, Teddy, so no problem there. And no offense, either."

"None taken," Teddy said. "I have great legs. And you and Katherine obviously have some sort of thing going on, so . . ." Teddy said, and I swallowed hard.

"It's not what you think," I lied, and I honestly don't even know why.

Robin's phone vibrated.

They read the message.

"Great, that's settled, then," they said, and switched it off. "Brian says get well soon."

"Wait a minute, no. I'm not going to be Teddy," I said. "Absolutely no way."

"Why not? It's literally one scene. And you know the words by now."

"It's not about the words. I don't want to be onstage. Like, ever."

"Come on, Tills, it's three minutes of your life," Teddy said.

"No. Teddy—"

"Just do it for Katherine," he said.

"I've already told Brian now," Robin said.

"I've been wanting to ask this for ages, but how do you know Brian?" Teddy asked.

"We're neighbors. We got close during the pandemic. Because, you know, Malcolm was in hospital for so long. We had Brian over for dinner a lot."

"Malcolm is real?" I asked.

"Why wouldn't he be real?"

"I don't know. I mean, we've never seen him."

"He was literally there yesterday."

"Where?"

"He was singing with Brian. You filmed him."

"No! The guy in the suit?"

"Yes."

"I thought he was an overdressed grandad or something."

"No, he's a flamboyant old queen," Robin said. "But anyhoo, Tills, you have to do it."

They looked at me, and then Teddy looked at me, and he looked all hurt and injured and tired and clean and soft, and I thought of his ruined Care Bears T-shirt and then I imagined Grace sitting at the table with us, eating toast, jam smeared on her lips and fingers, going: "What's it gonna be, Matilda?" and so I was just like: "Yes, fine, I'll do it."

———

Merely hours later, I found myself in a costume fitting, standing on the complete works of William Shakespeare that served as a foot-stool, with Robin kneeling at my elevated feet, taking up a pair of secondhand riding trousers, in the corner of Clapham Social Club.

"Even if you take them up, the weird leathery bit that's supposed to be inside my knees is literally around my ankles," I whined.

"That's coming off anyway," Robin mumbled through the pins they were holding between their lips.

I fanned myself with the script.

Even though the inside of the social club was always cool because it had no windows, I felt like I couldn't breathe.

The fact that Katherine had been completely standoffish didn't help.

And that's my biggest beef with fan fiction.

It may teach you a thing or two about cunnilingus and best practice during #friendstolovers, but every single story assumes that the rest of the sexed-out couple's life is lived in this hazy state of afterglow, and the truth is it's not.

I was secretly praying that Brian wouldn't get round to doing our scene, even though he said he would because, "Tilly's going to need a bit of extra rehearsal as she's never been onstage, okay." He also said it in a bit of a passive-aggressive way. You know, like people behind the scenes are lesser creatures.

He was working with the Phantom of the Opera and his wife, who must have had some sort of domestic dispute earlier that day, because they sounded aggressive singing their weird song from *Annie Get Your Gun* claiming "Anything you can do I can do better."

When the wife's voice failed in a moment of unmistakable real-life rage, Brian clapped his hands and went: "Thank you. Enough for today. And when you come back tomorrow, may I ask you to leave your personal problems at the door. This isn't about you two, this is about Annie Oakley and Frank Butler."

I looked at Katherine, and she looked at me, and I couldn't tell what she was thinking, which was even more annoying/heartbreaking now that we'd had sex.

I noticed once again her eyes were blue.

Funny how you know these things and then you notice them all over again.

Funny also how that can give you a stabbing pain in your solar plexus.

"Tilly, Katherine!" Brian shouted, and clapped his hands, and I was like, *Please no*. "We're going to rehearse you two first thing tomorrow, and after that, we'll do Maeve and Miroslaw, and then I'll do Katherine on her own after the break, and the rest of you can have your fitting with Robin, and as soon as you're done, you can all bugger off."

"Remember to bring your costumes. That's shoes as well. I want to see it all," Robin added.

"We'll run through it twice on Thursday," Brian announced. "So be prepared. We'll work on whatever needs to be worked on on Friday. You're off on Saturday, but I need you bright and early at the Criterion on Sunday, understood? Stage door opens at ten, and everyone needs to sign in, and I want you there, ready to work at ten. We'll be assigned a dressing room, and then we'll start the tech run. Now, tech runs are not for you, but for the crew, and they're long and tedious, and I don't want to hear a single word of complaint. No one is getting paid, and we're incredibly lucky to have been provided such a traditional theater. Bring food and water."

"Sounds serious," I said to Olivia, who had moved to stand next to me, wearing a corset that made her boobs look as big as my head.

"As serious as Cooper-Bunting being completely unexpectedly on team Adam and Steve rather than Adam and Eve," she said.

Olivia was still deadpan, and everyone looked at us, well, at me, because of course her face hadn't moved, and I looked at Katherine, and I don't know why I still thought it was funny when she looked at me like I was the worst person on earth, and then I was just like: "Excuse me," and I went to the toilet where I looked at myself in the mirror and I could not stop laughing.

Like, I was completely hysterical.

It was like those videos you watch on YouTube when newsreaders just lose it, and they have to just show ads, or the weather or something, because the person can't get it together, like, at all.

I heard people leaving, and I stayed in the toilets, and finally the door opened, and Olivia strode in, no longer in her corset, but in her blue WHSmith blouse.

"Mate, what is wrong with you?" she asked, but now she was smiling.

"I'm having a complete come-apart," I said, and wiped my eyes with toilet paper that promptly flaked off and stuck to my lashes, which triggered another round of hysterics.

"I can't believe you had sex with Cooper-Bunting," Olivia said. "Robin messaged me straightaway. Obviously."

"Obviously," I said, and coughed. "I think everything's been a bit much lately."

She got out her huge makeup bag and started reapplying literally everything.

"I've got seventy-three new followers on IG," she said.

"From the video?"

"Yeah, mate. Thanks for making me look so good."

"You are actually really good," I said to her.

"But am I good enough?"

I looked at our reflections.

"Isn't that everyone's question about everything all the time?"

"Did you actually go down on Cooper-Bunting?" she asked with a look of disgust on her face, and I was off again and LOLing so hard that I thought I might vom.

Scene 3

When Olivia and I finally came out of the toilets, everyone had gone, apart from Brian and Charles and Grandad.

"You ready to go?" I asked, and Grandad went: "I didn't know you were picking me up, Sarah."

"Let's go home," I said. "Do you need to use the toilet before we get on the bus?"

"I suppose I could, couldn't I? Better safe than sorry," he said, then pushed the door open and went into the gents.

I looked at Charles, and he was like: "My late wife had dementia. I know the disease well."

"I'm very sorry," I said. "I didn't know."

"The only consolation for me was that toward the end it's only hard for the family. Takes a person from you little by little, does dementia, and then one day they're just gone, even though they're still sitting right beside you. And you wish you could turn back time if only for five minutes, when they were still there, and tell them one last time that you adore them."

"I'm so sorry," I said again.

"No, I'm sorry," he said, and smiled at me, and I could barely stand it. "You've got all that ahead of you."

I dry-swallowed.

"My wife never wanted to be a bother. And she wasn't. It was difficult, mind you, but never a chore."

"How did you manage?"

"I didn't," he said, and I swear he got all teary, and I was like, *Please don't cry in front of me*, because seeing old people cry is literally the worst thing. "She had to go into a home in the end. I couldn't look after her. I'm all by myself, you see. Our daughter lives in New Zealand. I wouldn't have wanted to burden her, anyway."

"I don't think we can look after him when I go back to school and he gets worse," I said.

"There's no shame in asking for help," Charles said. "I had to learn the hard way."

"Really?"

"I fell asleep, in the afternoon, because we always have a nap in the afternoon, and when I woke up she was gone. Front door was wide open. Police brought her home six hours later. She wasn't wearing a coat, and it was January, and she'd gone up to the common and was talking to the pigeons. No ID, no nothing, just in her nightgown. Makes you wonder what's wrong with people who don't help an old woman wandering around Wimbledon Village in nothing but a nightgown in the middle of the day in January."

The gents' toilet door opened, and Grandad came strolling out.

"Ready to get on the bus?" I asked, and he nodded.

"I'll walk you," Charles said, and patted Grandad on the back.

"Do you remember when we went to New York?" Grandad asked Charles.

"No, I don't remember," Charles said, even though it blatantly wasn't him in the first place who went to New York.

"You do remember," Grandad insisted. "We saw Yo-Yo Ma at the Kennedy Center. It was marvelous. But I never liked American toilets, you know. When you flush, the suction is very aggressive. You remember."

"I do remember, Douglas," Charles said. "I do remember."

"Funny instrument, the cello," Grandad said.

"It sure is," Charles said, and then he waited with me until our bus came, and was like: "Do you want me to come with you?"

"No, thank you. I think I'm fine."

"Do you have help at home?" Charles asked.

"Sort of."

"Remember, there's no shame in asking for help, Tilly."

"Thank you."

"See you tomorrow, Douglas," Charles said.

"Okay, then. See you tomorrow, Dad," Grandad said to Charles, and got on the bus.

I made him sit by the window, and I sat on the aisle, and he didn't speak for the whole journey back, just sat there watching the world go by and humming that song from *Camelot*.

I linked arms with him, and I know he probably thought I was Grandma, but it didn't matter, because what mattered was that we were on the bus together, enjoying each other's company.

I got out my phone and said: "Let's take a selfie for Emilin," and Grandad repositioned himself and smiled, and we literally looked super cute. Except that I'd been crying from laughing and looked a bit knackered in general, but the smile was real.

Emilin messaged back straightaway: xx

Dinner came and went, Rachmaninoff arrived, and Grandad told us the story of him having no teeth yet again.

I had a shower and crawled into bed, and I swear I felt like I'd been awake for weeks.

I rewatched our video on YouTube, which made my soul really happy for a moment, because it actually was amazing.

I wanted to message Teddy, and I wanted to message Katherine, but I didn't want to sound needy, and so I ended up messaging Robin.

> Our video has over a thousand hits. That's insane.

> TBF, I think I've watched it about a hundred times. And I'd put my money on Cooper-Bunting and Olivia having done the same.

> Yeah, but that won't come to over a thousand.

No one will ever love you the way you love yourself.

OMG, that's so depressing.

Why?

Because I literally hate myself right now.

You don't.

I do.

Why?

I don't know. I don't think Katherine is talking to me, and everything is just a big mess.

You know what they say about sex ruining stuff.

But why does it have to ruin things literally the first and only time I have it?

Who said life is fair? Have you heard from Teddy?

No, why?

Just asking. I haven't.

He's probably sleeping.

Yeah. Sleep heals. That's why they put people in an artificial coma.

I want it.

I don't think you can request it.

I WANT IT.

Maybe meditate or something.

Meditation makes me antsy.

I'm sorry you're sad about Cooper-Bunting.

It's fine.

I know it's not and I hear you. Good night.

xx

xx

I fell asleep surprisingly easy but woke up at two from an anxiety dream where I was standing at the top of a hill, ready to throw myself into a ravine, and when I jumped, I woke up and was so full of adrenaline that I couldn't get back to sleep until almost six.

At eight fifteen, someone knocked on my door, and I sat up in bed, again, heart beating out of my chest and anxious as fuck.

"Tilly? You up?" Dad asked. "May I come in?"

I wondered if parents could tell you had sex sheets, but I was like: "Yes, come in."

His face appeared, but his body stayed outside in the hallway.

"I've just spoken to a colleague who has agreed to lend you Bottom's head."

"I'm sorry what?"

"Bottom's head," Dad said again, and you know when teachers are trying to clarify something for you by saying the exact same thing again, but louder? "The donkey. *A Midsummer Night's Dream*. Remember your friend Robin asked for it? You asked for it?"

"Oh my God, yes," I said, and shook myself fully awake.

"If you want, you can pick it up. We've got a matinee today, but we can go in early, and I can sign it out for you."

"Oh my God, yes," I said again, and pulled the charging cable out of my phone. "Let me message Robin. Can they come? Please, Dad, it would literally make their year."

"Fine by me. Come downstairs when you're ready. Ask Robin to meet us at the stage door."

I messaged Robin, who sent back a voice note immediately that was basically just them screaming, and then I went downstairs to make a quick cup of tea.

Grandad was sitting in the garden in his suit trousers and undershirt, and I watched Mum positioning the sun umbrella so that he was in the shade.

"Is he all right?" I asked Dad.

"He's not good today, Tilly. And your mother's teaching from home, so he can have a day off."

"You sure?" I asked.

"You can have a day off, too."

"Oh," I said. "It's . . . I don't mind staying here."

322

"No, Tilly, you've got rehearsal," Dad said.

"I'll message Brian about Grandad," I said. "We're only doing scenes today, anyway."

"Tilly, I don't know if it's good for him, you know. All that stress."

"Dad, he's not stressed—he loves it. He's got friends there. It *is* good for him. Also, we can't do it without him now, he's part of the company. We're even putting him in the program."

And as soon as I'd said it, I was like: *Shit, everyone is going to think I'm Theodore Booker, because his name is in the program,* and then I was like: *Do I need to mention this?* and then I got out my phone and sent Brian the most rambly message of all time.

"I think you should have a plan B," Dad said, watching me type away. "Regarding your grandad." And it was literally the weirdest thing ever to hear him say those words, because Mum and Dad and Emilin were people who weren't used to having to consider a plan B. Well, apart from during the pandemic when they had to work from home and Mum became some sort of ballet guru for people who were bored enough to take it up and also had big enough kitchens to do it in.

Mum came in, put some Bran Flakes into a bowl, and poured the tiniest bit of milk on top.

Dad and I watched her, and she must have sensed our alarm, because she was like: "For your grandad."

"He doesn't like Bran Flakes," I said. "He eats Frosted Flakes."

Mum kind of twitched, and I took the bowl from her.

"Thanks," I said, poured more milk, and started eating. "Don't you think it's really funny how Shakespeare called the person who was going to be transformed into a donkey Bottom? Like, Bottom, the ass?"

Mum and Dad looked at each other, then at me, and back at each other.

"You've only worked that out just now, haven't you?" Dad asked, and I was just like: *WTF?*

Scene 4

You should have seen everybody's face when Robin and I walked in with that enormous donkey head.

In fact, you should have seen the faces of the people on the 11:36 from Waterloo to Strawberry Hill when we boarded the train.

Because obviously, when you have a donkey head in your possession, you're not going to leave it in its impenetrable protective pouch, but you're going to set it free and start taking selfies immediately.

When we pushed the head through the doors of the social club, Olivia and Katherine and Miroslaw had already seen our IG story, but Brian literally screamed in delight, clutched his chest, and then fell on his knees and thanked us for organizing something "so utterly maaaaaarvelous," and then he actually cried. You know, like that judge on the pottery show who always cries when someone makes a really cute sink or something.

Miroslaw opened his arms to receive his costume, and he was just like: "That's one good ass," and I went: "And your character is called Bottom. Do you get it? Bottom, like ass. How hilarious is that?" And then Miroslaw went: "Yes, it's a play on words. I learned that in English class in Poland," and you know when you're like: *Fine, I'm the ass.*

He put it on immediately, and then Maeve insisted on trying it on, then we put it on Brian, and half an hour later I was just like, this could go really wrong, like, imagine the headlines: "COVID Outbreak at Amdram Society After a Dozen Actors Stick Their Heads Inside Ass."

Robin was so swept away by it all that they immediately changed their costume idea for the scene, making it more "modern" (a.k.a. gay—in every sense of the word), and Maeve was 100 percent there for it, which made me realize yet again that not all old people were stuck in their ways.

Robin said they wanted Miroslaw to wear a tight little pair of shorts, but that he could also just wear the cut-off black T-shirt he always wore and his boots, and Miroslaw was like: "Everyone will know I am a homosexual, no?" and Robin was like: "Your mother will be very proud."

We took pictures for the IG story straightaway, and hashtagged the shit out of it, linking it back to the flash mob.

We literally took the best pictures, some of just Miroslaw, some of Robin putting the head on Miroslaw and pretend-styling his artificial fur, then we took one of Maeve and Miroslaw pretending to be mid-scene, then we took one of Maeve and Miroslaw laughing with #bloopers.

When the general hysteria had died down, Brian called Katherine and me to the stage for our scene, and I felt like one of those donkeys they show on telly that are walking on wobbly legs, literally collapsing under the weight of all the things they're carrying, and then the voice-over says: "Have you got five pounds to help Trevor and his donkey friends?" and because you're sad, but you also don't have five pounds, you quickly change the channel.

I sat down on the pretend fallen tree trunk and watched Katherine walk over.

And if you think it's awkward being in close proximity to the person you've had sex with, who then flinched at your touch not five hours later outside St. Thomas's A&E and hasn't spoken to you since, imagine how awkward it was to be on a stage with them, having to put real life aside because you were there as different people.

I was like: *I hope she's learned to never have an affair with a co-star, because imagine doing that and then having to do a year-long West End run or, worse, having to work seven years on some TV show with them.*

And imagine having to look into that person's eyes and them being like: "But are you so much in love as your rhymes speak?" (when you've literally seen them naked, and all your insides are, like, sighing) and having to respond: "Neither rhyme nor reason can express how much."

Brian stopped us every two seconds, and he was like: "You need to listen to what the other person is saying. The audience can't know you've said the words a thousand times already. They need to think this is the first time you're having that conversation. Again from 'Love is merely a madness,' and, Katherine, darling, remember that Rosalind's in love, too. It's not just poor Orlando."

I know the whole thing was painful for me in so many ways, and it must have been painful to watch because Brian literally dismissed us twenty minutes later and was like: "Enough for today. I'll work with Katherine on the Scottish play now."

I went to the shop with Miroslaw.

He got a meal deal, and I got a banana Yazoo for me, a Dr Pepper for Robin, and a Ribena for Olivia.

When we got back and I saw Katherine onstage, it suddenly occurred to me that now I had to be in the show, we had no one to do the filming.

When I asked Robin to do it, they were like: "No way, I have to be backstage. What if someone pops a button?"

"No one's going to pop a button. And who cares if a button pops?"

"I care. I'm in the program as the only wardrobe person. People will blame me."

"Oh my God, no one is going to pop a button."

"Speaking of programs," Maeve, who was being fitted, said, "we're going to have to take out Theodore. I wonder if it's too late."

"Maeve, breathe out a minute, I can't get you undone," Robin said.

"That's because I've got such ample bosoms," Maeve said, and laughed. She shook the ample bosoms, and watched the bits that were visible above the corset jiggle.

"See? I've got to help Maeve change from this to the 'Send in the Clowns' gown. She can't go on singing it dressed as slutty Titania, can she? That would be dramatically confusing."

"Ohhhh," Maeve exhaled, and it was almost a sung note. "It would be dramatically different. But I can see Titania in Desiree and vice versa. Have I been typecast?"

The top hook of the corset flew out of its eye, and Maeve took in a deep breath.

"Better. Brian!" she hollered, interrupting his scene with Katherine Cooper-Bunting. "I've got a feeling I've been typecast, and I don't like it."

"What?" Brian asked, and took off his glasses to look across the room at her.

"I said I've been typecast."

"You're lucky I've cast you at all, knowing what a big pain in the arse you are. Now let me get on with things. And for God's sake, put your breasts away."

"You're going to have to change the program, you know," she said. "Because Tilly is now Theodore. You know what I mean."

"I've done it," he said, and put his glasses back on. "I'm having inserts printed. Really, woman, I don't know why I keep you around. But, if you want to be helpful, you can pick up the programs on Sunday morning. I'm having an early brunch in town with Malcolm."

"Oh, you're so romantic it makes me want to heave," Maeve said. "I can't get them. I'm staying in North London Saturday night."

"Anyone with a car willing to get them? It's only down the road from here," Brian asked, and looked around, and Katherine looked super annoyed that her scene got hijacked.

"We can pick them up," Miroslaw said. "My dad will drive me to the theater."

"Thank you, darling," Brian said. "It's all paid for. But I'll give you the invoice."

"You could at least ask me to have brunch with you, Brian," Maeve said as she hoisted her breasts back into her bra.

"Fine," he said. "Come for brunch. We've got a reservation at eight at the Sofitel."

"Uh, fancy."

"Maeve—"

"Sorry, carry on. Sorry, Katherine, darling."

As I was watching them, I was just like, that's literally Teddy and me in a hundred years. And then I wondered if Brian ever had sex with a man Maeve had fancied or vice versa, and, if so, how their friendship recovered.

"We'll have to ask Teds to film it," I said to Robin.

"With one arm?"

"Shit."

"We can ask Katherine's dad. It's his camera, after all."

"But he never used it to film others—he only used it to film himself doing a sermon."

"You just don't want to ask her," Robin observed correctly, which annoyed me. They held up a sheet for Maeve to get dressed behind, even though it was kind of too late for modesty.

"I'm not speaking to her at the moment."

"Oh no, have you two fallen out?" Maeve inquired.

"Not exactly," I said.

"Oh, life's too short for all that. Just kiss and make up."

Robin looked at me, grinning, and I looked at Maeve, and felt all the sadness in the pit of my stomach, and then Maeve went: "Oh. Oh dear. Well, there's many more fish in the sea. We'll find you one. But it must be difficult watching your friend with her. I'm sorry about that."

I looked at Robin like, *Kill me*, because whatever Maeve thought was going on was definitely not going on. Talk about people assuming Katherine's straightness.

I didn't bring up the question of the filming again—Katherine did. But not before throwing herself into the role as Lady Macbeth, and as I watched her, I finally got what Mum and Dad and Emilin and Grandad were all about, because no matter what personal disappointments or hardships you suffered IRL, you still had the work.

And it felt really unfair that Katherine could so easily disappear into it while I was left in the real world with a sadness I could barely describe.

"I'm sure we'll find a willing volunteer to film," Brian told Katherine, being all dismissive, which pissed her off, and she was like: "What's the point of all our hard work if we're not going to film it?"

"This isn't television, daaaaaaaaarling," Brian said.

"But we said we'd film it, and I really want it in case I need a self-tape in the future, and we've all worked really hard," Katherine insisted.

"We'll find someone," Brian said, and rolled his eyes, which she clearly hated. "But this is a live performance first and foremost, so excuse me for putting all my time and energy into just that."

She crossed her arms and leaned back in her chair.

She was beautiful when she was angry.

I stayed around when people were leaving, because I wanted to talk to Brian about Grandad.

He said not to worry about it, and if push came to shove, he could always "give Nora a bell," because he was sure she'd step in.

On my way out, I went into the toilet, and my heart literally stopped, because Katherine was standing there, leaning against the sink, clearly waiting for me.

"Can you maybe ask your dad if he'd film us?" I asked, because those were the only words on my mind that made sense. "That way he won't even have to buy a ticket."

She nodded.

Looked at her hands.

Looked up at me.

She opened her mouth to say something when—

"Anyone in there? I'm locking up!" Brian shouted.

We both flinched.

"Just a minute!" I shouted back.

Katherine clutched her chest and laughed. "He nearly gave me a heart attack."

"Same," I said, and took a deep breath. "Can I just say that I understand things change. But I still think you're beautiful."

She looked like I'd said something really complex, and then she went: "Tilly—" But I didn't let her finish, because really, it didn't matter.

I didn't want to have that conversation. If it had to be over, I wanted it to fade out gently. Until we didn't notice it was even there anymore, you know, and then one day it's just gone, and when you think about it, your first emotion isn't heartache.

I ran outside, and luckily the 219 was coming up the hill, and so I started running toward the bus stop with my arm out, signaling the driver I wanted to get on.

When I sat down, I broke out in a hot sweat from running and a cold sweat that came from the absolute devastation that was a broken heart.

I concentrated on my breathing. In and out, in and out. But I still cried.

"I hate you," I said to love.

Scene 5

That night I sat in my room in front of my mirror, and I was like: "What else could possibly go wrong?" which is a question you should never ask.

Everything was quiet. Like, no one was messaging me.

And time really expands when you're waiting for something, even when you're not sure what you're waiting for, which is why I decided to stalk all my friends individually.

I went into my WhatsApp conversations with people and checked if they were online, which is probably the lowest I've ever sunk in terms of level of loneliness felt and desperation to overcome it.

Teddy's parents came over at one point, and I heard Mum officially introduce them to Grandad, and then they all sat outside, and much, much later, when Dad got home, I heard them all laughing and being silly, which was nice, you know, because they were literally the best of friends before they fell out over something that wasn't anyone's fault.

I heard glassware clinking, and someone played *The Lark Ascending* on the piano, and suddenly they sounded like a bunch of drunk idiots watching a football match.

I watched Robin's IG story of them sewing tiny rainbow-colored stitches into Maeve's corset, and I commented on, like, every single picture, but they just liked it and didn't say anything back.

And suddenly there was a picture of Teddy in Robin's story.

He was sitting on their bed, looking happy.

My initial reaction was to comment on it, but not because I wanted to but because I felt like I had to, because I'd commented on all the other posts, and they didn't have to know that it made me feel even lonelier than five minutes ago.

I tried all sorts of replies, from heart emojis to lame exclamations like: "Aw!"

The thing is, even when you post things like that, and the words and pictures mean what they mean, it's all bollocks, isn't it, and everyone knows you're lying.

My arms and legs and eyelids felt like lead, and so I just lay there, imagining Katherine loved me back, and that Teddy was still my best friend, until I was too upset to be awake, and my brain mercifully checked out and let me fall asleep.

Scene 6

The next morning, I woke up 100 percent disappointed that this was still my life.

I did a line run sitting in front of my mirror in my bra and underwear playing Rosalind as well as Orlando. Then I got dressed and went downstairs.

Mum was in the kitchen doing pliés, one hand resting on the sink, the other arm moving around in orderly sweeps.

Grandad sat at the table eating a bowl of Frosted Flakes, ignoring her.

She'd cut a banana into tiny cubes for him that were already turning brown.

"Good morning," I said.

"Hello, Sarah," Grandad said, and smiled at me.

"That's Tilly, Douglas," Mum said, and stopped what she was doing.

Grandad looked confused.

"Mum, it's o—"

"No, it's not okay, Tilly," Mum said, all aggressive. "Sometimes I can't help but think he does it on purpose, you know. One minute he's perfectly fine, and the next he's talking nonsense, I . . . I just don't get it."

"Mum," I said, and gave her a death stare. "It's okay—it's just a name. It doesn't matter. He's not doing it on purpose."

"He's also right here," Grandad said, and got up. "Are you ready, then? We've got dress rehearsal."

"I'm coming, Grandad," I said, looking at Mum like *told you so*, and followed him out toward the front door.

"Douglas—" Mum said, but he slammed the door shut before we could hear what else she had to say.

When we got to Clapham, Teddy was there, and for a second I was annoyed he hadn't messaged to say he was coming, because we obviously could have taken the bus together, but then I realized that he must have spent the night at Robin's. He was standing behind the bar, cup of tea in hand, and talking to Robin, Olivia, and Miroslaw.

Katherine sat in her usual spot, reading a book, and because I had no idea where I should go, I went to the toilet.

I washed my hands for, like, five minutes, and then Robin came in and they were like: "There you are. Everyone's getting ready."

"I'm coming."

We started, of course, with "Seasons of Love," which Brian said I had to participate in now since it was an ensemble piece and I was in the ensemble, and when I tried to get out of it by telling him I didn't know the words, he went: "Don't be so utterly ridiculous, Tilly. Of course you know the words."

Then I was going to tell him I couldn't sing for shit, and he went: "It's for charity, for crying out loud," and then Malcolm, who was there and again wearing a three-piece suit, rolled his eyes at me, which I literally found so offensive, because he didn't know me, but I didn't say anything, just stood in Teddy's spot next to Miroslaw, who was like: "Just move your mouth."

"Yeah, thanks, I will."

"I know the words. We'll be fine. It's an important song. HIV is still very important. Living is very important. Loving is very important."

And then he winked at me, and I felt really stupid for being in a foul mood.

"You're important," I said to him, and he was like: "You're important," and then we laughed, and Brian clapped his hands to shut us up.

"Right," Brian said. "Finally. Now, a run-through means a run-through. We only stop if the set collapses."

"Are you seeing things?" Maeve asked. "There's no set."

"It's what we say in the theater, darling. So, unless the ceiling collapses, we are going to run through, okay? I don't care if you're not ready, I don't even care if you're not dressed, when it's your turn, you will be on the stage, understood? You'll get notes after."

Everyone nodded, nobody spoke.

"Very well," he said. He picked up his stopwatch and went: "And: curtain."

Grandad started the intro to "Seasons of Love."

The song went well, Maeve's *Sweeney Todd* went well, Katherine's Lady Macbeth went well. Then it was Charles's turn to sing that song from *Camelot*, but he got all the words muddled, and then he forgot the melody, too, and when it was time to sing another verse, he sang the one he'd already sung, and in the end, the song, whose central theme was Lancelot not possibly being able to leave Guenevere during any of the seasons of the year, turned into Lancelot only not being able to leave her in spring which was obviously a bit repetitive, as well as a lot less romantic. Charles was really annoyed about messing up, but Brian was just like: "Doesn't matter, next, next, next!"

Of course, the Phantom of the Opera was the one who ended up not being dressed, because he'd forgotten to put his cowboy boots on and was instead standing on the stage in a cowboy outfit and Crocs.

Then Olivia sang her song from *Oliver!* and I have to say she looked absolutely amazing. I'm not saying that tracksuits or exercise gear look bad on people, but when you then see them in actual clothes, they literally look like they're a different person.

Miroslaw and Maeve's *Midsummer Night's Dream* was outrageous. Imagine a donkey in tiny little shorts with a Polish accent giving it all that, and then Titania going: "What angel wakes me from my flowery bed?" and being completely over the top and stroking and kissing his nose. And when she went: "I love thee" in his ear, Miroslaw shook his head like he was still that goat from the day Katherine and I were horses, and he made actual donkey noises, which spurred Maeve on to fall even more in love with him, and it became so absurd and hilarious that Olivia laughed so hard she cried all her eyeliner off and had to reapply.

I looked proper ridiculous in the riding trousers, even though Robin had obviously mended them, and the sleeves of my shirt were so wide I don't know how they were ever fashionable, because they must have literally been in your dinner every single night, and no one had washing machines back then, so why?

Katherine looked incredible, of course, but she was all business.

Luckily, I didn't forget any of my words, but the strangest thing is that when you're on a stage and you know everyone is looking at you, time actually accelerates, and the next thing you know, the scene is over and you're getting out of your costume.

She didn't even look at me when we got off the stage, just went back to her seat and got out her notebook.

Olivia was next with her song from *Wicked*, and well, yeah, I mean, it was outstanding. Katherine never looked up from her notebook, and I was just like: *I get that they think they're rivals, but they're not because they'd literally never be up for the same role, like, ever, so they may as well support each other.* But what did I know about anything?

The last number in the show, "the grand finale, daaaarlings," was Malcolm's "Being Alive," and it was the first time we'd heard it performed properly, and it really was amazing, and Olivia ended up crying again, but this time not from laughter.

At the end, we all applauded each other and then Brian was like: "Thank you, everyone—that was a good effort. We'll have a fifteen-minute break. Please get changed if you haven't already, and then I'll give you your notes."

Everyone went over to the bar to make a cup of tea, where I ended up in line behind Katherine.

Her hair was still up in her Rosalind-pretending-to-be-a-boy style, and I watched the pulse in her neck.

I bit my lip.

She turned round and saw me.

"That wasn't too bad, was it?" I quickly asked.

"No, I thought it went all right."

"I hope I'm not, like, lowering your standard too significantly," I said.

"What are you talking about?"

"Well, you know, if you're going to use it as a self-tape. I hope I don't, like, make you look bad."

She looked at me as if she was annoyed, and then went: "Why would you make me look bad?"

"Well," I said, and took a clean mug from the drying rack, "I'm obviously not an actor."

"For someone who isn't an actor, you're actually all right, so stop being all weird about it."

She left me standing there, and when my tea was ready, I didn't even want it anymore.

Then everyone started to sit down again, ready for notes, and Charles came over and he went: "Have you seen your grandad?"

I looked around, and I couldn't see him.

"Is he in the toilet?" I asked.

"I've just come from there," Charles said.

It felt like the room was spinning, and my eyes wouldn't focus.

"Oh, fuck!"

"I'll have a look outside," Charles said.

I jumped out of my seat, spilled my tea, and burned my leg, but I didn't even feel it, and went after Charles.

He wasn't outside and there was no sign of him.

"Grandad!" I shouted at the heavens.

Scene 7

It was exactly like that feeling when you reach inside your pocket for your phone and it's not there.

Vomit-inducing, heart-and stomach-dropping panic.

I ran down Battersea Rise—I don't even know why I chose that route specifically—and I was just screaming: "Grandad!"

I ended up running all the way to TK Maxx, pushing past people, shouting abuse at them for wandering along the pavement four abreast at literally zero miles per hour.

I was sweating and my lungs were burning, and my brain was going: *You're going to have to call Mum and Dad*, and the thought of having to make that call somehow felt even worse than Grandad being missing.

I jogged back up the hill to the social club, where some of us were standing outside now.

Teddy was on his phone, and when he saw me, he put it away.

"I was just calling you."

"Is he here?" I asked.

"No, he definitely isn't. We've checked the whole place."

"Oh my God, Teddy," I said, and my hands were shaking,

and he took them and was like: "He's only been gone for ten minutes—we'll find him."

"I have to tell my parents. Maybe he's at home."

"Does he have keys?"

"No, but Dad's still home."

"All right, call him."

"He's going to kill me."

"This isn't your fault, Tills. Do you want me to call him?"

"No, I'll do it," I said, getting out my phone and calling Dad, and of course he didn't answer, and I had to keep calling him for, like, five minutes before he picked up.

"Why don't you ever answer your phone?" I shouted.

"What's wrong?"

"Grandad walked off, and we can't find him."

"What do you mean, 'walked off'?"

"'Walked off' as in he walked away from where we all are, and now we don't know where he is. Is he at home, by any chance?"

"No, he's not."

"But maybe he got on the bus and is headed that way."

Dad didn't say anything, and it made me really angry, because he's supposed to be the dad and have answers.

"Can you maybe go outside and stand at the bus stop?" I asked, and I could barely speak because my throat felt like someone was strangling me.

"Good idea," he said.

"Okay. And take your phone."

"I'll call you back in a minute, okay?" he said.

"Okay, we'll keep looking here."

I hung up and looked at Teddy. Robin had slung their arm around Teddy's elbow.

"Have you got a picture of him?" they asked me. "Because I'll post it on Nextdoor. People post about missing cats all the time."

"He's not a cat," I said. There was an awkward silence. "I'm sorry. I'll send you a picture. Thank you."

Brian walked up to us, and he was like: "Darling, we're fully committed to finding Douglas. He can't have gone far."

"What if he got on a train? He could be on his way to Brighton."

"Well, that would be wonderful, because he probably won't have a ticket, which means they'll be cross with him and soon realize he's not a well man, and they'll take him off the train and British Transport Police will probably drive him home."

"But what if he doesn't know where he lives? Oh God, I should have known. He's been getting worse; I knew he's been getting worse, and I've literally been ignoring Mum's concerns for ages. Why am I stupid?" I asked, and I honestly wanted to just die.

"We'll find him," Teddy said again, and squeezed my hand.

Charles came rushing round the corner, wiping sweat off his forehead with a handkerchief.

"No sign of him out back. You should call the police straight-away," he said, and everything became even more real.

"I thought you had to wait twenty-four hours," Robin asked.

"No, you can call them straightaway and explain that he's a vulnerable person. They'll look for him."

My phone rang, and we all jumped.

"Hi, Dad."

"He's not here, and I've waited for a few buses to go by, and nothing."

"Everyone says to call the police."

"Yes, I think we ought to. I'll do it right now."

"I think I'll have another look around the area here."

"I'm staying at home in case he shows up," he said.

"Okay. Call me if there's any news."

"Tilly, why don't you come home, too?" Dad asked, and again I felt like I couldn't breathe. "I'd feel better if you were here."

"Yeah, okay, I'll come home," I whispered.

"Good. Do you want me to get you an Uber?"

"No," I said, and swallowed hard. "I'll take the bus, I think."

"All right, baby," Dad said, and I wiped my eyes and hung up.

"Darling." Malcolm came up to us, phone in hand. "We've spread out in an orderly fashion. Maeve is walking toward Battersea with Olivia, Katherine is going across the Clapham Common way, Daniela and Thomas are walking toward Windmill Road, and Miroslaw is on the two nineteen to Wimbledon. I suggest Brian and I stay put in case he comes back here. Teddy has provided your address, which we've shared via

WhatsApp, so we'll know where to drop him off if we find him. Or when we find him, rather."

"Thank you," I said to him. "We haven't properly met. I'm Tilly."

"Malcolm," he said, and nodded. "And don't worry, we'll find him. Statistics say four in ten people who have dementia will go missing at one point, it's perfectly normal."

"How do you know that?" I asked.

"I work at the Office for National Statistics."

"Really?"

"No, I just googled it."

His phone vibrated, and he swiped across the screen.

"Katherine says she couldn't find him on her way home, but that she's going to look around Clapham Junction again."

"That's kind," I said. "I think I'm going to go home."

"I'm going to go to the station," Charles said. "One of the managers is a friend of mine. See if we can check CCTV."

"Thank you," I said.

I swung my backpack over one shoulder and went to the door expecting Teddy to be right behind me, but he wasn't. He was standing with Robin, and they were looking at a phone and talking.

I swallowed this new sadness, and it neatly settled on top of all the other sadness that had already piled up inside me, and started walking.

I walked to the bus stop, past the bus stop, to the next bus stop and on to the next, and then the next, and the next thing I knew, I was home, and my face was sunburned, and I unlocked the door, and Dad came jogging toward me, his phone in hand, and he was like: "Where have you been?"

And then he hugged me for ages.

"Two police officers came over," Dad told me. "They're out looking for him. All we can do is wait."

"Have you spoken to Mum?" I asked.

He shook his head.

"Why not?"

"Because I'm still hoping he'll show up before she gets back from work," he said.

"Do you think she'll flip?"

"Unfortunately, yes."

"I'm so sorry," I said, and sat down on the sofa.

"Tilly, you're not his carer."

"But I am."

"No, you're not," Dad said, and took my hand. "And we'd never ask that of you."

"I was distracted," I said. "And then he was gone. I'll tell Mum."

"No, I'll tell her," Dad said. "Look. It's my fault, really. Your mum's never been keen on having him here, and I'm afraid this proves her point."

"I thought she was all for it."

"She wanted him to go into an assisted-living facility. She said we couldn't do it."

"Oh."

"Well, the truth is we can't really afford to put him in one at the moment, anyway. Which is why she's been going like a lunatic to extend her Ballet at the Kitchen Sink project."

"You have to pay to go into a home?" I asked, because I never knew that. I thought that just happened to you.

"Unless you've got nothing and no one. But if you're in the early stages of dementia, you don't qualify for a place yet anyway."

"I thought Grandad had money."

"Of course he *had* money. But they didn't own their flat, and he was self-employed all his life and never bothered to pay into a pension. He gets state pension, but you can neither afford to live nor die on that, so I'm afraid that's not going to pay for a home. And his savings won't cover it if he's going to live another ten years. Which I hope he will."

"I've read that once people start really forgetting, they can die quite quickly," I said. "Like, within a year or two."

"I read that, too," Dad said, and patted my hand.

"The whole thing's so unfair."

"It is what it is, Tilly."

"I don't think I want him to go into a home, Dad."

"Oh?"

"Not yet, anyway."

Dad looked at me, then his phone. "I should call Emilin."

"No!"

"Imagine she found out Grandad went missing and we never called her."

"But, Dad—"

"It's not your fault, Tilly," he said.

I went to the kitchen to get a glass of water, and Dad called Emilin, who flew into a mad rage, and I could hear her even though she wasn't even on loudspeaker and Dad was all the way in the other room.

Dad kept going: "You don't have to come. What will you do here that would make a difference?" But ten minutes later, she'd decided that she was going to get the train from Norwich, where she was doing her lunchtime concerts that week.

About two seconds later, Mum got home, and as predicted, all hell broke loose.

I think when you live in a household where so few words are spoken, it's incredibly disorientating when someone suddenly starts ranting and doesn't stop. I felt like I was drowning in Alphabetti, and so I went up to my room, put my pillow over my head, and concentrated on not suffocating.

Teddy's parents came over a little while after the yelling was done, and I could hear them all talking in the living room.

Then the doorbell rang again, and it was the police.

I sat on the top step of the stairs so no one could see me and listened, but all they had to say was that they hadn't found Grandad, but that they were still looking, and they were doubling their efforts now because they didn't want him to be out there overnight because that was dangerous.

"Excuse me," said Teddy's voice, and my heart skipped a beat. He appeared at the bottom of the stairs, and when he looked up and saw me, he waved with his good arm.

I waved back.

"Well, no news is good news, I guess," Dad said to the police officers, and I heard the door shut.

Teddy was still standing there, and I was willing him to come and be with me.

He did come up, but only until he was eye level with me.

"We'll find him," he said, and smiled, and one of his dimples was trying to show itself, and I felt a tear threatening to plop out my eye, but I wiped it away before it could get anywhere.

"It's okay to be sad," he said, but he didn't move to touch me or sit with me or anything.

"I'm sad about everything," I said, and took a deep breath. *Dim drums throbbing*, I thought, and tried to project. "I'm sad about the whole Katherine thing, and I'm so sad about your accident, and that we've fallen out. I thought life after the plague would be so much fun, but it's been nothing but shit, and I hate it. I wish we were still in lockdown. At least we couldn't do anything wrong."

Teddy laughed and wiped his hand on his My Little Pony T-shirt, which I'd never seen on him before and therefore figured it must be Robin's, which made me even sadder because I'd been more than just replaced as a best friend—I'd been upgraded, because Teddy and I'd never worn each other's clothes.

"I think everyone needs a cup of tea," Teddy said. "Let's go and make some. Have you noticed our parents have made up?"

I nodded and wiped my eyes again.

"Hu-fucking-rrah," Teddy said, and we went down to the kitchen.

Teddy took drinks orders from everyone, and I put the kettle on.

I watched him put mugs out and distribute tea bags and spoonfuls of instant coffee.

Then he went to the fridge for the milk.

"I kissed Katherine," I said, and he said nothing, which was the absolute worst. "I also had sex with her."

"I know," he said, without looking at me.

"How did y—"

"Olivia made a joke about you two being the lesbian version of Adam and Steve. Anna and Eve."

"We hadn't planned it, and it probably won't happen again anyway, and if you want, I'll never see her again," I quickly added.

I watched him unscrew the red top of the milk and pour some into the waiting mugs.

"Why would I want you to never see her again?" he asked, and looked at me like it was the dumbest thing I'd ever said to him, which I don't think it was.

"She was supposed to be your girlfriend."

"But it turns out she's into you."

"She's not my girlfriend or anything."

"Tills, look, I don't want to be in love with someone who doesn't love me back. That seems, like, really stupid. And if you end up being with her, then I'm happy for you. But you lied to me, and that was a really shitty thing to do."

"I just wanted you to be happy."

"So you lied to me? That doesn't even make sense. You're my best friend. Did you think you could just sneak around forever and hope I never found out?"

"I don't know."

"I hate that you did that. I don't deal with betrayal very well."

"What can I do to make it up to you?"

He looked at me and huffed out a disappointed laugh, and I felt like actual shit.

"I don't know."

I nodded. "Is that why you've been hanging out with Robin?"

He shrugged. "I really like them."

"What, like-like them?"

"I don't know. Maybe. I don't know what to think at the moment."

"I'd be really happy for you."

The kettle boiled, and Teddy poured the water.

"I'm so worried about Grandad," I said. "Do you remember when he first got here? I was panicky because I thought I'd have to be there when he dies," I told him, and I said it extra quietly. "Like, that would be the greatest inconvenience of my life. And now I'm just terrified that I can't be there, and he'll be all alone. And scared."

Teddy put the kettle down and looked at me.

"He's fine, Tilly."

"You don't know that. Nobody knows that," I said, and my tears got bigger and rolled off my face. *Please hug me*, I thought.

"I love you," I said to him, but he didn't say it back.

Scene 8

Being helpless is an interesting feeling.

You mainly don't know what to do with yourself, which makes you miserable, and since misery loves company, you seek out other miserable people, which is how we all ended up at our house.

Charles arrived when everyone had finished their cups of tea and coffee, so we made more.

We had no snacks in the house, so Teddy walked to the corner shop to get Hobnobs and chocolate digestives and crisps, and when he came back, he brought Robin, who'd also wanted to see if there was any news.

At seven my phone rang.

It was Katherine.

Teddy, who was sitting next to me, saw her name on the display, and I put it away, and he went: "Just get it."

"Hi," I said.

"Hi. Any news about your grandad?"

"No, we're still waiting. But the police are looking for him."

"Can you send me a picture of him, because I told my parents, and they said they can share it on the parish Facebook page, and also with all the people at Stagecoach. Most are local, and loads of them have dogs, so they'll be out walking, and I know they won't mind keeping an eye out."

"Thank you. I'll send it you."

"Thanks. And I also need to talk to you."

"We're talking now," I said, feeling suddenly all feverish hot and cold.

"Not on the phone."

"Oh."

"But it doesn't have to be now, or even before the show, but I just wanted to say it."

"Okay," I replied, my stupid heart galloping now.

"I really hope they find him soon," Katherine said. "Will you message me if there's news?"

"Okay."

"Okay. Bye."

"Bye."

Brian checked in every half hour, and everyone from *Cupid's Revenge* must have been sitting next to their phones, because everyone replied with either a thumbs-up, or Thanks, or Thank you for keeping us in the loop, From Daniela and Thomas.

When Emilin arrived, I started crying again before she could even open her mouth.

Dad took her into the kitchen straightaway, where they had a whispery shouting match for ages, but when they came back out, they'd made sandwiches for everyone.

Emilin had to be the center of attention, of course—I think it has to do with her being a pianist, because these people expect everything to be about them. Which is probably why she gets on so well with the oboe, who understands his place is strictly in the orchestra, because who's ever written anything exciting for an oboe?

You know how you should never google things when you're having an actual crisis? Because Emilin was all over it. I think her handling of anything with a keyboard or touchscreen looks aggressive at the best of times because her hands have super-human strength and range of movement, but that afternoon she was like the Hulk, typing away literally like she wanted to smash the screen in.

She was going: "This website says if he's been missing for a few days, police or investigators may come and get his DNA. It says we shouldn't move anything in his room."

"Why would we go into his room? Stop exaggerating now," Dad said, and she clearly didn't enjoy being told off.

"It says they may also have to contact his dentist for dental records, so I better get all that out for you."

I was like: "Shut up! He's not dead."

And Emilin was like: "At what point have I suggested he's dead?" But she had suggested it when she said the thing about the teeth, and we all knew it, because she may think we're all stupid, but we're not, and I was just going to shout at her again, but Dad was like: "Enough!" and the whole room went quiet.

"Everyone needs to calm down," he said. "Why don't you go for a walk, Emilin."

I was crying again, of course, because the one thing that makes me cry above all else is someone else's rage, and I got up and walked to the kitchen to get more paper towels because I'd cried through a whole roll already.

I blew my nose so hard my ears popped shut, and because of that, I thought I was imagining things at first, but then I swallowed, and my hearing was restored, and there was the unmistakable tune of "The Teddy Bears' Picnic" wafting in through the open kitchen window.

I craned my neck, and Miroslaw's dad's ice-cream van was turning into our road.

I could see Miroslaw in the passenger seat, and next to him, in the middle seat, was Grandad.

I know I was screaming, because I could hear myself, and of course everyone came running, and I went through to the hallway and pulled the front door open and ran into the road, and Miroslaw was waving, and I was crying, and then Mr. Lewandowski honked the horn.

The rest of the evening is an absolute blur.

Probably because I was crying, like, a lot.

Miroslaw had told his dad that Grandad was missing and, apparently, they'd been driving around for hours, and they finally found him by the Wandsworth Common rail station, where he was watching trains, but when he saw the ice-cream van, he walked straight over to them and ordered a 99 Flake for himself "and one for my lovely wife," my grandmother, who's obviously dead.

They said they told him they'd take him home and that he didn't even resist, but just got into the van and said: "Are you having a good day, driver?"

He still looked confused, but when he saw me, his whole face lit up, and he was like: "Hello, my darling," and I hugged him for ages and then Dad helped me take him upstairs, where we gave him a bath, which should have been weird but really wasn't because you look at people differently when they need you.

Teddy's dad called the police to tell them Grandad was back, and then Teddy messaged everyone at *Cupid's Revenge*, and then everyone who was still at my house washed the dishes, and then went home.

I made Grandad a sandwich, which I took upstairs.

He was sitting up in his bed, Rachmaninoff was snoring by his feet, and he looked perfectly happy.

Maybe a bit sunburned on his nose.

I gave him a kiss good night, and he went: "Good night, Sarah," and Emilin looked at me, sad and happy at the same time.

I had a shower and got into bed because I was beyond exhausted.

I was already asleep when Emilin crawled into bed with me.

"Scoot," she whispered, and I moved over to make room for her. "Today wasn't your fault. I'm sorry if I was being horrid. But I was scared."

"It's fine," I mumbled.

"No, I'm really sorry. I know Mum and Dad are no help. We'll find a solution, I promise. I'll help."

"Thank you," I said. "I just wish Mum and Dad would inform themselves. And I don't mean randomly googling all things Alzheimer's. Grandad has this friend, Charles, at our play, and Charles's wife had dementia, and he knows firsthand what it's like, and he's been really kind to Grandad, and to me, and I just think it would be so helpful if Mum and Dad could at least talk to him."

"I think that's a great idea."

"It would be a start. Charles said that there's no shame in asking for help."

"He's right."

"Our parents are so incapable sometimes."

"How about I talk to Dad about it? Maybe we can have Charles over for dinner one night."

"I'd love that. Thank you," I whispered, and it already felt much easier to breathe.

"Oh no, poor Barnaby is all squashed behind the mattress," Emilin said, and freed him, shoving him at me. "Here."

"Thank you," I said, and hugged him.

"You okay?" Emilin asked.

"Yes, fine," I answered.

"Night night, love you."

"Night night, love you too. Do you think it's weird that Grandad always calls me Sarah?" I asked.

"I don't think it's weird at all," Emilin said. "You're just like her. You don't faff around; you tell him what to do. And you're the spitting image of her when she was a young woman."

Scene 9

Friday was spent trying to get over the whole ordeal.

Mum and Dad went to work; Emilin, Grandad, and I stayed at home.

Emilin played the piano for a couple of hours, and Grandad watched her until he nodded off.

On Saturday, Brian arranged a Zoom with everyone, because we never got our notes from the run-through. He didn't have much to say, just that he'd changed the order around "to make it even more entertaining, daaaaaaaarlings."

Katherine was inside the church, and you know how Zoom is great, because you can look at a person the whole time and they won't ever know it?

Which is actually completely creepy now that I've put that thought into words . . .

Teddy and Robin were at Robin's, because apparently, he was (one-handedly) helping them with last-minute alterations. Robin's bedroom was proper cool, all with fairy lights and big cushions and loads of plants and one of those mannequins you use when you're a seamstress.

The Phantom of the Opera and his wife were in their kitchen, and they couldn't work out how to unmute themselves, and you'd think watching that kind of drama unfold would become easier to watch with time, but it isn't so.

Miroslaw's mum walked past in the background, and Robin was like: "Is that Mrs. Lewandowski?" and then Miroslaw introduced her, and she was like: "Hello, good afternoon, I am Giannina," and it was the cutest thing ever.

Brian was like: "I've asked Nora to play the piano for us tomorrow, because I think Douglas has been through quite an ordeal. And I'm sorry, chums, since Nora only got the sheet music tonight, I don't know how good it's going to be tomorrow, but I'm asking you all to be very professional and flexible, okay?"

I was like: "Grandad is having a good day today, so you never know, he may be up to it tomorrow," and then Brian said: "We can always see how it goes when we get there in the morning."

When the meeting was over, I smiled at Katherine, and she was smiling, and I imagined it was for me, even though it probably wasn't, but I went to bed that night wanting to believe it.

I didn't even want sex with her, you know.

I mean, I did, but what I wanted more than anything was to just lie in bed with her, talk about nothing, laugh, kiss, or watch some crap on Netflix.

This made me happy, then miserable, then happy again, then miserable, and I thought, you know, why are there only two emotions when you're in love? And why are they on the exact opposite ends of the scale?

It's so stupid.

And so exhausting.

"No one ever said love was easy," the image of Grace sitting on the foot of my bed said, and I thought, *You know what? No one actually ever did say that.*

When I went downstairs on the morning of *Cupid's Revenge*, Emilin and Grandad were already in the kitchen having breakfast.

Grandad was all dressed up, and Emilin looked piano-recital ready.

"You off?" I asked her.

"I thought I'd stick around and watch your play."

"It's not really a play," I said.

"But you're in it. Consider it payback for the millions of times you had to watch me play."

"Really?"

"Tilly, you need to stop being so convinced that you're not worthy of anyone's time."

"I don't think that," I said, realizing it was exactly what I thought. "I just don't want you to do something you don't want to do."

"I just told you I want to come and see your play."

"But you need a ticket."

"We've bought tickets," she said, rolling her eyes.

"And Grandad is in it, too," she added, and stroked his arm.

"I'm the best thing in it," Grandad said. "But your sister isn't bad."

"Thanks, Grandad," I said. "But you've only seen me once."

"A natural, she is."

Emilin pulled up her eyebrows at me, and I shrugged.

Grandad, Emilin, and I took the tube together and arrived at the Criterion Theatre at a quarter to ten, and literally everyone else was there already.

Robin and Olivia were dragging three giant duffel bags with costumes from an Uber, and Teddy was wearing the donkey head. He was also wearing the Care Bears shirt the nurses had cut off him in A&E, which Robin had now mended in a dramatic fashion with thick green thread.

Brian, Malcolm, and Maeve arrived, looking ready to party, and then I remembered they'd been to brunch already.

A man at the stage door signed us in, and then the theater manager gave us a tour of the backstage area, pointed out all the fire exits, and showed us to our dressing room.

We only had the one, but it didn't matter, since most costume changes would happen in the wings and toilets that were closer to the stage anyway.

Robin was completely in their element, and already arranging for rails to be brought up so they could hang things.

The tech run was exactly as Brian predicted, completely tedious.

They didn't even need Grandad, and so he and Emilin went for a walk around the West End and ended up going for lunch somewhere nice in Covent Garden.

We didn't have to do anything either but stand/sit in our spots wearing our costumes so that the lighting people could light us and program their cues into a computer.

When I sat down on the pretend fallen tree trunk, which was a crate that day, it was the first time I really looked at Katherine.

And she at me.

"Hi," she said, and smiled.

"Hello, Rosalind," I said, because I decided to keep it professional.

She looked at her hands, then at me, and just when I thought she was going to say something, someone shouted: "Can I have you two looking straight ahead, please. I need faces."

Then it was scene change, and everyone was rushing again, and the next thing I knew, it was time for us all to get ready for the actual performance, and I don't know why it hadn't occurred to me that there would be people in the auditorium, but I suddenly got proper vom-nervous, and I had to clear my throat every two minutes. I remembered Brian saying the thing about keeping the voice healthy and not having dairy, and I immediately regretted the banana Yazoo I'd drunk during the break.

I was sharing a seat by the mirror with Olivia, wondering what else I could do with my face before I went onstage, when Emilin came into the dressing room.

She was like: "Grandad really wants to play, and so I thought I may sit with him by the piano."

"You have to tell Brian," I said, and powdered my forehead.

"I will. I'm going to have a quick look at the sheet music, too. In case Grandad needs help."

"We've got a lady called Nora coming if Grandad can't play," I said.

"He'd like to play, though," she said, and gave me that exasperated look, and I was just like: *Stop being a dick, Tilly*, and so I went: "Thank you. I think Brian will be happy with that."

"She's all right, innit?" Olivia asked when Emilin had disappeared.

"She's fine," I said, because after sixteen years of sisterly hostility, I wasn't willing to commit to anything more just yet. Even if she'd been nice to me in a roundabout way ever since the night Grandad was delivered back to us in the ice-cream van.

"Mate, you've gotta help me with something," Olivia said, suddenly all serious, lining her lips, and I was like: "What?"

"I'm planning on makin' a political statement. I'm gonna tear up this pretty dress, and I'm gonna paint myself a black eye."

"Brian's going to have a fit," I said.

"Yeah, but I'm not gonna stand there and sing about loving someone who abuses me without looking like it."

"I can't help you, because we've got our scene right before," I said.

"Mate, you can literally wear your costume under your

clothes for the opening. And then you just need to help me mess up my hair and take scissors to the dress."

"If I'm late, Katherine's never going to speak to me again."

"You two don't seem to be on speakin' terms as it is, mate."

I looked at her through the mirror.

She shrugged.

"She actually wants to talk to me," I said.

Olivia looked at me.

"I think she wants to end things," I whispered. "Not that anything's started."

"Clean breaks are good," Olivia said, and I knew she was right, of course, but I still didn't want it.

Not when we were so good together.

Because we were, when no one was looking, at least.

Maybe it was easier to leave an actual relationship.

Because you knew what you were leaving.

But with Katherine I knew nothing apart from our potential. And it seemed eternally unfair we shouldn't get the chance to see what we could be like.

———

Mr. Cooper-Bunting showed up at one point to set up the camera for his filming duty, which Katherine had clearly volunteered him for. He seemed really enthusiastic, which I put down to the fact that it was literally his job to be enthusiastic, because if even a priest couldn't be enthusiastic about life and death, the rest of us could just forget about it all.

Katherine herself was putting programs on each of the seats in the orchestra stalls, inserting the page that had my name in it, as well as the changes Brian made to the running order, Miroslaw was doing the same in the dress circle, and Teddy and Robin were doing it in the upper circle.

Grandad made it his business to walk upstairs to the box office to find out how many tickets had sold, and when he came back, he was like: "Ladies, gentlemen, friends, we've done it. We've got a full house."

Everyone whooped and cheered, and Brian cried.

Obviously, I'd never been in a show before, so I didn't really know what to expect, and I think I didn't really get how much adrenaline there was. Or would be. Not just for me, but for everyone, you know.

The stage management person kept making announcements over the Tannoy like: "Company, this is your one-hour call, your one-hour call to the start of the show," and life became so stressful.

Miroslaw was getting super nervous, too, and he kept pacing the corridor by the dressing room, wearing the donkey head and saying his lines really loudly.

Maeve intercepted him at one point, but because he hadn't seen her coming—it was so difficult to see from inside that head—he tripped over her elaborate skirt, and they both ended up in a heap in the hallway, and Maeve was laughing until she was screaming, and then Brian told them off for being careless, and said the volunteers from St. John Ambulance weren't arriving until the house opened, i.e., until the audience were allowed into the theater, and could they please pull themselves together.

We were told to be careful with spraying deodorant and hairspray, because apparently aerosols set off fire alarms and are responsible for nine out of ten theater evacuations in the West End, but Olivia didn't think that rule applied to her, and she was liberally spraying TRESemmé in the hallway. Katherine had a fit about it, and Olivia just went: "Oh, do fuck off, Cooper-Bunting."

Then it was like: "Company, this is your half-hour call, your half-hour call. The house is now open, the house is now open," and at that point, we weren't allowed to go onto the stage anymore, and apparently it was bad luck having a peek at the audience, and so I stood by the toilets, shaking, my throat still feeling phlegmy, and deciding whether or not I needed to be sick.

Emilin and Grandad came out of the stage manager's room, where they'd been chatting to them, and probably chilling out and laughing about us amateurs.

"You look pale," Emilin said to me, and then proceeded to pretend spit over my shoulder three times. "Toi, toi, toi," she said. "I hope you'll love it."

"Not vomming will be enough of an achievement today," I

said, my voice all wobbly and coated from banana Yazoo, and I was like: *Why did I treat those dumbass exercises as a massive joke?*

"Dim drums throbbing, in the hills half heard," I projected down the corridor.

Miroslaw brayed.

Grandad stepped up to me and was like: "You ready, Tilly?" and I was like: "Absolutely," which was obviously a lie, because I regretted every single choice I'd ever made that had led me to now be standing in the backstage hallway of the Criterion Theatre, about to go onto the stage.

I quickly reminded myself that I was doing it for charity. And for Teddy. And for Katherine. And that I'd never have to do it again.

Then we had the five-minute call, and what felt like three seconds later, they called: "Act one beginners to the stage, please, that's all act one beginners to the stage."

Which obviously meant all of us, because we were starting with "Seasons of Love."

And the weird thing about being that kind of nervous is that you literally forget how to do anything. We'd been told how to line up, and let's be honest, lining up is not rocket science, and yet suddenly we couldn't do it and Brian had to angry-yank us back into the correct order, which was pathetic, to say the least.

And being in the wings in a big theater is basically the strangest thing.

You're standing there, in complete darkness, and all you can hear is the breathing of the people right next to you and behind you, and the disembodied chatter of the audience.

And your insides are humming with a confusing mixture of anticipation, excitement, and terror, and you know there's no going back, and you can feel your heartbeat everywhere in your body.

When the house lights went down and the lights onstage came up, it was our cue to go, and so we filed onto the stage, and the audience applauded.

Emilin—who is graceful only onstage, I noticed—led Grandad to the piano, Brian gave the sign, and we were off.

I just stood next to Miroslaw and tried not to sing too loudly, because I obviously don't know how to, and being on that huge stage, you couldn't hear yourself at all, which I found completely confusing.

And here's another thing you'll never know until you're actually on a stage during a show: You can't see the audience at all. So, if you think you can go to the theater and make eye contact with someone onstage, you're fundamentally mistaken. They can see fuck all.

The song came and went, Brian gave his "welcome, everybody" speech, and we rushed around getting into costume for our first scenes.

I quickly stripped down into my ridiculous riding trousers and enormous shirt, put my hair up, and ran to Olivia, who was in the accessible toilet, already giving herself a black eye with the help of a mahoosive makeup palette.

"It looks amazing," I said.

"Cheers. Can you ruin my hair?"

"How?"

"Just ruin it, mate. Shit, I forgot the scissors. Quick, can you rip this dress?"

I tried, but the material was unrippable.

"Fuck," I said, and yanked again.

"Get scissors, quick," Olivia said. "Where are we, anyway?"

We listened to the loudspeakers that were transmitting the goings-on onstage.

There was applause, and then I heard the sounds of Grandad on the piano.

"Shit, 'Some Enchanted Evening,'" Olivia said. "Hurry."

I ran out of the toilets, ran into Katherine, who was like: "Where are you? We're next."

"I need scissors," I said.

"What for?" she asked, and looked me up and down.

"I'm helping Olivia with a thing."

"Oh no," she said. "She can't—"

"She is."

"But—"

"You know she's right," I snapped at her, because of course Olivia was right. It was the absolute morally correct thing to do. And how could we as women not support her cause?

"Maeve," Katherine called suddenly, and together we sprinted to the dressing room. "Maeve, we need scissors," Katherine said, and Maeve didn't ask, just dived into her toiletries bag, boobs literally hanging out of her corset, and held out a pair of scissors.

"Ladies, you need to go to the stage," she said, and looked at us.

"You need to help Olivia," Katherine said, and put the scissors back into Maeve's hand.

"She's in the accessible loo," I said, and Maeve, who was already making her way there, hoisted herself into her costume.

I looked at Katherine and went: "Let's go."

"One more thing," she said, grabbed an eyeliner from the makeup table, opened the lid, and drew a mustache on me.

I was temporarily paralyzed by feeling her breath on my face.

Her lips looked so soft, and I got dizzy, and my heart ached.

"Perfect," she said, and smiled at me. "Now we can go."

We ran down the corridor, past the accessible toilet where Maeve was going: "Cooper-Bunting sent me with scissors?" which really made me LOL.

We'd barely got to the wings when the audience broke into applause.

Charles came off, and we had to go on, and my last thought was literally: *I'm not going to live through this.*

I sat down on the fallen tree trunk/crate next to Katherine and cleared my throat.

Katherine looked at me.

"Sorry," I actually whispered, and she gave me a death glare.

Then she transformed into Rosalind in front of my eyes, and she smiled at me, her face glowing. Ethereal, I thought. Then we were off.

Everything was going so well until we got to the point where she said her line: "I would cure you if you would but call me—" And here she came really close to my face and stage-whispered, "Rosalind" across my lips, which wasn't rehearsed and therefore threw me, and not just that, but someone from the audience was wolf-whistling, which made other people laugh, and I was completely pulled out of the scene, which made me forget all my words.

And so we just sat there.

And my brain wasn't even trying to find the lines anymore. It was thinking about nothing at all.

I could hear rustling in the audience, and someone was giggling in a nervous way, and then I heard the words: "Now by the faith of my love" gently floating at me from stage left, and it was Teddy, who was prompting me.

"Now, by the faith of my love, I will," I said, and then we rushed through to the end, because I think we were both afraid I was going to have a complete neurological shutdown again.

We got a huge applause anyway, which was great, and I can say I'd never been so happy in all my life for something being over, but I didn't really have time to think about it, because

Olivia was next with her song from *Oliver!* and when she walked onstage, people literally gasped.

Her performance was obviously musically flawless, but Maeve had also done quite a number on Olivia's dress and hair, and watching a beaten-up woman singing the most beautiful song about how much she loves the man who'd beaten her was possibly the most uncomfortable and heartbreaking thing I'd ever seen.

Katherine and I watched from the wings, and I watched Brian, who was standing across from me in the wings stage right, and at first he looked a bit annoyed, but then he just crossed his arms and kind of watched her, and when she was done, he shook his head and clapped.

Katherine and I ran back to the accessible toilet with Olivia and doused Olivia's eyes with micellar water, and she started again with her face, and I brushed out her hair and made it *Wicked* ready.

Robin appeared with Katherine's Lady Macbeth nightie, and Katherine stripped down to her underwear at which point I turned my back to her because I wasn't a weirdo, and no meant no.

She had to go, and I was still brushing Olivia's hair, and Olivia went: "Mate, go and watch her. I know you want to."

"I'm fine," I lied.

"Mate, did COVID teach you nothing about hashtag NoRegrets?" Olivia asked, and I put down the brush.

"Can you do this on your own?"

"Yes, mate. Fuck off now."

I ran back upstairs and squeezed into the wings behind Robin and Teddy, who were standing huddled together, holding hands.

"Hi," I whispered in Teddy's ear. "You saved my life."

"I know."

"I owe you."

"No, you don't."

The thing about stage presence is that Katherine had it. It was like a thing that was on the stage with her. A physical something that gave her gravitas, and made the onlooker stop breathing.

Like, she was in control of the space and all its energy, beyond compelling.

When she was done, there was a lot of whooping and cheering, and she smiled a proper Katherine smile before she came into the wings.

The Phantom of the Opera and his wife were next, and the thing was they may have been shit, but that somehow made them completely entertaining, and loads of people laughed during the song, and I was like: *They're going to go on* Britain's Got Talent, *and then perform at* The Royal Variety Performance, *and only because they're actually awful. #life.*

Olivia was next with her song from *Wicked*, which was absolutely amazing.

Grandad proper hammered the piano, and Olivia became this different character, and I swear everyone actually screamed when she finished, and the small children in the audience, who at that point I assumed were all Cooper-Buntings, 100 percent wanted to be like her.

"People will always love a singer more than an actor," Katherine said from right behind me, having appeared out of absolutely nowhere.

"No, they don't," I said.

"They do, just listen to them."

"It's not a competition."

"Everything's a competition," she said. She was still wearing a fake-bloodstained nightgown.

We took a step back to let Olivia pass, who was coming off stage. "Bitches," she said, beaming.

"I'm sorry I forgot my lines," I said to Katherine. "I hope it didn't ruin the video for you."

She shrugged. "If it looks bad, I just won't use it," she said, and I was like, *Ouch!*

Then she walked out of the wings and into the hallway.

I followed. "I'm sorry you're angry. I honestly completely lost the plot when that person was heckling us."

"I'm not angry about that," she said, and looked at me like I was an idiot. "I'm really annoyed you told literally every single person in the world that we had sex."

"I didn't—"

"You did. And literally five minutes after it happened."

"When?"

"In the hospital."

"I only mentioned it to Robin becau—"

"I told you that I'd only just figured out that I like girls. It wasn't for you to tell anyone."

"I never—"

"And five minutes later, everyone else knew, too."

"I never even thought abou—"

"It's great that you've always known about your sexuality, but has it ever occurred to you that not every person is like you? Like, I have no intention of keeping it a secret or anything, but *I* want to be the person to tell people."

"I'm sorry."

"I'd have been so annoyed if my family had found out from someone else before I had the chance to tell them. They probably would have thought I didn't trust them, which obviously is not at all the case."

"Have you told them?"

"I told them that night. I came home crying, and they sat me down because they thought something awful had happened. And it really wasn't how I wanted to tell them, you know. I was going to tell them that I'd met someone—you— and that I was happy. It was supposed to be a nice moment, and not rushed and with them being worried and me blubbing in the kitchen."

"I'm so sorry."

Katherine shrugged.

"What did they say?"

"My parents don't care if I'm gay or straight or whatever."

"I thought it might be tricky with the church and all."

"Yeah, because Jesus really hates it when people love and respect one another," Katherine said, and huffed.

"I'm an idiot," I said, and I really felt it.

She looked at her fake-bloodstained hands.

"But I really like you," I said.

She looked up at me. "I really like you, too."

"So, maybe, not like right now, but maybe we can, I don't know, go to the Globe again or something. Like, on a date. Sometime."

"I'd like that," she said. "But, Tilly, this time, no secrets. We tell everyone."

"We'll post it on IG."

"Maybe not everyone. But, you know, Teddy."

"Of course."

"Deal," she said, and held out her fake-bloody hand.

"Deal," I said, and shook it, and then we kept shaking hands, and I was just wondering if maybe we could hug when:

"Coming through," Maeve hollered from the other end of

the hallway, leading Miroslaw, who was already wearing the donkey head, toward the stage.

"Oh, have you two made up?" she asked. "Good, I love a happy ending."

"What is happening?" asked Miroslaw.

"Nothing, darling, keep walking," Maeve said. "Fools in love, is all."

Finale

Maeve and Miroslaw were hands down the stars of the evening, and I don't think either Olivia or Katherine even minded, because Maeve and Miroslaw's performance was outrageous, and the audience were beside themselves when it was over.

After Malcolm's song, which was supposed to be the grand finale, all the Stagecoach kids from the flash mob, whose families had booked tickets to see the show and had therefore significantly contributed to the full house we were experiencing, came out from the audience and onto the stage under the elaborate leadership of Nora, and then everyone sang "Seasons of Love" again, and when they brought up the house lights, we saw that everyone in the audience was on their feet, which was amazing, and clapping along, which was cringe.

Brian cried, and then Malcolm cried, then Maeve cried, and Olivia cried, and Teddy and Robin were just hugging each other and jumping up and down, and I couldn't stop smiling like an absolute lunatic.

I hugged Grandad and Emilin, who took a bow together. Emilin, who obviously had a lot more experience at this sort of thing, was waving at people in the audience, and I saw that it was Mum and Dad, and so I waved, too, and Dad blew us a kiss and was filming on his phone.

Backstage was chaos after, and we were laughing and shouting over one another as we were packing our stuff, and then Miroslaw got up on a chair and was like: "Everyone! You have to go to the front of the theater. We have a surprise."

When we rounded the corner by Lillywhites, dragging the bags of costumes and still hyper AF, we saw a huge crowd of people on Piccadilly Circus, all queuing in front of an ice-cream van that had hoisted the British and the rainbow flag.

"Surprise," Miroslaw said. "It's two pounds for ice cream, and the money goes to the Acting for Others charity."

Brian, who still hadn't recovered from being emotionally overwhelmed by the surprise "Seasons of Love" megamix, just grabbed him and hugged him, and I don't know what he was saying to him, but whatever it was made him cry even harder, and Miroslaw looked serious but happy.

Mum and Dad and Grandad and Emilin were almost at the front of the queue, and Teddy's mum and dad were a couple of people behind them, and I ran over to hug them, and they told me well done. Then they lied about not having noticed I forgot my words, which was kind.

Mum was like: "Maybe you can take some acting lessons," and I was like: "Not in a month of Sundays."

Turns out acting is so much harder than I thought, and

I'd probably have to give up Yazoo, and because life is stressful enough, I literally have zero desire to add further anxiety-inducing activities to it.

I was really proud of everyone, you know.

Imagine being old like Charles and getting up in front of hundreds of people and singing. That's, like, a pretty big deal if you ask me.

Miroslaw's mum and dad were proper sweating, and I was like: "Hello, Giannina. Hello, Mr. Lewandowski," and he went: "Call me Jakub," and gave me a 99 Flake.

Dad paid for the ice creams, and when he gave Mum hers, she was like: "I didn't really want one, Roger," and then Emilin went: "Jesus Christ, Mum! It's for charity—just have the damn ice cream and be happy about it," and Mum did, and I think she was.

The Cooper-Buntings looked like the Von Trapps from that film *The Sound of Music* about the nun and the Nazis. They didn't stand neatly in order of height, though, but looked like this mad scurry of people. They all had ice creams, too.

When Katherine saw me looking, she smiled and waved, and I waved back. Then she said something to her mum, who looked over at me, smiled from one ear to the other, and waved. Then her dad waved, too, but he nodded, like: *We already know each other.* Katherine said something to her sister, Stella, who looked at me, and suddenly all the other siblings were craning their necks, looking at me, and waving, too. The littlest one, the one who'd been cutting strawberries the day I collected the camera, waved like a madman.

I wondered what Katherine had said to them, but I guessed it was maybe about us going on a date or something, and even though I'd already had sex with her, this made me feel nervous all over again. Then I wondered if one of the Von Trapps turned out gay, and if their coming-out was as wild and joyful.

Everyone was kind of mingling, and the whole thing turned into an after-party.

I spotted Teddy and Robin standing in the entrance to the Criterion Theatre, and they were still holding hands, and Robin was poking his dimple one minute, and then they were kissing the next.

Nora was all over Grandad, and Emilin was clearly all for OAP love, which made Mum look the most uncomfortable she'd ever been, which was great for me, and I was really hoping Emilin would suggest having Charles and Nora over for dinner.

And on that note, I saw that Dad was talking to Charles, and they looked all kind of serious, and I knew that Emilin must have spoken to Dad about what's next with Grandad like she said she would, and I was suddenly so grateful for her.

Olivia was sitting on the steps of the statue and actually signing her name in the program for all the Stagecoach kids who were posing for selfies with her.

Maeve had decided to help in the ice-cream van, and so Jakub and Giannina were taking a break, and they had their picture taken with Miroslaw and the rainbow flag in front of the big lights at Piccadilly Circus.

At one point Robin was like: "You guys, we have to take a picture underneath Eros because, how funny is that?" and so Katherine and Teddy and Robin and Olivia and Miroslaw and I all posed, and Emilin took pictures with everyone's phones, which was a bit silly, really, because we were clearly all going to share them on IG anyway.

"Oh my God, do you get it? It's Eros," I said, like, five minutes later, when I finally properly looked at the statue. "Guy with the love arrow. He gets you when you least expect it. It's literally Cupid. As in *Cupid's Revenge*."

They all stared at me, and I was just like: "I literally only just got it," and of course everyone was laughing, and then Teddy pulled me into a sideways hug with his good arm and went: "Matilda."

"Why am I stupid?"

"It's probably hormonal."

"You're too kind."

"That's me."

"I suck," I whined, and pulled him closer.

"You do."

"Do you think you can ever forgive me?" I asked. "It doesn't even have to be today; I just want you to know that I'm so sorry and that I don't want to lose you."

"Try not to lie to me again like that."

"I promise."

"Because I don't want to lose you, either."

He kissed the top of my head, and I felt hope blossoming there and spreading out warmly and gently.

Katherine and I ended up taking a couple of selfies together, too.

But instead of just posing, she gave me a proper kiss, and it was the perfect moment with her lips on my lips, and the taste of vanilla and chocolate, and the heat of the concrete radiating upward, and the sound of buses and cars and motorcycles, and people talking in all different languages, and laughing, and the smell of London at the height of summer.

"Remember when we were horses?" I asked, and she laughed as the setting evening sun reflected in her eyes.

Acknowledgments

My biggest thank-you goes to my friends, both near and far. I'd especially like to thank Brittain for her continuous and seemingly inexhaustible love and support, and for always making sure I eat food that has nutritional value (and cake!). I thank Luci for always so graciously offering her presence, wisdom, laughter, and encouragement.

I thank my agent Rachel Mann, who is not only an excellent agent, but also an excellent human.

Thank you to my parents for everything.

I'd also like to thank the whole team at Macmillan, especially my editors.